THE BACK DOOR TO HEAVEN

THE BACK DOOR TO HEAVEN

BOB ALLEN

Purpletooth Publishing

ISBN #979-8-89282-088-2 (Print)

ISBN#979-8-89282-089-9 (Ebook)

Published by Purpletooth Publishing, Chicago, Illinois

Publication services provided by Fort Raphael Publishing Company, Chicago, IL, www.FortRaphael.com

Cover designed by Touchstone Graphic Design

This is a work of fiction. Names, characters, places, and incidents are either the product of the author's imagination or are used fictitiously. Any resemblance to actual persons, living or dead, events and locales are entirely coincidental.

CHAPTER ONE

The crocodiles waited patiently beneath the low-hanging branch of the tree. Each baby egret that fell from the giant nest triggered a free-for-all among the crocs, roiling the water to a muddy hue, and when the fracas died down, the remnants of the prize, mostly just feathers, would float away in the lazy current.

The birds attempted their maiden flights, but each attempt so far had failed, much to the primal delight and benefit of the crocodiles below. The baby birds grew hungry and desperate as they waited for their mother to return. She had not returned to the nest for at least three days, explained the narrator in his slow and deliberate British accent.

It could be assumed that something fatal must have befallen her, for it is extremely rare that a mother egret would abandon her nestlings. The hunger prompted the failed attempts to fly. The next bird had hopped onto the rim of the nest, flapped its wings, and paused. The shot on the television slowly closed in on the bird as it surveyed the situation at hand. The close-up showed the bird, a scrawny specimen with what seemed to be a bad punk haircut, and appeared to catch the fear in its oversized, glossy, black eyes.

Finally, the bird fluttered its wings and left the nest. It plummeted like a rock into the water below. It continued to flap its wings, but the rapid beatings on the water did not lift the bird as it had hoped but instead acted as a dinner bell for the six-foot-long crocodiles that lazed on the riverbank. The bird was an easy meal. It exploded like a ripped pillow at a slumber party as the crocodile snared it in its mousetrap-like jaws. The remainder of the crocs loitered about, sensing that there may be more.

"And they were correct," continued the narrator.

One by one, the baby birds would hop onto the rim of the nest, flap their wings and drop to their deaths below. Finally, the last bird in the nest took its position on the edge just as his siblings had done, but this bird took its time, or at least the editing made it seem. It studied the scenario closely. It looked down to the water, looked up to the sky, and even looked straight into the camera, which was back to its close-up shot.

The nature program gave the impression that somehow this one would be different, that this bird would make it and fly off into the lush green of the woods on the riverbank to find food, live, and have its nestlings. It would never abandon them and leave them in a do-or-die situation.

The bird leaped from the nest, its wings seemingly beating faster than any of the prior attempts of the others, hovered briefly, dropped down a bit but rose again, "Actually flying!" the narrator exclaimed. But from the right side of the picture appeared a set of airborne crocodile jaws. The bird's fate was the same as its siblings.

"Why do you play this shit?" asked Tom Sullivan from his bar stool.

"Because I've been watching you for the last twenty minutes, and your eyes haven't moved from the TV once, that's why," replied Mike McGurn, sole proprietor of McGurn's Tavern. "Besides, it's interesting stuff. Would you rather I put Oprah on?"

"Just asking, that's all."

Mike turned his attention back to the Tribune, spread out across the bar. The neon glow from the beer signs illuminated the faces of the small crowd of daytime regulars in an almost surreal aura, an aura that seemed routine to them. Harold and Sven sat at the end of the bar. That was their corner, at least during the day. They both were retired from a blue-collar life that had produced nice pensions and a wealth of stories that interested only them.

O'Reilly was there also. Although not a daily communicant at the bar, he was certainly there enough to qualify as a regular. He sipped his third Cutty and water while gazing up at the TV. Usually, after four or five drinks, O'Reilly would get up from his bar stool and say something about his wife while heading for the door, to which Mike would respond with a cheap imitation of a laugh and say, "Take care partner, see you next time."

There was also Stutterin' Dave, who was an employee. Dave sat at a table next to the electronic dart board, taking a break with a bag of pretzels and a soft drink. He was a bit slow, and Mike kept him around to lug cases of beer up from the basement and sweep the bar. It seemed like Dave had been around since day one and was a fixture there, like the autographed softball from the 1982 Murray Park championship team that sat atop a beer mug over the cash register.

Like the signatures on the ball, Dave's young physical features were fading to a grey, bumpy mass. He was now grizzled and overweight and would pass for a regular if not for the soft drink in front of him.

Tom grabbed his bottle of beer, his fourth, from the bar and walked over to the electronic dart board, grabbed the darts, and went to the throw line. He didn't bother to put any money in the machine, as no one did unless a tournament or wager was involved. He flicked his first dart at the board—double sixteen. The second dart failed to hit the board and bounced to the floor. The next dart flew past Dave's right ear, causing him to flay about in a mad scramble, strewing his pretzels about the tabletop.

"Hey, Davey. You better move. I don't think I got it today," laughed Tom.

Dave collected his pretzels and moved farther away from the dart board to the next table while Tom retrieved his darts. Mike glanced up from his paper. Tom took his spot at the throw line and launched an even wilder throw that caused the now-vigilant Dave to take evasive action to avoid getting hit in the forehead. The scramble brought the rest of the bar's attention to the scene, followed by Tom's mad laugh.

"Tommy!" snapped Mike, "Don't start that shit now!"

Tom's attempt to disrupt his boredom failed miserably, causing him to feel even more restless as he returned to the bar. He ordered another beer and turned to gaze out the window, past the neon 'Miller Lite' sign that overlooked busy Seventy-Ninth Street. It was late afternoon on a raw and gray Thursday in January. Outside the window, it looked like a grainy old black-and-white photograph that had survived a basement flood.

The cars and road had a powder-like salt residue that left a jagged, thin white line along the side of the vehicles and on the street. The light was fading, and the cold wind, The Hawk, swooped down the street and down the collars and coats of a group of waiting bus riders shivering at the stop on the corner. Tom hated this time of year, not because of the dour aesthetics but because nothing ever happened. There was no buzz, no action.

Everything moved in slow motion, and a malaise came over Tom as he turned back to his beer at the bar. He picked up a book of matches that lay there and individually lit each match until it burned to his fingertip. He dropped the charred match into an ashtray.

Mike had finished the paper and started to prepare for the evening crowd. It was Thursday, and the Hawks were on, so he was expecting decent business that evening. He began to fill the beer cooler in front of Tom.

"You okay, Tom?"

"Gimmie another one," replied Tom.

Mike reached down, pulled a bottle of Old Style from the cooler, opened it, and placed it before Tom. He grabbed two dollars from the small pool of cash lying on the bar, went to the register, and brought back a quarter.

"How's your dad been doing?" asked Mike.

It was small talk but purposeful small talk as Mike tried to get a read on Tom. He sensed his restlessness. He kept an interest in Tom, not because he particularly liked him; he thought Tom was an asshole, but out of respect for Tom's father, Pat Sullivan. He knew that Pat and Tom's relationship could be tense, but he also knew that Pat would appreciate it if you cut his kid some slack, so he did.

"He's doing okay," said Tom.

"I expect he'll be dropping off some signs for the windows soon."

"Yeah, I guess so."

Tom gazed at the last match between his fingers as it burned out.

"You been knocking on doors?" asked Mike.

Tom was a precinct captain in the ward and knew he was behind on his work.

"Yeah. Every night," Tom said, lying through his teeth.

It seemed to Mike that Tom wasn't interested in small talk or anything else. He wished Tom would leave the bar.

As if he read Mike's mind, Tom took a long final swig from his beer, rose, and walked silently out, leaving behind a half beer, two dollars and change, and an ashtray full of smoldering matches on the bar.

Tom pulled his collar up, walked headlong into the swirling snow, and headed up Seventy-Ninth Street to his parked car. The snow was a pain-in-the-ass type of snow, not heavy at all. It blew into his eyes. It caused him to squint as he tried to avoid a direct hit to the cornea.

"Tommy!"

He heard someone call his name. He turned around and saw Bernie Palis and Steve Dalton standing in front of McGurns.

"Yo," said Tom.

"You coming or going?" asked Bernie.

"No. I'm done. Going home."

Steve and Bernie looked at each other in a knowing and apprehensive manner. Tom caught the exchange and wanted to be in on whatever Steve and Bernie had.

"What?" Tom asked.

They looked at each other once more as if drawing mental straws as to who would tell Tom the news they had.

"What? Come on, what the fuck is going on?"

Bernie drew the short straw. "Uh, listen, Tommy, man, I don't want to be the one who tells you this, but we saw Bedrun at your house a little while ago."

"When?"

"Just a little while ago. About a half-hour."

"Is he still there?"

"I dunno. We were driving by when he went into the gangway. He knows my car, but I don't think he saw it."

"Is he still fucking there?"

Bernie tensed up. Steve took over the responses.

"I don't know. He may be."

Tom stood silent other than emitting a large exhale. Knowing Tom as they did, this was the reaction that Bernie and Steve had feared. They stood speechless, looking at Tom for some clue as to whether they should run or at least find some cover, but Tom's mind was not on either. He shuttered his eyes, and focused on the thought of Bedrun doing Janice. In his house. In his bed.

"I'll fucking kill him!" he said aloud. Like a bull about to make a run at a toreador, Tom snorted, turned toward his car, and walked off.

"Oh shit," said Bernie.

* * * * *

Sheila Perkins sat in the living room of her bungalow, watching the local newscast when she heard the ravings of Tom Sullivan as he exited the home next door. These sounds were not new. Sheila was aware that Tom and Janice could get loud during their arguments. Occasionally, during the summer when windows are open, a projectile could be heard crashing against the wall amidst the yelling. Today she heard muffled shouts of Tom threatening and calling out for Janice.

She wished they could keep it down.

The fights were less frequent since the divorce when Tom moved out, but they would still have the same marital intensity. Sheila knew the routine. She would go over after Tom left and try to console Janice, who would be in tears trying to explain the cause of the current battle.

Sneaking a peek through her front curtains, Sheila watched as Tom slammed the front door and headed to his car. She also saw a bloody towel wrapped around his clenched fist, trying to put the club-like hand in his coat pocket. It scared her. She had never confronted any injuries in her role as an after-the-fact sympathizer, but this latest episode did not look comforting. He got in the car and drove off, the light, dusty, snow peeling off it as it sped down the street and around the corner.

Sheila picked up her phone and dialed Janice's number. Six rings and the answering machine. She grabbed her coat, went to the kitchen drawer, and took out a small set of keys that Janice had given her. She walked out her front door and up to Janice's, where she rang the doorbell three quick times before using her key. The door opened to the dark living room.

"Jan?"

Not getting a response, she continued deeper into the house. The soft light over the stove illuminated the kitchen.

"Jan?"

She proceeded further into the kitchen, where she found the light switch and flicked it on. She saw a large hole in the wall. Blood was splattered around it. Startled, she quickened the pace of her search.

"Jan! Jan! Answer me, please!"

Getting no response, she began to check the other rooms. She looked into Janice's room and the toy room, finding no one. Entering Tommy Jr.'s room, she saw clothing strewn about amid toys and books, and a heap of blankets on the unmade bed. Nothing seemed abnormal.

But suddenly, the blankets moved.

She raced to the bed and pulled back the blankets to find Tommy Jr. beneath them with his hands, feet, and mouth bound with duct tape, his eyes wide with fear.

"My God," gasped Sheila.

She could not remove the tape with her hands, so she ran to the kitchen to look for something to cut the tape. Rifling through the cabinet drawers, she recoiled when she found more blood drippings in the first drawer. She grabbed a pair of scissors from the drawer and went back to Tommy Jr. As she cut through the tape, she noted that the child seemed excited but not overly afraid or panicked, which she sadly speculated was what happens when family squabbling becomes old hat. A door slammed. The boy's hands and legs were free, and she slowly removed the tape from his mouth.

The first words from his mouth hardly surprised her.

"Daddy mad! Daddy mad!"

"It's okay, honey. It's okay. Daddy's gone now. Do you know where Mommy is? Is mommy home?"

"Yes, Mommy home."

"Okay. Stay right here. I'll find Mommy. You stay put, Tommy, okay?"

"Okay."

Having searched the entire house floor, Sheila opened the basement door, flipped on the light switch, and cautiously descended the wooden stairs.

"Jan?"

She walked about the unfinished basement. She could see the entire room from where she stood. The furnace sat tucked into the corner of the room, flanked by a washer and dryer. She approached the furnace area and noticed web-like, dark streams that snaked across the concrete floor. She followed the streams and found two bodies propped up against the wall behind the furnace, each with at least one bullet wound to the head. One was Janice. The other was a male that she did not know, but his right hand twitched. Whoever he was, he was still alive.

CHAPTER TWO

Homes with broken doorbells were a pain in the ass. Pat Sullivan first knocked on the storm door and waited for a response. Getting none, he knocked on the inside door. He felt like he was storming a castle. Boom. Boom. Boom. From the inside, it probably sounded like a police raid or a Trick-or-Treater from Hell.

The respondent answered by peeking through the door window and then momentarily disappearing as the locking mechanism rattled to life and the door swung open, revealing the master of the realm in full view.

Pat was bundled up in his pea coat, hat, and scarf while holding a clipboard. His head would be enveloped in the billowy steam of his breath while silhouetted against the night mercury vapor streetlight.

Houses with broken doorbells were incomplete. All the landscaping, watering systems, painted trim, plastic gnomes, and lawn jockeys do not say anything about the owner when they are missing, but a doorbell that rings when pressed speaks volumes. It shows the owner had some pride, mechanical aptitude, or a brother-in-law in the trades.

Still, Pat was a true believer. If the doorbell was working on even the most neglected home, Pat felt that maybe the owner had just come upon some hard times and would surely bounce back because he had pride and that despite everything else, he made sure his doorbell worked.

Some houses in his precinct even had a doorknocker which is supposed to replace a working doorbell and add a bit of class to the homestead.

"Wrong," thought Pat. The banging of a doorknocker is a medieval and barbaric method that alerts the master of the castle that someone is waiting for them at the front portal. Historically it had a role that extended beyond merely summoning the lord of the house. The loud bangs at the door would help the lord to determine how he would react to the unknown visitor. Fast and hard knocks signal urgency, whereby, depending on his current fiscal or political situation, the lord would either quickly answer it or beat it out the back door. Alternatively, the lord would just let the hired help attend to it if the knocks were slow and easy.

Not so with a working doorbell. Each buzz or ring of a working doorbell is identical. Whether it be a process server, Death, or the Avon Lady, the sound is the same each time. The owner needs to learn the purpose of the visit, which adds a sense of mystery to each arrival.

Pat had time to ponder such things as he made the rounds of his precinct, up and down the city blocks and the front steps of each house. By election time, Pat would talk face-to-face with each voter household. This was how he had worked his precinct for the past thirty-two years, face-to-face, person-to-person.

"Old School". That's what the kids called him. He didn't mind. He took it as a compliment. He believed in the 'old school' as a method and philosophy, and most of the kids did too. He knew all the registered voters in his precinct. Mostly, his visits were just reminders to the regulars to vote and see if anyone in the household needed absentee ballots. Usually, the absentee ballots were for the kids away at school or in the service. He liked to keep atop the situation with the kids and get them to vote regularly as soon as they were of legal age. For all the idealism and verbiage that spouted from these kids, they tended to only vote in the presidential elections. Pat ensured they were aware of the municipal and county elections and, for the most part, had trained the kids well.

After tending to the voters' needs, he would leave them with the endorsed party slate, printed up on beautiful four-color brochures with pictures of each candidate smiling, and asking for the voters' help, and telling them that together they will face the future, blah, blah, blah. He never read the stuff; he just handed it out.

Pat made his way up the front stairs of 7719 S. Hamilton, a well-maintained brick bungalow. Since this was the home of Wally Perick, it had a working doorbell. Pat pressed the illuminated button above the storm door handle. The button went dark momentarily as a two-tone chime rang inside the house. A few seconds later, Wally answered the door.

"Patrick, my friend. Come in."

Wally retained an old-world accent despite having lived in this country for thirty-one years. It was the only thing he kept after leaving Poland. Walteslave Perickovichski arrived in America with his youth, a strong back, five bucks, and nothing else. Now he had a beautiful family and a nice home with a working doorbell.

Pat entered the home and removed his hat.

"Hello, Wally. It's that time again."

"I know, my friend."

Wally did not throw the term 'friend' around loosely. Pat knew and appreciated that fact.

"Well, I'm just here to see if we can count on you and your family on election day," Pat said.

"You can. Of course, you can. We will be there."

"Will you need an absentee ballot for Joe, Eva, or Michael? Will they be away at school?"

"Only Joe and Eva. That damn Michael does not go to school anymore."

"Oh?"

"I'm afraid that Michael does not like to work. He is a lazy bum." Wally's voice rose a bit as he talked about Michael.

Pat attempted to re-direct the conversation. If Wally got going, they would end up drinking his homemade wine in the basement, and Pat had promised Mary that he'd head straight home tonight.

"That's too bad. Okay then, I'll leave these two forms for Joe and Eva. I can pick them up later."

"Yes. Yes. No problem. Patrick, can you stay for some wine?"

"Uh, sure."

"Good."

"But just for one."

"Yes, of course, just one. Come this way then."

Wally walked through the kitchen, down the main hall to the basement door. The bungalow layout was familiar to Pat because he lived in the same type of home. It was familiar to everyone who grew up in the city. They went through the kitchen, past the bath, just before the rear bedroom, down the stairs, and into the wonderful world of Wally Perick. A full basement was painted and dry, with Wally's work area off in the corner.

It consisted of an old couch, two chairs, and a large table that supported a percolating water-cooler bottle full of the next batch of wine. The area acted as a lounge area for Wally and his guests. A rudimentary man cave that was Wally's World. Pat was a welcome guest.

Wally grabbed a bottle from the top shelf, opened it with a cork-screw, and poured the wine into two tumblers. In all the times Pat was a guest of Wally's, he had never seen a real wine glass.

"Salute."

"Slainte'."

The drinks were topped off after the toast. Pat sat on the couch.

"This is good stuff, Wally."

Pat wouldn't know a good wine if it bit him on the ass. As far as he was concerned, if it didn't smell like vinegar, it was good stuff. He took another drink and glanced at his watch. He was going to try this time to get home.

"So, how are things, Patrick? How is the family?"

Pat knocked on the wooden surface of the end of the table. "As good as they can be."

"That is good, Patrick. You are a good man. You work hard and have a beautiful family. That is good."

"How about you, Wally? How are things?" Pat took another drink and settled back. He expected a long answer.

"Some things are not so good, Patrick. Michael is having some problems."

"I'm sorry to hear that. What type of problems?"

"He has met a woman. A woman who is the devil."

"Aren't they all?"

"This one is different. She has him under her control."

"How so?"

"He is always there. At her home. He does whatever she wants. He seems helpless."

"Maybe the kid is just infatuated with her. You know, the kids at that age."

"You mean pussy-whipped?"

Pat chuckled. It didn't seem natural to hear that colloquialism through an old-world dialect.

"Yeah, I guess so. Pussy-whipped."

Wally laughed. "It is true. I learn American expressions, but 'pussy-whipped' is the same all over the world. A young man can get caught up in what a woman offers. This does not exist only in America. Only 'pussy-whipped' does. Why are Americans so vulgar?"

"I have no fucking idea," said Pat. He took another sip of wine.

"He does not come home at night. His job calls here in the morning, looking for him and asking where he is at. I tell them that I do not know, but of course, I do know. He is with that woman."

"Have you ever met this woman?"

"I saw her once. Michael came home for something one time. I see her as she waits in the car. I do not see too much, but she seems older than Michael. Much older. And the car is very expensive."

"Well, Wally, it could be just a phase. Like a lotta kids his age, this is the fun part of their lives. You know, sow some wild oats."

"I do not like this phase. I have raised two other children and have never felt this wild phase from them before."

Pat didn't know how to respond, so he finished his tumbler of wine. Wally instinctively reached over to refill. Pat instinctively accepted.

"Patrick, I ask you for a favor. Michael needs to come home and start his life. He has been out of school for over a year now. He has no interest in college or school or anything like that."

"How can I help?"

"I think I need something to bring him home. Something to attract him. A job. A good job with a future. I was wondering if you could help me in this respect. I want him to work for the city and have a good job. A secure job with benefits and decent money. Can you help me?"

"I can certainly see what's available. I can't promise anything."

"I understand. And I want you to know how hard this is for me. I have always supported you and whomever you supported, Patrick. I have never asked you for any favors, and I never wanted to. Politics is the same everywhere, and I have no problem with that. For every goat or chicken it cost my family in the old country, it cost me a raffle ticket or donation here. It is the same. Only the consideration is different. However, I believe in you. You are a good man; whoever you support is a good, hard-working man like yourself. I will support him."

Pat finished his second glass of wine, reached for the bottle himself, and poured another refill.

"If I had something to bring Michael home, a reason, I think he would leave that woman and start his life. Like his brother and sister."

"Let me check into it. There may be something. You know, of course, that there will be a certain amount of work involved. And those raffle tickets."

"I know, Patrick. I know how it works. How many tickets should I buy from you?"

"We're not raffling off anything right now, but we will be. You can count on that."

"What a country, Patrick. What a country." They both started to giggle, helped along by the wine buzz. Giggling was Pat's cue.

"Wally, I appreciate the hospitality but must get home. Mary is expecting me tonight at a decent hour."

They both rose and shook hands. Wally escorted Pat to the front door.

"Patrick, my friend, I will be seeing you."

"Yes, I will be in touch. I'll come back for the ballot forms."

Pat stepped out into the crisp night air, turned up the collar of his coat, and tugged his hat down over his head. The night was cold and clear. Pat felt a bit flush. The wine seemed to warm him as he began his six-block walk home, a lone figure trudging down the sidewalk, clipboard wedged between his body and arm with his hands in his coat pockets, thinking about doorbells.

When he arrived home, Pat hung his coat and hat in the front hall closet and surveyed the usual scene in the living room. The television was on. Mary was sitting in her customary place at the end of the couch, nursing her evening cup of tea, while Claire slumped awkwardly in the corner chair, looking angry and bored.

"Hello, everyone," said Pat as he leaned over and gave Mary a peck on the cheek.

"How is it outside?" asked Mary.

"Brisk and healthy. Is Curtis in bed?"

"Yes, and don't go in there. He was a pain to get down tonight," said the suddenly animated Claire.

"Okay. Okay. I'm just gonna peek in."

"No, Dad. Please."

"All right. I'm gonna go downstairs and finish this stuff," he announced as he waved his clipboard.

His buzz from the wine had him feeling good, so he grabbed a beer from the "icebox," his archaic term for the refrigerator, and headed for the basement door. He stopped at the door, then tiptoed down the hall two doors down. He cracked the door open and stuck his head into the dark room. Two tiny eyes peered back at him through the bars of the crib. Curtis was almost four years old and still slept in the crib, more because of lack of space than any maturity issues.

"Hey Buddy, I'm home," Pat said, thinking he was being discreet.

"Hi, Grandpa."

"Okay, good night now."

"Grandpa?"

"Yeah, Buddy?"

"Can I get a drink of water?"

"I'll get it. Be right back."

Pat backed out the door and turned to find Claire's scowling face almost directly in his.

"Dad, what are you doing? I asked you not to do this."

"I'm just gonna get him some water. I'll take care of it."

"You bet your ass you will," Claire loudly whispered and turned.

Pat went to the bathroom and filled a small cup of water. He returned to the bedroom to find Curtis standing up in the crib.

"Here you go, Buddy." He handed the cup of water to the child. Curtis took a small sip from it and handed it back to Pat.

"Thank you, Grandpa."

"Sure, sure. Now go to sleep, or we'll both be in trouble."

"Why?"

"Because you should be asleep."

"But I'm not tired."

"I know, but we all have to do things we don't like doing. Lay down now."

Curtis obliged as Pat tucked him in.

"Good night, Buddy."

"Good night, Grandpa."

Pat backed out of the room and went down to the basement. It was finished years ago in a style that reflected the era. One could picture a group of neatly manicured teenagers sitting on the carpeted floor, poodle skirts arrayed, amongst a scattering of 45 RPM records while sipping bottles of Pepsi through a straw. The knotty-pine wood paneling was all the rage then. Pat remembered how good it felt when he completed the remodeling. He had enthusiasm then; the fire burned.

The basement had two rooms. One room was for laundry or minor home repair projects, while the other was finished with the dated paneling and was used to host graduation, communion, and birthday parties. Pat once wished he could have a TV to watch the Bears, but the reception was horrible down there, and he never got around to getting one even after he got cable TV. He did keep a little corner for himself. An old desk and lamp set off away from the laundry. This was his version of Wally World but not nearly as exotic as there was no wine, and the seats were unupholstered.

It didn't matter to Pat anyway. He very rarely had anyone down there anymore. He used it now to keep his precinct records together and as a refuge, away from the family and the rest of the world. He might listen to a Sox game or talk radio or sit silently. Some nights he would sit and listen to the sounds of the laundry. The dryer would drone on with an occasional disruption of the rhythm by a loose penny that someone left in the pocket of their pants, a soothing and relaxing sound. In contrast, the washing machine had a grinding, mechanical sound with a different, more industrial rhythm, a blue-collar mantra.

There were no sounds this evening. The furnace intermittently clicked on and off, but he was oblivious. He took the voter lists from his clipboard, checked off each address he had visited that evening, and compiled his results into a compact summary which he would turn into the ward office the following day.

He headed a crew of six people who would delve into the ward and work on whatever project was the order of the day. These projects varied from street and curb repair and pothole filing to snow removal. This was what Pat liked most, the varied aspects of the job. He had been offered inside jobs several times, but with the money equal, he chose to stay outside.

With the paperwork done, Pat kicked back and sipped his beer. It had been a long day. He thought about Wally and his request for his son. He could put in the good word for the kid, but he had some reservations. If this kid was the lazy bum his old man said he was, what good was he to Pat? The last thing Pat wanted was to have to stick his neck out for this kid and then find out that he was a lazy bastard. Then what? Fire him? That may cause some problems with Wally.

He would have to meet the kid and take him on the rounds one night to see how he did. He would hate disappointing Wally if this kid wasn't up to it.

The Pericks have lived in Pat's precinct for a quarter century. Newlyweds Wally and Maria Perick had bought their home in the early 70s when Pat was promoted to his precinct captain position. As soon as they moved in, Pat warmly greeted them with a welcome basket of bread, salt, wine, and political literature. He got the idea from the movie *It's a Wonderful Life* and added his twist with the literature. He wanted the newcomers to at least know who he was and where he was coming from.

The Pericks appreciated the gesture, and from that day forward, Pat was golden. On many occasions, Pat would find himself testing the latest batch of wine made by Wally, giving his approval after numerous toasts.

Through the years, they had toasted Mayor Daley, the White Sox, Bears, and the Fifty-First Ward organization more times than they had cared to admit. He genuinely liked Wally and his family. They were his first success story, and he could count on at least four votes from the family in every election. He wished more families like the Pericks would move to his precinct.

It was getting more challenging every year to make his target of at least eighty-percent voter turnout. That was the golden number in the world of ward politics. A consistent eighty-percent turnout would ensure Pat's good favor with the ward boss. However, now he had to work harder every election as the ward changed.

What was once a solidly white ward was now becoming a minority-majority, but not just one minority. The influx into the ward's north side was predominantly Hispanic, mostly Mexican, and from the east came the blacks, the African Americans as they now wanted to be called. This double-sided pressure was forcing the prior white majority to the city limits on the southwest side with nowhere to go.

The cops, firemen, teachers, and city workers all had to reside in the city or lose their jobs. Something had to give. The border blocks became integrated with the white folks with no other options. This was Pat's precinct.

Each block became more diverse over the years, and Pat had accepted it as the way things are.

More and more, Pat theorized, the distinction between neighborhoods would be more economic than cultural. The middle-class blacks and Hispanics wanted the same thing that the middle-class whites wanted, a decent place to live and raise a family.

Pat was growing weary of the whole thing. The years had accumulated, and he was about to reap the benefits of all his work for the City of Chicago, particularly the Fifty-First Ward. Retirement was on the horizon. This was his last aldermanic election before he and Mary would ride off into the sunset.

They were planning on looking at some property in Wisconsin, far enough away from the city but close enough for the visits with the grandkids, to maybe build a small cottage-like home for just the two of them. He smiled as he thought about it because he was starting to feel like it would happen. Mary proposed the idea. At first, he wasn't sure about the whole thing, but it grew on him and was currently in full bloom. One more election and then less than a year later, he would be done, done with it all.

CHAPTER THREE

"I heard Daddy yelling. He was mad."

With those words, Chicago Police Detective Larry Wiggin had his probable cause and dispatched a car to pick up Tom Sullivan as a person of interest in the murder of Janice Sullivan and the attempted murder of her associate.

He believed the male victim was Charlie Bedrun, a local hero just released from Stateville after a two-year run. Charlie was one lucky son of a bitch. The bullet he took to the head did not kill him but placed him in Christ Hospital, unconscious and tubed to all sorts of life-sustaining liquids and machines. Wiggin had no idea of his medical condition yet and would have to wait to talk with him, so, for now, he would have a friendly chat with Tom Sullivan when they brought him in.

Tommy Jr. had told the nice policeman what he had heard and seen while, still unbeknownst to him, his mother was being murdered.

"I was sleeping. Someone taped my hands, like this!" He put his hands together as if he was starting to pray.

"Was it Daddy?"

"Yes."

"Did you see him?"

"No, I was sleeping, remember?"

"Then how did you know Daddy tied you up?"

"I heard him yelling. He was mad."

"Was this after you were sleeping?"

"Yes."

"Did Daddy wake you up?"

"Yes. Daddy was mad."

"How mad was he, Tommy?"

"Real mad."

"Did you ever see him this mad before?"

"Sometimes."

Wiggin had already been to Janice Sullivan's basement and found what looked like a classic drug hit. Both bodies were bound and shot in the head. Janice's wound went clean through her head from the right side. Powder burns indicated it was fired from close range. Bedrun's wound looked like a glancing shot. It penetrated the skull but entered and exited in the rear. A sloppy job thought Wiggin. The shooter was either rushed or an amateur. Or both.

Tom Sullivan was certainly at the house near the time of the shootings. The eyes of Sheila Perkins and the ears of Tommy Jr. confirmed that. After Wiggin had surveyed the scene, Sheila was the first person he interviewed. She described the dark home as she entered and saw the blood-splattered hole in the wall. She re-enacted her struggles with the duct tape as she tried to remove it from Tommy Jr. She also voiced her strong opinion of Tom. She wasn't a big fan.

Per Sheila, Tom had a raging temper and would fight with Jan at the drop of a hat, which fits the scenario here. But Wiggin needed more. He also learned from Sheila that Tom liked to hang out at McGurn's during the day. He stopped there on his way back to the precinct.

A report on Bedrun was already on his desk when he returned to the precinct. The prints matched Bedrun, who was in and out of jail since he was 16. He had left Stateville three weeks before after serving time for a drug possession conviction.

Although no drugs were found at the scene, which was expected after a hit such as this, there was some paraphernalia and scales. The equipment found could hardly sustain a large-volume operation, it was enough to establish that the other victim, Janice, could have been dealing with small amounts, possibly for rent money.

Wiggin's educated guess was that Janice may have been a classic wrong-place/wrong-time victim, not involved in the underlying dispute. The wild card was the husband. His presence turned the case into a domestic disturbance matter. He gets wind that his old lady is seeing somebody, and being the hot head that he is, goes over there, finds them in a compromising situation, and then bang-bang.

There's your motive, opportunity, and probably a half-assed defense for temporary insanity. Two eyeballs and four ears put him at the scene at the time close to or right at the shootings. Wiggin, however, did not feel locked in. He put the report down and squirmed in his chair a bit.

They picked up Tom at his apartment. He was sleeping his buzz off when the knock-and-announce squad arrived. He pliantly went with them.

Wiggin found Tom in the spartan interrogation room at the Area Headquarters. Assistant States Attorney John Mullin was already there. The room contained two chairs, a table, and a large two-way mirror that allowed anyone to view and hear Tom's statements. Mullin was there strictly to determine whether charges would be brought against Tom. Wiggin did not doubt that they already had enough to bring the charges. Anything else that Tom said would be icing on the cake.

"Tom, Janice is dead, but I'm sure you know that," said Wiggin.

"What? What do you mean?"

"She's dead, Tom. Found her and her friend in the basement. Both were shot in the head. You were there. Want to tell us about it?"

"Janice is dead?" Tom dropped his head and held the bridge of his nose with his bandaged and manacled hand.

"You have an accident today?"

Tom lifted his head, not knowing what Wiggin meant.

"Your hand. What happened? Did you fight with someone today? I'll bet that's your blood splatted on Janice's kitchen wall."

Tom realized what Wiggin was driving at. "Hey man, I was there, but I had nothing to do with this. This is crazy. She was my wife."

Mullin chimed in. "Did you know Charlie Bedrun?"

"Yeah, what about him?"

"Did you know he was at Janice's house?"

Tom squirmed in his chair. "No."

"No?"

"Yeah, that's what I said. No."

"Well, that's funny," interrupted Wiggin, "because Steve Dalton and Bernie Palis told me something different. I talked to them at McGurns. They told me that they told you Charlie was there. They also told me you threatened to kill Bedrun when you left the bar. Are they lying?"

"Fuck you; I'm done. I'm not saying anything else. I want a lawyer."

"Suit yourself, tough guy. But he better be fucking good because he's gonna have a tough case."

Tom closed his eyes. He realized that Janice was gone and he was being accused of killing her. "I loved her. I loved her," he repeated to no one in particular as his body jerked in spasms when he started to cry.

"Get this fucking loser out of here!" yelled Wiggin.

CHAPTER FOUR

Eddie Byrne's shiny black Lexus pulled from the alley into its customary spot behind the Fifty-First Ward office. With briefcase in hand, he exited the car and entered the building through the rear door. He proceeded past the makeshift dining area, which doubled as a storage room.

The room acted as a haven for cheap lawn signs, each with Eddie Byrne's smiling face and name on the front. The signs were stapled to wood slats that sink into voters' front lawns displaying their aldermanic preference.

Eddie continued through the back room and entered a partitioned area used for office space. Desks and chairs were strewn about, indicating that the layout was temporary. Normally the desks and chairs did not belong there. They were on loan from a local construction company with extensive dealings with the city.

This was the nerve center of the *Citizens for Byrne* campaign headquarters. Strategy and coffee brewed every hour. Election posters hung on the walls along with ward maps and voter registration lists from nearly forty precincts. Handwritten on each list was a mark next to the address of each voter who had been contacted. Campaign literature costs money, so it made no sense to revisit the already enlightened.

Eddie weaved his way through the orderly mess, nodded to his staff, who were mostly busy on the phone and entered his private office at the end of the corridor just outside the war room. That's where he found Walt Zeal, Billy Lopresti, and Warney Richmonds, his right-hand man, discussing a pressing election matter.

"Who the hell has been stealing our lawn signs?" Warney asked loudly to anyone who would listen.

"Where at?" asked Walt.

"East side, in fifteen, twelve, and thirty-one."

"First I heard about it. Maybe Robin's people?"

"Yeah, but who?"

"I don't know," pitched in Billy, "but if I find him, I'll cut his balls off."

"Hey guys, give me a minute, will you?' said Eddie as he entered the room.

The three recognized Eddie's way of telling everyone to get the hell out. He seemed to be in one of his mysterious moods again, so they cleared out without any of the banter that morning greetings generally consisted of. With a quick wave, Eddie closed the door behind them, took a seat behind his desk, reached into the bottom drawer, withdrew a bottle of Dewars Scotch and a glass, poured out two fingers, and slammed it down. He loosened his tie and poured another drink, and sipped it. He gazed straight ahead, staring at nothing while at the same time trying to see everything.

He remembered having a lucid vision at one time. He knew what he wanted to accomplish and had a solid map etched in his mind like stone. Idealistic? Yes, of course, but not stupid. He did not enter the world of Chicago politics without knowing that there would be many unsavory alliances. Sometimes you just had to hold your nose and extend your hand.

His first election was exciting, and he reveled in it. He slept on a cot in the back of a storefront at his campaign headquarters on Seventy-Ninth Street. Every day he would wake up at the crack of dawn and greet commuters at the train station or meet the ladies in the beauty parlors and the men in the taverns. Flesh-to-flesh campaigning, he liked to call it.

But times change. Appease the masses; that was always the case, but now there were so many damn sets of masses. It became more of a juggling act than a singular act of appeasement. Issues important to one group were issues the other groups opposed. Somewhere in the middle is where Eddie sought refuge. The one thing he learned in sixteen years of public service is that you can't please everyone. Someone will always feel slighted; thus, one must always continue to watch one's back. In law school, they taught him to "think like a lawyer," but he received no formal education on how to "think like a politician". That he learned on the job. Despite all this, he still felt a bit of the fresh idealism from his first term. He wanted to do the right thing and felt that the basic duty of the alderman was to provide essential services: street paving, snow removal, tree trimmings. He made damn sure that they were distributed evenly throughout the ward.

He tried to be fair and deal with the entire ward in an even-handed manner, but it was becoming more challenging. Like any politician, Eddie had to follow the money. Campaigns cost a lot of money, and the money became the key to any chance he had of moving up the political ladder, maybe to a countywide office.

With the money came the special favors that were expected in return. As a result, the ward services tended to become lopsided, and suddenly, it became an issue for his challengers. He had to campaign harder for this election than his first. He was spending the political capital he had accumulated through the years, getting outside help for the streets and the like. He was sweating this one out, leading him to align himself with certain entities in the ward that he normally would not associate himself with.

Some of these associations were just plainly needed, like help from outside the ward. Some others were relationships that Eddie hoped he would not have cause to regret. He took another sip of scotch and looked at his watch. The Reverend Zuko was due in his office in fifteen minutes.

Pat Sullivan entered the ward office through the front door. It was later than he wanted it to be. He got off to a slow start that morning. When he woke up, Mary was still asleep, which was extremely rare. He asked her if she was feeling all right. She groggily responded in the affirmative. Not believing her, he made some toast and tea and brought it to her in bed.

"Stay in bed today. I think you might be coming down with something," he gently ordered before he left.

He continued into the office past the long Formica counter in the lobby and into the rear office area to a community desk situated in the corner. He sat down and spilled out the contents of his clipboard, voter lists, each marked and tabulated with the total drawn at the bottom of each in red ink. He made copies of the lists for his records and placed the originals in an "IN" box attached to the wall next to the desk.

"Good morning, Pat."

He turned and saw the young and lovely Marita before him extending a Styrofoam cup of coffee, black, no sugar, to him.

"Marita! You are so good to me. How are you this morning?"

"I'm fine, Pat. Here's your coffee."

"Always thinking of me. God love ya."

Pat genuinely liked Marita. She had joined Eddie's staff about four months before. He loved her attitude, young, pretty, and with nothing but future in front of her. He guessed that she was probably about twenty-two years old and Hispanic. He would never ask a lady her age or racial background. Just not the gentlemanly thing to do.

"Before you leave, he wants to see you."

"Okay. I have to load some signs into the car. I hear him in there now with someone. Will he be long?"

"Probably not. His meetings with Reverend Zuko usually don't last long."

"Who?"

"The Reverend Zuko."

"Who's he?"

"I think he runs a shelter or something on Halsted. I know he takes a lot of literature with him every time he comes here."

"Okay, I get it-friend of Eddie. I'll get my stuff in the car and come back in. I need to pull around to the rear."

Pat brought his white Ford Taurus to the rear of the building and backed in to make loading the signs into his trunk easier. As he reached for the door handle to enter the building, it swung open, revealing a large, dark, and formally clad man with a cologne-stained air of self-importance about him. He looked down at Pat, glaring, then instantly smiled broad.

"Excuse me, sir. I did not realize you were there."

"That's all right," said Pat.

The man was dressed in all black, with a cape draped over his massive broad shoulders, half concealing a silk shirt and neatly pressed pants. A large cross, centered in the middle of his ample chest, was dangling from a gold chain around his neck. He held in his right hand a glossy black cane that was topped with the gold figurehead of an animal with its mouth open and exposed fangs. Pat could not figure out what type of animal it was, but whatever it was, it was pissed off.

From beneath a large black fedora, his long black curls glistened and extended to his shoulders. On his cape, he wore a campaign button that read "Byrne for Alderman" with Eddie's smiling face peering right back at him.

"My name is Reverend Zuko," he said, extending his catcher's mitt-sized right hand.

"Name is Pat Sullivan. Pleased to meet you," said Pat as he allowed his right hand to be swallowed up in the Reverends.

From behind the Reverend, exiting the door, were four black men, each dressed as impeccably as the Reverend but without the extravagance. Each also wore a campaign button. They brought out boxes of literature and put them in a Cadillac Escalade that was parked next to Pat's car.

Pat deducted that they were on the same side.

"What area are you guys working? I don't want to overlap you guys or anything. We have enough work to do without having to do it twice," said Pat.

"I heard that, my brother. We will be working the east end of the ward. But my real work does not end there. My work, brother, is worldwide. To all of mankind, wherever he may be situated, from Galilee to the China Sea. From Ohio to Kosovo. From Mandaly to Bombay. But for brother Byrne, the Lord and his foot soldiers will be working the east side from Racine to Halsted."

"That's good to know," said Pat, "I'm just west of you in the nineteenth precinct."

"Well, God bless you, Brother Sullivan. May your efforts be strong, and the fruits of your labor be satisfying."

The Reverend then got into the back seat of the Escalade, followed by his crew, and drove off. Pat watched, not sure if he comprehended what he had just seen. Oh well, he thought to himself, any friend of Eddies is a friend of mine. He finished loading his car.

Eddie sat in his office. He always needed to wind down after a visit from Zuko. He reached back down to the bottom drawer, poured another glass of scotch, and sipped it.

There was a knock at the door. Eddie capped the bottle, put it back in the desk, and downed the rest of the scotch from the tumbler.

"Come in."

The door opened, and Pat walked in. "Hi, Ed. You wanted to see me?"

"Did I? Oh yeah, yeah. Come on in, Pat. I'm going to get some help for you. I want you to know that it's coming. We are going to put at least three workers in most of the precincts. We need to hit every fucking door in this ward."

"I don't need any help, Ed. I hit every door in my ward anyway. You know that."

"I do, Pat, I do. I was looking out for you, that's all. How much time do you have left?"

Pat looked at his watch. "One year, ten months, three days and, um, fourteen hours and thirty-two, no, thirty-three minutes."

"That's what I mean. It would be a shame to get sick or hurt or something being so close to retirement. I'm trying to cover your back, Pat, not break it. You deserve it."

"Thanks, Ed, I appreciate it, I do. But I would just as soon do this last one by myself. You know, go out in a blaze of glory."

"Okay, partner. Suit yourself."

"Is that it?"

"Yeah. How's everything at home? How's Mary?"

"Good. She was a little under the weather this morning, but she'll be fine."

"And Tommy?"

"I don't know. I haven't talked with him in a while."

Eddie noticed Pat's reluctance to talk about Tommy and steered the conversation away. "I got a couple of tickets for the Hawks this Friday. Are you interested?"

"No thanks. I'm not gonna give Wirtz a cent of my money, even if they are free. I'll read about it in the news tomorrow. By the way, who was that walking out of here with his posse just now?"

"The Reverend Zuko. He runs a soup kitchen on Halsted," Eddie replied nonchalantly.

"He seems quite the character," replied Pat as he glanced at the glass on the desk. "Little early for that, isn't it?"

"Early is relative to the person who has risen," said Eddie.

Pat gave a confused look in response and shrugged. "Okay, well, I gotta get my day started. I'll see you."

Eddie gave a wave as Pat walked out of the office, closing the door behind him, and reached back down to his bottom drawer again.

Mary had tossed and turned, getting little sleep that night. Pat woke her at six. She sat up slowly in bed and accepted the toast and tea Pat had offered her. She forced herself to stay awake, not wanting to deny Pat his act of TLC nor wanting him to know that she was sick.

Pat set the food on a serving tray on the nightstand beside the bed. The tea was steaming hot, and the toast was a tad burnt with nothing spread over it. Mary issued no complaints as she knew she would not touch any of it and would go right back to sleep the minute Pat left. This quickly became her normal routine when Pat left in the morning.

Every day was different depending on what Claire and Curtis were up to. Generally, she would find herself asleep on the couch or lying across the bed for just one good nap. Lately, she found herself napping longer and with more frequency. Today she would try to take a long nap as Claire and Curtis were going to the mall and would be gone for at least the morning. She had to steal naps here and there to keep up with her day as the chemotherapy was now taking its toll on her.

Mary firmly believed that the Church and family were above all else. Nothing else mattered or was relevant in her life. The older she became, the more resolute she was about this belief. It was all simple and basic to her. God had a plan for everyone, and she was living the script out.

That was why her reaction to the doctor's news that she had breast cancer was so calm. It was God's will. God's plan. God's doing.

Six months earlier, Mary's doctor had found a sizable lump in her left breast during a routine examination. A biopsy revealed it was cancerous and metastasized to her liver, spleen, and lymph nodes. She decided to keep the diagnosis and treatment secret from the rest of her family, for she thought it would do no good to have them agonizing over her. She thought it would be treated like any other ailment and, with a heavy dose of prayer, would go away like a cold or the flu.

When she started the therapy treatments, she explained to Pat that the redness of her skin was related to the blood pressure medication she was taking. When she started to lose her hair, she wore hats. Pat never said anything about the hats. But she was skeptical, so she flat-out told him that she was starting to appreciate the vanity and stylishness of hats. He shook his head at the revelation because it was never like Mary to be stylish. However, it made her happy, so he never thought twice about it.

Finally, when hats alone could not hide her hair loss, she bought a wig that was as near and close to her regular hair color and style as possible. Despite her apprehensions that Pat would see through the wig ruse, he never did.

The days of intimacy with her husband were long gone. Although they slept together every night in the same bed, Pat had not tried to make love to her in years, and Mary never instigated anything. In the past, when they were intimate, Pat would always start things by reaching over in the middle of the night and just touching her on her arm, his signal that he was ready. She responded immediately, like she was constantly awaiting the magic middle-of-the-night touch. Mary never refused but never embraced the ritual, either. She considered it her duty and was to be there when her husband, this man she made a vow with before God, called and reached out in the night.

When they made their vows forty-five years earlier, she promised to "love, honor and obey" and obey she would. However, through the years, the midnight touches from Pat became rarer until they ceased altogether, becoming a distant familial memory to be stored in a shoe box like old report cards or locks of baby hair.

The treatment continued for five months as Mary kept secret both her doctor's appointments and prayers for a cure. She believed these secret treatments and pleas to the Lord would work, the disease would be discharged from her body for good, and her life for her family would continue as usual. She prayed constantly. God works in mysterious ways, and somehow this would be a test for her, a test she would pass with faith and prayer and a wee bit of help from the medical community.

Unfortunately, the treatments were not much help, and the stubborn evil disease would not recede from her organs. Hence, her doctor presented her with a choice, she could continue the treatments which were not working, or he could open her up and attempt to remove the deadly growth from her body. The percentages either way were not good, he explained. She had a twenty percent chance of survival from the surgery.

The treatments did not affect her condition, and the doctor made it seem like they would be a waste of precious time. Mary was not concerned with numbers or odds; they would take care of themselves as this was all part of God's plan for her. She calmly asked the doctor when she would need her decision. He responded, "The sooner, the better." She knew she could not make such a decision without Pat's input. Her secret would have to be revealed finally.

She woke up that day intending to discuss the matter with Pat.

To continue the chemotherapy may be less of a burden on her family. Her friend, Bessie, would drive her to the doctor, and she would be home before anyone found out where she was, but she knew she would be neglecting her family to a certain extent by feeling tired and nauseous all the time from the treatments.

She also wondered how long it would be before Pat found out about the wig she wore. Plus, the chemo treatments were just not working. Her chances were probably better with the surgery, but she did have concerns regarding the actual procedure; she had never had so much as a broken bone or a stitch in her life, so her fear was based on the unknown. She also knew that she could not make the decision considering only herself- she needed to decide how it would affect her family.

She kept the family together as it was, for despite her day-to-day chores and gestures that conserved their family unit, she also knew that she was the icon that acted as the center of their family life. Rarely did she ever get into an argument with Tom or Claire regarding their actions or duties. Pat was around for that. She was the mediator between Pat and the kids, oh-so-subtle but oh-so effective. If Pat ever figured out her role, he never let on. Maybe he knew, but Mary didn't care, it worked, and the family was still intact. Tenuous but intact.

She would opt for the surgery, but she would have to tell Pat as soon as possible.

She thought that decision was more difficult to execute than to make as she sat in her bed next to the tray of uneaten breakfast. The whole issue tired her out. Everything tired her out now. Slowly her eyes closed, and she turned over and went back to sleep.

Mary had slept for nearly two hours when she was stirred by two little feet tromping towards her and a gentle tug on the sleeve of her nightgown from her grandson Curtis.

"Gramma, gramma. Wake up. Look what I have."

She found herself face-to-face with the bulging eyes of Kermit the Frog, the latest prize from a happy meal.

"Oh, that's nice," said Mary. "Let me get my glasses." She slowly reached over to the nightstand, buying some time to get her wits about her, before putting them on. She took the figure from the boy and studied it.

"Kermit has such big eyes, and he sure is green."

"Yeah, and I ate everything today. Just ask Mommy."

The boy melted Mary's heart every time she saw him. A little big for his age, Curtis had beautiful light brown skin and a close haircut, barely allowing a trace of the hairline to develop. His father, Adam, whom neither Pat nor Mary had ever met, was long gone. A subject that remains open with Claire.

Claire entered the room. "Were you sleeping?"

"No, I'm awake now. It's okay." Mary looked up at Claire. "Are you hungry? I see that Curtis ate. I can fix you something."

"No, lay back down. I'll get something. It's time for his nap anyway. You've been tired lately, huh?"

"I think I may be coming down with something. I haven't been able to get a full night's sleep lately."

"Do you want me to call Dr. O'Hara?"

"No, there's no need. I'll be all right. I was going to get up now anyways."

Mary swung around the bed and placed her feet on the floor while reaching over to grab her slippers. She overextended herself and fell onto the floor with a loud thud.

"Mom! Are you all right?"

More embarrassed than hurt, Mary replied that she was "Just fine" and attempted to lift herself. She realized that she could not get up by herself. Claire lifted her back up to the bed.

"Are you sure you feel okay? Did you hit your head?"

"No, no, I'm fine. Hand me my slippers, would you?"

Claire bent over and put the slippers on Mary's feet for her as Curtis chimed in. "Gramma, what happened?"

"Nothing honey, I'm okay."

"Just how did you fall, Ma?"

"Just got a little dizzy, that's all. Help me get up."

Claire extended her hand to Mary and pulled gently.

"Come on, I'll guide you. Where do you want to go?"

"Stop, let go of my hand," Mary said softly.

Claire obliged and allowed Mary to proceed by herself. She wobbled for three steps and started to teeter towards the dresser, quickly saving herself by grabbing the dresser top with a desperate clutch.

"Okay, that's it," Claire said as she reached for Mary. "You're going back to bed. Both of you can take your naps together here in the same bed. Curtis, get your shoes off."

"I want my blankie."

"I'll get your blankie. Ma, do you want your blankie too?"

"Very funny," replied Mary as she lay back down.

Mary stared at the ceiling after enduring her daughter's maternal instincts. Curtis nestled close to her in the natural cradle formed by her arm and body while still clutching Kermit the Frog, his gentle breathing keeping rhythm with Mary's heart. She thought a child's innocence was the purest thing in the world and deeply loved her grandchildren.

She would have to be around to help nurture this child. God love Claire, but she was still a child, learning and innocent to a certain extent. Mary had to live through her sickness. She would have the surgery, and Pat would have to be told. Mary fell asleep.

CHAPTER FIVE

Pat got home early. He had gotten a disturbing phone call earlier in the day. He sat at the kitchen table, nursing a beer and gazing straight ahead. Curtis came into the room with Kermit the Frog, his prize from McDonalds, to show Grandpa.

"Grandpa, look what I got."

Returning to earth, Pat acknowledged Curtis's presence as he took the toy from the boy. "What is that? A frog?"

"It's Kermit."

"Oh yeah. I see it now. Wow. That's a neat toy."

"Come on, kiddo. It's bath time. Let's go." Claire said as she entered the room, holding onto a pair of Curtis's pajamas.

"Do I have to?" pleaded Curtis.

"Yes, you do. Now."

Curtis obliged and marched to the bathroom with Claire. Suddenly the boy turned around, scooted around his mother, ran to Pat, and hugged him. The act caught Pat in mid-drink from his beer can, and the ensuing jolt of a three-year-old boy with a head start caused him to spill some of the beer down the front of his shirt and on the boy.

"Great. Now you smell like a lush. Get in the bathtub," said Claire.

"I love you, Grandpa," Curtis said while finishing the hug.

Pat smiled, wiped the beer from his chin, and suddenly felt a wave of emotion sweep over him that he tried to control. "I love you too, Buddy," he whispered back.

Pat nonchalantly wiped a small tear from his right eye. He took another sip of beer and listened to mother and child as they had a small but significant bonding experience. With the water running in the background, he overheard them talk.

Claire patiently answered Jesse's questions on various subjects ranging from the day's activities to the color of the sky. Her voice had a tone that expressed maternal manners that he had never noticed before. It was ripe, full of wisdom and guidance that only a parent could possess. He wondered where she acquired this trait. He tried to recall if he had bathed his children when they were Curtis's age. He couldn't, and it bothered him.

He remembered the night Curtis was born. Claire was sitting upright on the couch in the living room. She and Mary were watching "Wheel of Fortune" and settling down for the evening when Curtis signaled his arrival. Like a crack fireman hearing the alarm bell, Mary sprang into action. She directed Pat to get the pre-packed overnight bag into the car and go out and get it started while she assisted Claire by helping her off the couch and draping a coat over her shoulders. The hospital was a twenty-minute drive. Pat drove while Claire and Mary sat in the rear seat. Claire's contractions increased.as he drove. Pat swore he had never heard such moaning. He weaved through the light traffic faster than normal but drove with caution. He got an adrenalin rush when he turned right on a red light, hand despite the sign posted at the intersection that such a move was prohibited. He almost wished a cop would pull him over so he could get an escort to the hospital and follow the lit-up squad car through red lights and stop signs. That would have been fun. But no such luck. He continued his fast pace to the hospital with his daughter groaning in the back seat.

"It's okay, dearie," comforted Mary as she dabbed a moist cloth on Claire's forehead.

"Ma, I have to tell you something."

"Save it dear. Save it. You need your strength. Don't speak. You need to rest up between contractions."

"But ma, it's about the baby. I..." Claire could not finish her sentence as another wave of pain arrived, contorting her face into a picture of twisted agony. She grabbed her mother's hand and squeezed tightly, making Mary wince for a quick second.

"Not another word. We are almost there. Be quiet, Sweetie," Mary consoled.

Pat arrived at the hospital's emergency entrance and watched as the orderlies whisked Claire and Mary off, leaving him to park the car. Twenty minutes later, he found them in the birthing room, a startling difference from when the last time Pat attended such an event. The room looked like it could be in someone's home. There were patterned drapes on the windows, wallpaper on the walls, nice-looking furniture, a couch, and a television. Hell, this room reminded him of the Motel 6 they used to stay at on vacation.

While Pat marveled at the new world of birthing, Claire lay in the bed holding on to Mary's hand while she continued the excruciating cycle of pre-birth. She was silent as Mary had directed in between contractions. She closed her eyes each time and tried to sleep, hoping the entire process was a dream from which she would wake up and find herself alone and happy, lying in her bed in an apartment in the Lake View area. She no longer tried to tell her mother about the baby, about Adam. She would soon find out.

Pat got comfortable on the couch in front of the television. After getting accustomed to the moans that arrived every two minutes, he watched as a Marine from Bakersfield, California was about to buy a vowel.

While Claire rested between her contractions, Mary motioned him to the hallway.

He dutifully followed.

"Shouldn't we contact Adam?" said Mary.

"Yeah, I guess. But how? Do we even know where he's at?"

Mary shook her head. This was terrible. A man was about to become a father and would not even know it.

Suddenly it dawned on Pat that he had never met Adam. A meeting was arranged a few times, but they had fallen through for what Pat thought were legitimate reasons. Adam couldn't get off work, or he was visiting his sick father.

"Can Claire give us his number?"

"I don't know if she has it on her. Not now, anyway. She is about to give birth to your second grandchild. She's a little busy right now."

Pat felt he had asked a stupid question and tried to let it go, but he suddenly felt uneasy about the whole subject.

"Well, I guess there isn't anything we can do right now. I'm going to get a paper and sit in the lobby."

"No, don't bother. We could be here a long time. Why don't you go back home, and I'll call you when the time comes."

"All right then. Call if you need me."

Driving home, Pat decided to stop at McGurn's and kill some time. It would be at least a couple of hours before he heard any word, and he had nothing to do at home. When he entered the bar, it was just about empty. Otis Morris, a regular, sat at the bar. Stutterin' Dave sat in the corner. He smiled when he saw Pat walk in. McGurn was behind the bar leaning over his *Tribune* sports section. Pat took a corner stool near the window where he could see the television. He wanted to see if the Marine from Bakersfield had won any money, but McGurn had on another animal movie. This time, the subject was the Serengeti Plain and what would become of the creatures when the dry season arrived, and the water hole dried up. "Like a jungle at closing time," thought Pat.

McGurn came over with a coaster and a smile.

"Howarya, Pat."

"Okay, Mike. Waiting on some news from Claire. She went into the hospital with labor pains. Mary is with her now."

"That so? Well, this one's on the house, Grandad. You want a shot of something?"

"No, I'll wait on the shots. Don't want to jinx anything. I'll have a beer."

McGurn took a beer glass from below the bar and tilted it under the tap. When the glass was full, with a small head of foam, McGurn considered it a masterpiece. A perfectly poured beer was put in front of Pat.

Pat took a sip as the phone rang behind the bar. Pat's thoughts went back to the hospital and Adam. Strange shit. He never met the guy and never talked with him, yet here I am, the grandfather of his kid.

Pat's courtship of Mary was far more traditional. He even asked Mary's father for her hand in marriage. She was worth it. She was a star. A glowing, shining, glimmering bright spot on a dark landscape. He fell in love with her the day he first met her.

He used to say that it was like he got hit over the head with a two-by-four. The rituals and customs then were different. He was about to head off to Korea, courtesy of Harry Truman, when he met her at a St. Rose's Church Hall dance. He cut a heroic and sharp figure in his uniform.

He was not concerned about her age then. She was 16 and he was twenty, about to ship out for two years of active duty. This was how loved worked. He would leave, do his job for God and Country, come home to his young bride-to-be, and start a family and homestead. That was the way you did it then.

McGurn came back from the phone. On the television, a pack of hyenas chased down an old lion whose better days were well behind him.

"Any word yet?"

"No, nothing. I don't expect to hear anything for a while anyway." Pat took another sip of beer. "Hey, Mike. Do you remember when you first went out with your wife?"

"Which one?"

"The first. The one you thought you would spend the rest of your life with."

"Well, yeah."

"Was it good? Was it real? Did you think you set for life?"

"Yeah. It was good, and it was real, and yeah, at the time, I thought it would go on forever. Tells you how much I know. Fucking bitch."

"Do you think kids feel the same way today?"

"What do you mean?"

"Do the kids feel the same way today? When they meet, do they feel like they are on top of the world? Do they know that when they make a vow that it's for the long haul? It takes a lot of effort and work to be with someone for life."

"I dunno Pat. Some do, I would think."

"Yeah, some do, but it seems to be the exception now, not the rule. Now, when couples tell other people that they've been married for ten or fifteen years, they're looked at as if they are a fossil. You know what I mean?"

"Maybe, maybe not," replied McGurn. "I agree that it's a whole new world out there now, especially with the kids. They got shit that we never had to worry about, but on the other hand, common sense is no different. Common sense is still the same now as it was back then. Kids shacking up with other kids and having kids. You're almost proud now if your kid is married when they have their kids."

Realizing that he had described Pat's current situation, McGurn turned contrite. "Sorry, Pat."

"It's okay. I was just wondering if it was me or what." Pat finished his beer. McGurn grabbed the empty glass and filled it with another perfect pour.

"It's not you, Pat. Don't worry about it. Kids today are all doing it."

Despite McGurn's efforts to ease his mind, Pat still felt confused and ill at ease. This feeling had gnawed at him slowly during Claire's pregnancy, always present but never critical. Tonight, it manifested into some reflective beast searching for sustenance in the form of answers.

Pat felt he had been a good father. He was around most of the time if he wasn't working. He did have to work long hours some-times, but he had to put food on the table and shelter over his family's heads.

Wasn't that what he was supposed to do? Wasn't that the role of the male in any species?

Throughout centuries of human existence, the male of the species hunted or foraged. What he brought home would provide food and clothing for the family. The female would care for the home and offspring. These were the roles as they evolved, and no one questioned them, until now.

Pat had other questions.

Could he have made a difference in his kids? Would his kids have turned out differently if he had been around more or if he paid more interest in them while they were young? Would Tom have turned out differently if he had gone to his little league games?

Many a night, Pat would come home after a ten or twelve-hour day, and the kids would attempt to show him a finger painting or some homework from school. He would dismiss it and ask Mary to serve him dinner. Afterward, he had a can or two of beer, watched the late news, and went to bed.

Did he cheat his children?

He didn't feel too good about the answers forming in his head. A second voice tried to counter everything.

It could have been worse. Neither of your kids turned into a drug addict or an axe murderer, and they still call occasionally.

Although Tom could be a hothead and an occasional asshole, he was a good kid. He finished high school and, with Pat's help, went to work for the city. He has been there for almost ten years. He got married to a fine girl and has a beautiful family. He works hard. He's had some problems with his marriage, but he loves his son.

Does that make him a bad guy?

Early in Tom's life, after the doctors had told Pat and Mary that he would be their only child due to Pat's weak bullets, they discussed a course of tough love for the kid to avoid any issues with Tom becoming a spoiled only child. Tough love was not in Mary. Pat knew that all along, for she only had unconditional love, the maternal blinders that every mother develops for their children.

Could that whole thing have backfired on him? Could he have gotten closer to the kid?

With Claire, Pat at least tried for a while. She was their miracle baby. After Tom was born, they were not having any luck with child number two, so they went to see the doctor, who told them about Pat's lack of ammunition. However, eleven years after Tom, along came Claire. It was a surprise to both of them. Mary was 43 years old. Pat was concerned about both mother and child's health. Mary had a tough time with the birth, about 23 hours worth of trouble. He remembered that he held his breath for what seemed like the entire period.

He exhaled when the nurse came to the waiting room to tell him that both mother and daughter were okay. The relief that he sensed was one of those times when you recall how you felt. He remembered the distinct hospital aroma that lingered in the waiting room, the drab sand color of the walls, and the large mole the nurse had on her right upper lip. He left the hospital vowing to be the best father a kid ever had.

How long did that last? A year or so?

Work, elections, and general life took his time away. He fell back into his old habits and before long, he was back to dismissing the homework and asking Mary for supper. The miracle baby had become routine.

McGurn filled Pat's glass again, and Pat emptied it again before leaving the bar. Upon his arrival home, he scrounged about the cabinets for an easy and quick meal when his eye caught the blinking red light of the answering machine. He pressed the message button and heard Mary's voice.

"Pat, we need you down at the hospital now. It's about nine-thirty. Claire and the baby are fine, but we need you at the hospital as soon as you get this."

She sounded tired. Oh well, supper would have to wait. He and Mary could stop somewhere on the way home. He drove to the hospital. Mary met him at the entrance.

"How is everyone?" Pat said.

"Fine, fine."

"Boy or girl?"

"She had a boy."

"How big was the lad?"

"Nice size, eight pounds six ounces."

"Good then. Where are he and Claire?"

"Claire is asleep in her room. The baby is in the nursery."

"Can we go up and see him?"

"I suppose we can go up. If you like."

Mary's response struck Pat as somewhat cold and matter-of-fact. After they checked in at the front desk, he followed her to the elevators. She walked in silence.

They entered the sterile neon-lit hallway leading to the nursery windows. Mary produced a slip of paper with the name "Sullivan" written on it and displayed it through the window to the nurse on the other side of the glass.

The nurse reached into a crib, pulled out the bundle, gently placed it in the crook of her arm, and approached the window. Pat smiled as the nurse approached.

"She has the wrong one!" roared Pat.

The tiny face that peered back at them from beneath the sterile blanket belonged to a black child. Pat laughed louder as he attempted to point out to the nurse her mistake.

"Wrong one!" Pat mouthed for the nurse, "You've got the wrong baby."

"Pat."

"You... have... the... wrong... one," Pat slowly and distinctly mouthed to the nurse.

"No, she doesn't," said Mary softly.

Pat continued to laugh at the nurse with the bundle behind the window. He turned to Mary, "Tell her she has the wrong one."

Mary solemnly shook her head.

"What?"

"No, she doesn't."

The smile slipped from Pat's face and was quickly replaced by a look of confusion mixed with a bit of fear. "What do you mean?"

"Pat, that baby is your grandson."

He could not comprehend Mary's last statement. It was not logical or reasonable. "What was that you just said?"

"That child is your grandson. That is Claire's baby."

"Oh, bullshit! What the hell is that? We're gonna sue this hospital for mixing up these babies!" He walked towards the elevators.

"No way! No damn way!" he muttered to himself. Raising his voice, he turned to Mary. "We gotta talk to the hospital manager. Come along, Mary!"

She stayed put.

He turned again to her, "Come on, will you? Let's go and straighten this out."

Mary and Pat were then in their 43rd year of marriage. Pat had never heard Mary utter so much as the word "hell," much less any other expletive. But right then and there, she told him, "This child is your fucking grandson, whether you choose to believe it or not!"

At that moment, the truth hurt. The double blast of Mary's cursing and the brutal news about the child smacked Pat back to reality. He paused, looked down at his shoes, and then turned back to Mary.

"Okay then. What time should we be back tomorrow?"

A loud voice from the bathroom brought Pat back to the present.

"Curtis! See what you're doing? You're getting water all over the floor!"

Pat shook his beer can and realized it was empty. He got up to get another one when the front door opened. Mary bundled up in her coat and scarf, stepped into the kitchen. She seemed surprised to see Pat drinking beer in the mid-afternoon.

"What are you doing here?" she asked.

Pat reached into the refrigerator, shut the door, and returned to the kitchen table.

"Sit down, Dear. I have something to tell you."

"And I you, as well. I suppose it's good that you're home now because I need to go over something with you," said Mary. She unbuttoned her coat and draped it over one of the kitchen chairs.

She had decided it was finally time to go over her life and death options with Pat and explain her sickness.

"Tom's in a little trouble," Pat said.

Mary's eyes hardened.

"Jan and a friend of hers were found shot last night. Jan is dead. Tommy was seen there just before it happened," he continued.

"What are you saying?"

"They've accused Tommy of the murder."

Mary felt her knees buckle. She grabbed the back of the chair for support. Pat helped her sit down. Trying to collect her wits about her, she placed her hands on her temples and closed her eyes, like a medium trying to see into the future. For a minute, she thought she was going to be sick. A rush of nausea rose in her throat, which she quickly stifled. Pat still had his hands on her shoulders, holding her steady as he tried to anticipate her reaction. Finally, she opened her eyes and looked up to Pat.

"My God," she paused and returned to the table, "This is untrue. It can't be."

"It's not. We both know that," Pat said in a consoling tone.

His response did not please her. She was well aware of Tommy's temper, and forgetting her own situation, anger replaced her queasiness.

"Tommy has a temper, yes, but he is not capable of this type of act. I will not believe it. We will fight this to the end!" roared a now livid Mary.

"I called Eddie. He's going to get back to me with the name of a lawyer."

"What's wrong with him? He's a lawyer! Why can't he defend Tommy?"

"Well, the election coming up, ya know. I don't think he wants this type of publicity."

"Publicity? You mean to tell me after working under him for over fifteen years that Mr. Politician doesn't want publicity? That's a crock, Patrick Sullivan!"

"I know, I know," pleaded Pat, "but he's going to get us the best one available. We'll beat this. I've got to go to the bank and get Tom's bail money and the lawyer's fee."

"How much is this going to cost?"

"I don't know. The bail has yet to be determined, but the lawyer will need fifty thousand dollars."

"Fifty-thousand dollars! Jesus, Mary, and Joseph! That's all we got!"

"We've got equity in the house, and I can borrow on retirement. We'll be okay."

"What about your retirement? You were going to retire next year."

"We'll see, we'll see. Mary, if I have to work, I have to work! We can't leave Tommy sitting in that jail with all those criminals. It's just not right."

Pat left the room and grabbed his coat from the front closet. "I'll be back as soon as I can," he called as he left through the front door.

Mary's mind was now changed about the course of the treatment she would have to take for her disease. Her mind was now focused on the family crisis.

CHAPTER SIX

Early in his life, Joe Hinckley wanted to be a professional athlete. Which sport didn't matter. He was good at all of them, especially the big four: baseball, football, basketball, and hockey. He was an athlete whose prowess and agility transcended the abilities of any other player. His grace was evident whether he was deking the helpless defenseman on the ice or completing a no-look pass to a power forward on his wing.

The only question being which sport would be lucky enough to merit his presence and reap the benefits of his star power. It was his destiny, he thought, a pre-ordained edict by the jock gods who had reached down and touched him and infused him with the skills no other mortal in the park could possess.

Then he got fat.

Hinckley was not big-boned or husky; he was flat-out fat and knew it. At first, he was not concerned. He was a growing lad and needed the extra pounds to continue his athletic endeavors. Being a jock would consume and burn any unneeded fat and give him more power to knock down any would-be tacklers on the gridiron. He could mix it up under the boards or drive the ball through the power alleys of White Sox Park. Power was good, he thought; it separated the men from the boys.

He learned, however, that he lost speed and quickness with more power and bulk. He found that his finesse was slipping, and his behind-the-back passes started to end up four rows up in the bleachers. Ground balls started to elude his outstretched arms by inches. His coaches told him to shake it off and move on, but as he entered high school, he needed bigger clothes and …lunches. He thought all he needed to maintain his athletic prowess was to start working out in the weight room and maintain a regular exercise routine.

One day, he came home, sat at the kitchen table, and watched his mother prepare the evening's supper. His mother was a huge woman. He had never seen her in this light before.

Mom was mom, a shapeless staple of the home with no physical characteristics to speak of, at least to Joe. He looked at his mother closely and started to connect the dots on the whole gene pool thing.

When his father came home from work an hour later, Joe studied him as he had earlier with his mother. He concluded that his father was also fat. His father's navel peaked out from under his tee shirt like an eyeball returning Joe's stare, and to this day, he believes that it winked at him.

Later that night, upstairs in his bedroom, he stripped down to his undershorts and stood in front of the mirror hanging on the wall over his dresser.

Joe recalled the scene from "Saturday Night Fever" when John Travolta posed in front of his mirror. He started to mimic Travolta's postures, but he could not get the look that he wanted. He peered into the mirror and closely examined his physical features. He realized that he had his mother's eyes and nose, his father's receding hairline and both of their waistlines.

Joe felt a sense of blighted hope start to fester at the bottom of his gut as he turned out the lights. He lay on the bed in the dark room. The revelation sank in that he would probably not be the Bruce Jenner of his generation that he had always thought he would be. The future was now a foggy window of destiny that he could do nothing about.

From then on, his workouts did not have the fire nor the regularity required of a future sports star. His interest in sports waned. He attempted to play high school football his freshman year. He was a practice player whose most important contribution to the team, other than getting the crap knocked out of him by the first stringers, was to weigh down the blocking sled for the offensive line to push around the field. He had yet to pick up a football since that year.

Joe reflected on his childhood and brief athletic career as he sat behind the steering wheel of his City of Chicago-issued SUV at 82nd Street and Francisco. The vehicle was parked at the curb, under a large tree covering him from the mercury vapor streetlights overhead. He had caught on with the city, worked in the rank and file for a couple of years, and was now a supervisor in the Streets and Sanitation Department, Fifty-First Ward, courtesy of his supreme support of incumbent Alderman Eddie Byrne and various election campaigns.

The only light in the vehicle was the glowing tip of his Marlboro Light, which flared when he dragged on it, eerily highlighting his puffy facial features. He was now a healthy five foot eight inches, his father's exact height, and had thin wispy, dishwater blonde hair, an attribute his mother passed to him, and toyed with the 250-pound mark on the bathroom scale, a legacy from both. His hair had inevitably receded and followed the same route of retreat as his father's, forming matching widow's peaks on matching oval heads. He had accepted his genealogical lot in life a long time ago. He only started thinking of his physique because a potential physical confrontation was looming on his immediate horizon.

A lone figure appeared at the end of the block, walking from house to house and leaving leaflets at each home. He rolled up the leaflet at some houses and stuck it through the front door handle. At others, he would drop it in the mailbox, which Joe knew to be against the law. He would set him straight if he were one of his guys.

Joe continued to watch as he made his way to the house that Joe was parked in front of.

Joe got out of the SUV and approached the figure, who was a male, black, twenty-five-year-old. His name was Orvin Rodrik. He was a precinct worker for Joe, or so Joe thought. Orvin carried pamphlets and campaign literature for Dale Robins, a challenger for Eddie's aldermanic seat. Joe was dismayed.

"Hey Orvin, what you got there?"

Orvin turned and was surprised to see Joe. He attempted to hide the literature behind his back, but realizing how stupid it looked, he shrugged and handed a pamphlet to Joe. "Here, see for yourself."

Joe knocked the pamphlet from Orvin's hand and asked, "What the fuck are you doing?"

"What the fuck do you think I'm doing? I've gotten fucked over by Byrne for the last time!"

"Fucked over? You're lucky to be working at all, you piece of shit!"

"Hey now, no need to get that way. I carried my precinct for that mother fucker every time. I don't know what the fuck he wanted."

"You didn't carry shit. You got fifty votes per election, big fuckin' deal. We used to find literature dumped in the garbage over there all the time. Who are you trying to kid?"

"Look, Joey, your guy has some problems. The 'hood is changing, and Byrne isn't. He's white, and he's gonna stay that way for the rest of his life. Ain't nothing he can do about that."

Joe knew Orvin was right. Eddie Byrne was as white as new underwear, and the ward demographics were changing. The reality was one thing, but loyalty was something entirely different.

"After all the shit he did for you, you're gonna jump ship on him now? What's up with that?"

"Hey, I gotta look out for what's best for Orvin, man. You know that, Joey, you did the same thing."

"Fuck you, Orvin!" Joe was getting frustrated. Orvin was right again. Joe had bailed on Ray Sienski in 1991 when Byrne challenged him as the "outsider" and, luckily for Joe, won. Orvin was making sense. Joe couldn't have that. He slapped the literature bundle from Orvin's hands, spilling them onto the sidewalk.

"Oh? You gonna be like that then?" Orvin said in a pitch three octaves higher than his normal conversational voice. "Fuck you then."

Orvin started to walk away. "Fuck you and Byrne! Fuck you and the organization!" He pointed his finger at Joe as he continued his retreat.

"Fuck you and anyone who looks like you!" He got braver the farther he got away from Joe.

"Fuck you, Byrne, the organization, and your FAT ass!"

Joe exploded like a sprinter. Orvin turned and bolted. Quickly gassed, Joe ceased his chase when the gap between him and Orvin quadrupled. Orvin streaked to the end of the block, and fired one last verbal salvo, "YOU FAT FUCK!" and disappeared around the corner.

Joe turned to go back to his SUV. He picked up a piece of the scattered literature on the sidewalk and looked at it. A large black and white photo of Dale Robins, taken during his college days and wearing a Chicago State basketball jersey, looked back at him. Underneath the photo was Robin's campaign slogan in large type, "FOR WHAT IS OURS! VOTE FOR ROBINS!".

Joe crumbled it up and threw it back onto the pile on the sidewalk. He then stepped on it, wiped his feet as if scraping poodle excrement from the bottom of his shoe, and returned to his vehicle. His anger in check, he quickly drove away from the scene of the grassroots political discourse.

CHAPTER SEVEN

The following day, Pat arrived at Eddie's office with a slight head-ache and a cashier's check for fifty thousand dollars made payable to Bernard Tannenbaum, Attorney at Law. The situation at hand, and perhaps the extra beer from the night before, had caused a slight, throbbing, and stubborn sensation in the back of his head. He had taken two aspirin earlier, which did not ease his apprehensive feeling about the meeting with the lawyer and Eddie.

Tannenbaum was the criminal defense attorney recommended by Eddie. Pat had no other recourse than to listen to Eddie's advice on the whole issue.

"I know a guy..." were the first three words to come out of Eddie's mouth when he told him the news of Tommy's arrest.

Eddie sat behind his desk in his usual coiffed manner. Bernie Tannenbaum sat on the leather couch, dressed as nattily as Eddie. It was tough to tell who was the politician and who was the lawyer.

"Pat," said Eddie as he rose from his desk, "this is Bernie Tannen-baum. Bernie, this is Pat Sullivan, Tommy's father."

Tannenbaum extended his right hand. "Pat, nice to meet you under the circumstances."

"Hi, Bernie," Pat replied, sitting in the chair before Eddie's desk.

"I have to run some errands," Eddie said. "Pat, you're in good hands. Bernie is a great fucking criminal lawyer. Listen to him and do what he tells you. If anyone can help Tommy out, it's him. Believe me."

Pat obediently nodded.

"If you need anything, just call me; gotta go," and Eddie left the room.

Bernie got up, moved behind Eddie's desk, took out a yellow legal pad and unscrewed the top from an expensive-looking pen.

"Mr. Sullivan, I know this is a tough situation. I have taken the liberty of looking at the police reports on this matter, and I think we may have a shot at beating this thing. I need to ask you some questions."

"Pat. Call me Pat."

"Okay, Pat. First off, tell me about Tom. Why wouldn't he have done what they have accused him of?

Pat took a second and silently mulled the question over. He had never thought about why Tommy *wouldn't* have killed his wife. He could only come up with the standard parental answer.

"Tommy is a good kid," he paused, trying to get the right words in place. "He has a...trait, I think, that allows him to get a little hot now and then, but I have never seen it to this extreme. I mean, he has a good work ethic, he loves his son, he supports him and sees him, to me, that is a good man."

"Okay, okay. What was his relationship with Janice like? Did they live together before they got married? Did they date for a long time? I know that they got divorced, but was it messy?"

"They fought a little. I know that. About what, I haven't a clue. I don't think Tommy had a drinking problem or anything like that, and I know that he never hit her, at least as far as I could see. I know Janice did not want to work full-time while Tommy Junior was small. Tom might have had a problem with that. He never told me anything about it anyway."

"Were you aware that Tom had an Order of Protection entered against him by Janice?"

"Uh, no. What was that all about?"

"Six months ago. Tom threatened her that if he ever found out that she was seeing someone else, he would break her arms; at least, that was what Janice stated in her complaint."

"I was not aware of that. That doesn't sound good, does it?"

"It doesn't help. Were there any other issues that you were aware of?"

"Issues? No, I don't think so. He was still on title to the house, and they were to sell it when Tommy Junior got to be eighteen, but I think they both agreed on that."

"What about the drugs?"

"What drugs?"

"They found drug paraphernalia at the house. Scales and baggies and things like that. Nothing big, but it seems that maybe Janice was moonlighting a bit by selling pot from the home. Were you aware of anything like that?"

"Jesus Christ, no. I never suspected anything like that. I knew they liked having a good time, but nothing like that."

"Was Tom ever involved in anything like that?"

"Drugs? Jesus no. I never saw any sign or anything like that. Like I said, I know he likes his beer and all, but…"

"All right. Tell me about Janice and her family."

"She was a neighborhood girl. I liked her. I thought that she would be good for Tommy. He had met her at a local party, I think. She grew up in a single-parent home. I had met her mother only once before they got married. She was a cleaning woman, Polish, first generation. She worked downtown at night, cleaning the offices. She died about a year before Tom and Jan got married. That's about all I know about her family, to tell you the truth. She had no brothers or sisters that I am aware of."

"But tell me what she was like. Did she goad Tom or incite him in any way?"

"Let me tell you this. I liked Jan. Yeah, she and Tom would argue a fair amount of time, but it was just your normal stuff. Maybe Tom would come home late after work occasionally, but honestly, I thought they were solid."

"When did they get married?"

"I think it was in 92 or 93. She was pregnant with Tommy Junior at the time, but she didn't show or anything. She was just a couple of months pregnant."

"So they had to get married."

"No. Who gets married for that anymore? No, I think that they really loved each other. I think that they wanted to get married. The kid just hastened it."

"What about this, Charlie Bedrun? Did you know him?

"The guy was there with Jan? Is that his name? I never heard of him before."

"Well, Charlie was not a nice guy. He has a history of drug dealing and gangbanging. That's what we are looking at now. He had just gotten out of the joint less than a month ago. He wasn't a heavy player or anything. Was Tom involved in any of that stuff?"

"No. I can say that. I would be shocked to hear of Tommy's involvement in anything like that."

"Okay then. I will be at his bond hearing tomorrow morning and try to get some statements. Tommy Junior is still with DCFS; I'm sure the police have talked to him about this. Will he be living with you?"

"Yes, of course. What's next?"

"Well, I'm sure the police have tried to talk to Tom already. I will go down to County now and see Tom myself to hear what he said to them and talk to him about his side of the story. It's still a fact-finding kind of stage right now. I'm also sure the State's Attorney has already filed charges against him. And then there will be a bond hearing in the morning."

"What's that all about?"

"The court will require some money to ensure Tom's presence in court if they release him."

"How much?"

"That's what the hearing will be all about, if they even give him a bond. Murder is a very serious charge. We have to argue that he is not a flight risk and not a risk to the community while he is out. The court may put some conditions on the bond. Would it be all right if he stayed with you if need be?"

"I'll find the room if I have to. I'll get the money together also. Anything else?"

"For now, that's enough. The hearing is tomorrow at nine in the morning."

"I'll be there."

"All right then. I'll be off to see Tommy. Did you bring the retainer?"

Pat reached into his coat pocket and pulled out the crisp white envelope the bank had given him with the check inside. "There you go, Mr. Tannenbaum."

Tannenbaum glanced at the content of the envelope and slipped it into the right inside pocket of his suit jacket. "Thanks, Pat."

Par stood up and turned when Eddie entered the room, back from his errands. "Everything work out between you two guys?"

Tannenbaum and Pat nodded. As Pat started towards the door, he paused and turned around. "You asked me why Tommy couldn't kill Janice. He wouldn't because he loved her. He really loved her. He never stopped loving her, even after the divorce. I could tell. That's why he couldn't have killed her." He then turned back to the door and left the room.

"Can you help the guy out?" Eddie said.

"Interesting case. We'll see," Tannenbaum replied as he reached into his suit pocket, pulled out a check for $25,000 made out to Eddie Byrne, and placed it on the desk in front of Eddie.

"Thanks for the referral, Eddie."

"Anytime, my friend," said Eddie. "Anytime."

* * * * *

Tommy Junior, or TJ as the Sullivans called him, blazed his red fire truck through his imaginary roadway on Pat's living room floor. His cousin Curtis followed behind, giving chase with his decal-spattered monster truck. TJ was on an extended sleepover and was now having fun playing with his cousin at Grandma and Grandpa's house. Grandma told him that Mommy and Daddy were taking a little vacation for a few days, and TJ would stay with his cousin. This worked for TJ as he liked Curtis, and they kept each other company when the adults had adult things to do, like meetings with lawyers, chemotherapy treatments, and bond court hearings.

While TJ and Curtis played on the floor, the other members of the Sullivan family sat scattered in the living room like the toys on the floor. The bond hearing was the following day, and everyone was tense about the outcome. Claire wanted to see her brother again, home and with the family where he should be, until these awful lies against him were rebutted. Pat sat in his overstuffed wing chair in the corner, mulling what this bond would cost him, and Mary sat with her own secret.

Tannenbaum had called and told Pat to have $60,000 waiting. If that weren't enough, Tannenbaum would have a quit claim deed prepared and ready at the courthouse. Pat would be able to put up his home as additional security for the bond. The money was about half of what Pat had in his retirement accounts. But he would be all right, he told himself, because the money would be returned to him after Tom went back to court and defended himself against these unthinkable charges. He looked at it as a short-term loan to his son. What could go wrong?

Mary was in her own sphere. She wanted to share her dark secret of even more misery confronting the Sullivan family. She was going to tell Pat the other day, but as she looked at him sitting in his chair in the corner and watching his vacant eyes, she knew he had enough on his plate right now. She could tell that this whole situation with Tommy was tearing him up.

He had gone to see Tannenbaum and given him the money needed to prove that Tommy was no killer. It was required to clear the Sullivan name, something worth far more than any amount of money. She knew that Pat had worked long and hard to accumulate that money for their retirement, and she also knew that Pat was looking forward to it, but there was no question that the money had to be used to help Tommy.

She had a disturbing thought. Like Pat, she also looked forward to their retirement. The money they had saved, and his retirement fund, were sufficient to allow them to live a comfortable lifestyle. But she felt conflicting emotions as she reviewed their priorities. Would she even be around to partake in the retirement pie? How fair would it be to Pat? She was determined to pray tonight, seeking an answer.

"Are you going with me?" Pat asked.

Mary snapped from her trance. "Where?"

"To the court. For the bond hearing."

Mary shook her head. "I'm afraid I can't bear to see Tom like that. Handcuffed and treated like a prisoner." While true, she could not go if she wanted to as she had a scheduled chemo treatment in the morning.

"I understand," said Pat, while not actually understanding, "It'll be me and Mr. Tannenbaum then."

CHAPTER EIGHT

Joe Hinckley pulled to the curb in front of his pride and joy, a three-flat apartment building. He made his biggest hit on the gambling boat in Joliet three years before and used it for the down payment on the building instead of giving it right back to the casino as he had done previously with his winnings. When he finally closed on the property, he felt like he was on top of the world.

He lived on the main floor of the building, between the elderly Patroski's, who lived below him, and the young newlyweds, the Andersons, on the upper floor. With the rent he received each month from the tenants, he could make his mortgage payments and live almost rent-free in his building. On occasion, he was forced to make expenditures, the biggest being the re-tarring of the flat roof a year ago. All-in-all, he felt good about his investment.

Despite some late-night noise from the newlyweds above, both tenants were ideal and paid their rent on time.

He had heard horror stories about bad tenants who didn't pay timely rent or keep their apartments clean. He felt fortunate that he did not have to experience any of that. Joe believed proper screening of prospective tenants was the key to any landlord-tenant relationship. Of course, he had never screened a tenant in his life as he inherited the Patroski's from the former owner, and the Andersons were friends of a friend who just happened to be looking to rent until they were ready to buy their own home. In the world of residential leasing, Joe had it good.

The building itself was solid. It had oak hardwood floors and trim and was built in the 1930s from depression-era labor. The various owners kept it in good shape and performed regular maintenance. Joe, being a precinct captain, made sure that all three doorbells worked.

The building sat on a block of three flats. They all had the same layout and were made of faded red brick with octagon fronts and flat roofs. Owners' families occupied some apartments, but most were rent-paying tenants. It was not uncommon to see an unfamiliar face on the block, which was fine by Joe.

Joe kept up the maintenance traditions of the previous owners and was determined to keep it that way. He lived for few things. He was never married and only rarely dated. His last date was more than two years ago with a friend his cousin had set him up with. Nothing ever clicked, and it was just as well to Joe. He told himself that women were a pain in the ass, always taking your time and money.

Rarely did he go on vacation. If he did, it was usually to Las Vegas for an intense and mostly losing gambling foray. His only socializing was to spend a few evenings a week on the gambling boats in Joliet. He liked to gamble, primarily blackjack and poker. He knew he had probably lost more than his fair share over the years. He rationalized that he knew the parameters of what he could afford to lose.

He was still hoping for the Big Hit, where his picture would appear in the next morning's newspaper with the casino manager and an oversized check made out to him with many zeros.

His other nighttime meanderings usually involved some aspect of his position as a precinct captain, knocking on doors and passing out literature or attending fundraisers and meetings. These were the things that Joe lived for, his job, his building, and a regular date with his fickle gal, Lady Luck.

On the weekends, he usually was involved with some home project, repairing, updating, fixing, or just plain tinkering. This was his life, the only life he knew. Of course, he had some friends at the tavern he could shoot pool with or watch a Bears game. But these were merely acquaintances, not buddies. If he ever needed help with a project at home, he could undoubtedly get the manpower at the tavern, but he had to pay them an hourly wage. Buddies get paid in pizza and beer; acquaintances get paid in cash.

He entered the building and slowly walked up the stairs to his apartment. He was tired from passing out literature. The Orvin episode from the night before still weighed on him more than the fatigue. He tossed his keys on an end table and plopped on his couch. Instinctively he clicked on the TV. The Orvin encounter had planted some seeds that were beginning to take root in the pit of Joe's stomach. He needed bodies to help him work his precinct, and if Orvin left, would there be others? How many more could defect to the Dale Robbins camp?

Joe knew Orvin was not the leader. He was following someone else. He wondered how many others in the ward would defect and who led them.

Dale Robbins was the first real serious challenger to Eddie Byrne in at least the last four elections, sixteen years. Eddie knows how to play the game, but the bottom line in every election is, are the people working? Is the economy good? Do I have a job? The current economic climate in the area could have been better.

The ward lost three factories and two warehouses in the last four years. In their place stood less than one hundred percent leased strip malls and other retail establishments, which do not pay either in taxes or employment near what the defunct factories and warehouses did.

There were new issues confronting Eddie, and Joe had sensed Eddie's apprehension. The black population had spread rapidly and was almost a majority in the ward. Dale Robbins preached a single issue: "Black majority, black rule."

It alienated much of the rest of the ward, the whites, and the other emerging force, Hispanics, primarily Mexicans. They were moving into the ward at an identical pace as the blacks, lacking only their sheer numbers. Joe thought they would probably be a more significant force in four years, but now they had to focus on Dale Robbins.

Robbins was no dummy. He was young when he cut his teeth as a volunteer for Harold Washington, Chicago's first black mayor, learning from the ground up about grass-roots politics and forming coalitions with neighborhood organizations and churches. He had worked hard to put himself in his current position. He emulated the persona and charisma of Washington by turning himself into an affable yet organized candidate. His public speaking rallies were filled with humorous anecdotes and clever rhyming catchphrases. They resembled a church-like revival with frenzied gospel fervor.

Robbins was following Washington's plan like a contractor follows a blueprint. Joe admired Robbin's political savvy, yet at the same time, he feared the fallout if Robbins won. Joe's city job would be placed in jeopardy, and if that happened, so would his beloved building and world.

Joe was in a comfortable niche that would be lost if Robbins beat Byrne. No more SUV. No more crew chief. No more importance in the ward. Joe felt good about being able to walk into the Alderman's office at just about any time and have a chat with Eddie. He took pride in knowing the alderman personally and knew he could play that card if needed. Not many people can say they can hang with the alderman, but Joe Hinckley could. He did not want to lose that. He couldn't lose that. Dale Robbins would have to be defeated.

A knock at the door interrupted Joe's musings on the current local political situation. He opened the door to find Greg Anderson, his newlywed tenant, standing there.

"Hi, Greg. How are you?"

"Good Joe. I came to tell you that Carol and I found a house. Out in Tinley."

"Oh, well, good for you. Bad for me, I guess. I think you're about to tell me something else."

"Yeah, well," Greg looked down at his shoes. "We are going to sign a contract tomorrow with closing in about a month. If you don't mind, we hope to be out of here in early March, but we'll pay for the whole month."

"Okay, fair enough. Hey, well, good for you guys. I can't say I didn't know this was coming."

"You've been a good guy, Joe. You have a great building here, and I don't think you'll have any problem getting another tenant in here."

"No, I shouldn't. Well, okay then. I may want to show the apartment to possible tenants, but I'll give you guys a heads up."

"No problem. Thanks so much, Joe. We really appreciate all of the help you've given us. Well, I'll be seeing you."

Greg headed up the stairs as Joe closed the door behind him.

"Fuck," Joe said to himself. On top of the election, he now had to find a new tenant. That meant putting an ad in the *Daily Southtown*, interviewing prospective tenants, running credit checks, and all the other bullshit that went along with the process. This was going to take valuable time which he did not have. For the first time, Joe would have to get his own tenants and dreaded the thought of tenant screening and the potential of making the wrong decision.

First things first. He needed to give the apartment a fresh coat of paint and make any repairs required after the Andersons moved out. It's a lot of work. He went to the kitchen, grabbed a beer, and returned to his regular position on the couch. He could do nothing about it now, so he would drink tonight and worry about it tomorrow.

* * * * *

"What the fuck happened?"

"What do you mean?"

"He survived."

"What? Alive survived? Like, he's still living?"

"Yeah, he's still alive, man."

"But I shot that fucker in the head."

"See, you fucked it up, asshole!"

"Shut the fuck up and get off the line!"

"Fuck you, man. You fucked it up."

"With no help from you."

"I held up my end. Don't lay that shit on me, man."

"Both of you, shut up." There is an awkward pause.

"I'm not laying any shit on you, man."

"You're the one who shit in his pants."

"Shut up, man!"

"He what?"

"He shit in his pants, man. Like a little fucking baby."

"You did?"

"Well, the dude scared me when he came in. I wasn't expecting that."

"You're such a pussy!"

"Well, at least he didn't see me."

"He saw you?"

"No. I don't think."

"You don't think?"

"Well, I peeked out the front window when he got there."

"Did he see you?"

"No. I don't know. I don't think so. Probably not, but I doubt it, you know?"

"THAT'S IT! Both of you shut the fuck up now!"

Obedient silence. Pause.

"Now, the two of you morons are going to finish this job. Without shitting in your pants. Do you understand?"

"Yes."

"Yes. Si. We'll finish it. Where is he at?"

"Christ Hospital. Room 810. Listen to me, both of you idiots. This will not be tolerated again. It has to be done quickly and quietly, or there will be problems for everyone concerned, including the both of you. Do you understand me?"

"Yes"

"Si Si."

"Don't fuck it up again."

CHAPTER NINE

"People versus Thomas Sullivan."

The Bond Court Clerk called the case and started a chain reaction when the bailiff opened the side door of the courtroom and
shouted, "Sullivan!" The name was loudly repeated down the hall.
It could be heard over the noise made by the shuffling of feet by the
shackled inmates. Each repetition of the name 'Sullivan' that echoed
down the line made the hairs on the back of Pat's neck stand up.

Cook County Jail and the Circuit Court of Cook County, Criminal Division, share the same hopeless square mile. The Court House
itself was erected in 1929 with a classic four-column entranceway
that looms over everything in the residential neighborhood. The
guard towers overlook the jail portion of the complex.

On one side of the street are well-kept homes of working-class
people. On the other side, a guard with a semi-automatic weapon
peers down from behind aviator shades. Among the much less news-
worthy, Richard Speck, John Wayne Gacy, and the fictional Bigger
Thomas all heard who they were and how they got that way in this
Courthouse, and the long introspective journey was about to begin
for Tom Sullivan.

Below the somber gray skies, the wind churned up California
like a shotgun blast of little needles, each searching for a bare patch
of skin to embed itself. Pat's cheeks turned to a raw sanguine shade
as he struggled against the fast-moving winter barrage while walking

toward the Courthouse entrance. He dared not take his hands out of his coat pocket to adjust his collar because he clutched a certified check for sixty-thousand dollars. If the wind blew that away, that would be it for both his retirement and Tommy getting bonded out of jail.

He clutched his coat tighter as he made his way up the stairs to the entrance, where he quickly glanced up at the impressive set of columns. He was too cold to be humbled, and he immediately entered.

Bond Courtroom 205 was a small windowless room on the first floor with enough space for a small gallery. The wood partition that separated the gallery from the bench was a classic waist-high, dark wood railing that had seen better days. Small bits of plaster were missing from the corner of the ceiling, and plaster patch areas were visible all over the walls.

When Tom's name was announced, Bernie Tannenbaum approached the bench, where he found both the Assistant State's Attorney and the bond court judge waiting. Judge Stokely sat above the proceedings from behind the bench. Pat strained to hear the preliminaries from his seat in the third row.

"Bernie Tannenbaum for the Defendant, your honor."

"Good morning, Mr. Tannenbaum," returned Judge Stokely.

"Julius Harris for the State, your honor."

As if on cue, Tom Sullivan appeared from the side door, his hands cuffed together in front of him and wearing a bright orange jumpsuit with 'DOC' printed in large black letters on the back. He looked down as the bailiff directed him to his spot in front of the bench and next to his attorney. He glanced back at Pat with a look that Pat had not seen since Tommy was a boy, a scared and confused look that could only be given to one's father. Pat nodded back to Tom, hoping to convey a sense of strength and a bit of resolve.

"Mr. Harris, now I've already looked at this matter. Do either of you have anything to add?"

"Yes, your Honor," started Tannenbaum. "I want the record to reflect that Mr. Sullivan has family contacts in the area, a loving family that will see to it that if Mr. Sullivan has any physical difficulties in making any of the required court appearances, they will certainly assist him in any way he needs. I can back this up, Judge, because the defendant's father is here and would be capable of posting a reasonable bond for the release of the defendant from custody."

"Counsel?"

"Judge, that's all fine and good," said Harris, "but nowhere in the statute does it state that because the parents of the defendant put up his bond money, it should be a factor in determining whether bond should be given or not."

"That's true, Judge," countered Tannenbaum, "but my purpose in alluding to it is that it pertains to the totality of the 'flight risk' of the defendant. My point, Judge, was that because of the loving and close nature of the familial relationship here, Mr. Sullivan would never risk his father's well-being by fleeing."

Tannenbaum's words struck a dormant chord in Pat that had not been stirred for quite a while. He wiped it away from the corner of his eye. He would be there for his boy, he vowed. Whatever it takes.

"Well, I'm going to grant the bond," said Judge Stokely. "But I want it to be high enough where the defendant understands the gravity of this by being here for every hearing and on time. His appearance will not be waived for any of the proceedings, and I set his bond at one and one-half million dollars."

Tannenbaum quickly responded. "Your Honor, I respectfully ask that you reconsider. Mr. Sullivan, the defendant's father, is a city worker and may not have access to that amount of funds."

"I'm sorry, Mr. Tannenbaum, but from what I understand, we have a dead body and the possibility of another one. The defendant is fortunate that he is even eligible for me to consider his bond at all. Bond at one and one-half million dollars. Call the next one."

With a quick tap of the gavel on his bench, Judge Stokely moved to the next case. The bailiff grabbed Tom's arm and led him back to the prisoner hallway. Tannenbaum motioned to Pat to meet him in the hallway.

"How much equity do you have in your home?" asked Tannenbaum.

"It's paid off. Why?"

"They're going to need one hundred and fifty grand for his bail."

"Holy shit, man. I don't have anywhere near that. I brought the check for sixty grand like you said, but that's it."

"I was maybe being too optimistic. The Judge looked at Bedrun's medical report and he's not doing well. This is potentially a double murder; if that happens, forget any bond."

Tannenbaum reached into his briefcase and pulled out a legal document. "I prepared a deed to your home. You'll have to sign it over to the court. After Tom makes all his hearings, you will get it back."

"So I get this back after this is all over?"

"Yes. As long as Tom makes it to court."

"You bet your ass he will."

* * * * *

Outside on California Avenue, Pat waited in the freezing wind outside the main gate of the Cook County Jail. The razor wire that lined the top of the wall wavered back and forth in the wind like the jaws of mad dogs. Pat stared at the chain link barrier, hoping for a glimpse of his son in street clothes.

The chain link barrier slid sideways via a motorized device. From behind it walked a tired and humbled Tom Sullivan. Tom and Pat hugged each other. They stayed embraced for a full minute before finally looking at each other; the tears had already welled and receded. Pat pointed in the general direction of his parked car. They both walked side-by-side for an entire block before speaking.

"Thanks, Dad," Tom said in a cracked low voice.

"It's quite all right, laddie."

"Is TJ at home?"

"Yes. He's been staying with us. He doesn't know anything. Mommy and Daddy are on vacation for a while."

"Thanks again."

The route home took them south down California to 71st Street. Pat looked at the signs on the shops and stores and couldn't read them. Carniceria, Cerveza Fria, and Carne Asada were the most prevalent words on the signs.

"Boy, this area has changed."

Tom gazed out the car window. "Yeah. Been like this for a while now."

As they passed Archer Avenue, they came upon Kelly Park, once renowned for its sixteen-inch softball teams, the best in the country. Now, three soccer fields were laid across the park like bland serapes, covering the remnants of the small softball diamonds.

"Geez, this is kind of startling if you haven't been down here in a while."

Tom chuckled. "You gotta get out more, Pops."

As they approached 67th Street, they came upon the northeast border of Marquette Park and the monument to some Lithuanian aviators. Pat had always remembered the memorial but could not for the life of him remember what achievement deserved such a prominent honor.

The monument was the size of a small, sloped one-car garage made from granite or some other shiny rock. It sloped down from its top, creating a large and dangerous slide, much to the neighborhood children's delight. Etched into the front were the aviator's names and a depiction of an aircraft that looked like the Spirit of St. Louis... but wasn't. There was also a description of the aviator's heroic feat that Pat had never read. The neighborhood kids of today, black and brown, were now climbing about the monument despite the windy conditions outside.

Pat recalled that the area was once called Little Lithuania. Driving around, you could still see remnants of the Lithuanian heyday here, but nothing matched the strip down 69th Street twenty-five years ago. Hell, the President of Lithuania lived in this area. It must have been something then. He wondered if the Lithuanian president had moved out with everyone else or if he bailed out early. And what about this monument? The whole Lithuanian neighborhood moved out, and they left behind their monument. What kind of crap is that to leave the monument behind?

"I wonder why they didn't take the monument?"

"Huh?"

"The Lithuanians. Why didn't they take their monument with them when they left the neighborhood? They just left it here for the black kids to climb on now. Look at that."

Tom looked out his window at the monument. "Well, for one thing, it looks pretty fucking heavy."

"Yeah, but you can cut it up or something. There's a way to do that, you know."

"Yeah, yeah. I'm just messing around. Maybe they just didn't want it."

"Well, that's a shame. You just don't leave something like that behind."

They rode the rest of the way in silence. Tom gazed out the window and dragged on a cigarette while Pat drove on. Finally, they pulled up to the house. Pat walked behind Tom as they trudged up the steps to the front door, where Mary waited for her son. As Tom opened the door, she hugged him and held on.

"Come on now, let's not put on a show for the neighbors now," said Pat.

That night, for the first time that Pat could remember, the entire family sat around the front room watching TV, eating popcorn, and interacting like a sitcom family. Pat felt as if he could let his guard down. He wrapped himself in the warm scene like a wooly blanket, watching Mary revel in the simple family picture, which made him feel even better. He realized that this was one of the short times when holy and good things converge. Even though they may last mere hours, they somehow make you feel that all the troubles and the bullshit were worth it.

CHAPTER TEN

Tom fidgeted in the plush leather chair; his movements made flatulent noises as he adjusted. He was uncomfortable sitting on this type of furniture. It seemed that the only times he would find himself seated in a chair like this was when he was waiting for a decision or words from someone on high, like a principal or a doctor. Or a lawyer.

Bernie Tannenbaum's office furniture was made from dark cherry wood, highly glossed with blood maroon leather coverings, set off by brass tacks. Bookshelves containing law books with identical spines surrounded the room. Bernie sat behind his desk and looked down at Tom.

"Tom, have you thought of taking a plea?"

"What do you mean?"

"The State has a lot of evidence. Granted, all of it is circumstantial, but a lot of evidence nonetheless. I'm still in the process of getting the police reports and statements from the State."

"What can we do?"

"Counter it. Counter it all. For everything the State offers, we offer a reason or explanation. If our responses are reasonable, we may be able to get our reasonable doubt. But to do that, we must get out ourselves and take witness statements and evidence."

"What about DNA?"

"What about it?"

"I've heard of cases where guys spend a lot of time in jail and are let go because of DNA. What's that all about?"

"DNA helps to eliminate suspects from the scene. Your DNA is all over the site; remember, you used to live there. DNA isn't a factor here."

"I can't do time. I had nothing to do with this."

"That's why we must explain the evidence the State has. You were placed at the sight at the time of the crime by two witnesses, your neighbor, and your son. Okay. We cannot deny that based on that evidence, can we?"

"No. We can't."

"Right. So, we have to explain why you were there at that time in a plausible and reasonable manner so the jury can understand and appreciate. Now, let me ask you straight up, why were you there?

"I was going to kick Charlie Bedrun's ass!" a quickly agitated Tom answered.

"No," Bernie replied while shaking his head.

"Tom, I've done a little homework on you. I've asked around about you, who you are, what type of guy you are, you know, that type of thing. Depending on who I talk to, I generally get the impression that you are a good and upstanding citizen, and like any other good and upstanding citizen, you have a quirk or two. Nothing exceptional, mind you; everyone I talked with about you had expressed surprise about what you are accused of. However, there was a consistent tone from everyone that you are a stubborn guy who can fly off the handle now and then. Is that something you can agree with?"

"I guess so. That may be right."

Bernie got up from his chair and sauntered over to one of the classic wood windows in his office. He opened it halfway, reached into his shirt pocket, pulled a Marlboro Light from a pack, lit it with a disposable lighter, and blew the smoke out of the open window.

"It's a no-smoking building," he explained. He quickly took two drags and tossed the butt into a glass of water that sat on the windowsill.

Tom tried to readjust silently in the chair. Sensing Tom's uneasiness, Bernie smiled, shut the window, and returned to his chair.

"Here's the deal, Tom. I don't want to scare you or anything. This is beatable, but we must know what we have and what we are defending against here. Let me ask you again, why were you there?"

Tom squirmed again in the chair. "I was concerned?"

"Are you asking me or telling me?"

"I'm telling you."

"Well then, fucking tell me. Tell me you were concerned about the mother of your son and that you had a reason to be there out of this concern because someone had told you that a man of suspicious character was seen lurking about the home where both the mother of your son and your helpless child were living. Tell me that you were very clear about this. Tell me that your faculties were on the level with yourself when you went there. Tell me the truth!"

Suddenly it dawned on Tom that he may be in a fight for his life. He knew the truth, and maybe Bernie did also, but he may have to explain the truth to twelve strangers, twelve fucking strangers who did not know who he was, and that he could never do what they have accused him of doing.

A bead of sweat emerged from his hairline and sat there glistening like a prism as the smoky sunlight pierced it. Bernie saw it as a sign that Tom was getting his message.

"Let's try it again, Tom," said Bernie in a softer tone. "Why were you there?"

"I had heard," he began slowly, "that a bad dude was, uh, seen hanging around my home. Where my wife and child lived. I was concerned about them, about their well-being." Looking up at Bernie but not necessarily seeing him, he continued his timeline as if in a stoic trance. "I pulled up in front of the house. I saw a curtain move in the front window, like someone was watching for me, keeping a lookout. I ran up the steps and banged on the door a couple of times; then I opened it with the key."

"You weren't supposed to have a key," interrupted Bernie.

"I didn't have one. I knew Jan had a lock-out box that was under the mailbox. I grabbed the key from there."

"Okay. You walked into the house; what did you see?"

"It was getting dark. There were no lights on. I walked in and through the living room and into the kitchen."

"What did you see in the kitchen?"

"Again, nothing. I poked my head into each of the bedrooms and didn't see anyone there. TJ's room was a mess, as usual. I had no idea he was lying in that bed, under the blankets. I thought everyone had left, honest to God."

"Did you call out to anyone?"

"Yeah, yeah. I was yelling the minute I got into the house."

"Were you mad when you were yelling?"

"Mad as hell, no, not mad, I was...anxious. Anxious and concerned about Jan and TJ."

"Did you go down to the basement?"

"No."

"At all?"

"No. I yelled down there and went about halfway down the stairs, but I didn't go all the way down."

"Why didn't you go down to the basement?"

"Well, if they were screwing, it wasn't in the basement; there's nothing to do it on down there. It's just the furnace, washer, dryer, and TJ's toys. There was no real reason to check down there. It was just the basement, and besides, I could pretty much see everything from the stairs."

"Explain the blood in the kitchen."

"I hit the wall. Hard. I was pissed and just punched the wall after I didn't find anything. I was mad. I cut my hand open and went into the kitchen drawer to get a towel. My knuckles were bleeding all over the place."

Bernie sat back in his chair and loosened his tie. He jotted notes on a yellow legal pad that sat in his lap. "What about the neighbor? She says you and Jan had some pretty good fights before."

"We had spats."

"Spats? She got an order of protection against you, which, by the way, you violated by going to her house that day."

Shaking his head, Tom did not have an answer, but he tried anyway. "Yeah, I got hot once in a while. I regret every instance, but it was a passion, not hatred. There's a difference."

"When you were leaving, your neighbor said she saw you put something in your pocket, like maybe a gun."

"No way. I didn't have a gun. I was trying to stick my hand in my pocket so no one would see the blood. I knew Sheila might be peeking."

Bernie furiously scribbled notes on the legal pad.

"Are we going to beat this thing?"

Looking up, Bernie took off his glasses, dug into the corner of his right eye with his index finger, rubbed whatever matter he found between his fingers over the floor, and leaned forward at the desk.

"Sure. We should be able to, but I cannot promise anything. Not now, anyway. I have to verify what you just told me. My investigator has to talk to witnesses, and I'm still waiting on documents from the State. I'll have to talk to people myself and get out to the crime scene."

"What if we can't? What am I looking at? Level with me."

Bernie rose and strode over to the window again, opened it, and lit another smoke. He exhaled but didn't seem concerned if the smoke made it out the window.

"Right now, a life term."

"Right now?"

"Yeah, the State has to ask for the death penalty. They haven't as of yet."

"Why haven't they?"

"They are still looking at the facts too. They have to make sure they have all their ducks in a row before they go asking for the ultimate penalty."

Tom pulled out a cigarette and tried to light it, but his hand shook so much that the flame went out before he could make it happen. Bernie walked over and held his lighter under Tom's cigarette. Tom inhaled deeply as he wiped the now numerous beads of sweat on his forehead with the back of his hand.

"Tell me about Bedrun," Bernie continued.

"He was a fucking creep. A low-life piece of shit. I knew he was a dealer, just a small time. I'd see him now and then and never paid him any mind. I had heard that he did some time."

"Is there anything else you want to tell me?"

Loudly squirming again in the chair, Tom shook his head and replied, "I don't think so."

"Okay, then, Tom. That's it for now. I've got some work to do on this file. I need you to keep in touch. You got the next court date, right?"

"Yeah, I got it."

"Okay, it's your arraignment. We'll plead not guilty, but you have to be there. I'll see you then unless something pops up."

"All right, got it." Tom rose from his chair and walked to the window, where he deposited the butt of his cigarette into the cup. He heard the soft hiss of it extinguishing itself in the now brown, ashy water.

"I'll be there," he said as he put on his coat and left.

* * * * *

Dearborn Street in late January can be brutal. The wind sweeps down the man-made canyon of architecturally protected buildings that once qualified as skyscrapers. The wind caused Tom's eyes to tear up as he walked down Dearborn to the El. He was making the most challenging decision of his life. Like the wind that blew down Dearborn, Tom's thoughts were funneled and channeled to an acute apex, but unlike the wind, Tom's freedom was in jeopardy.

He walked to the station and got on the elevated train.

The contents of Pat's stomach were a twisted mess. His worst fear was now being realized. The Honorable J. Stokely had just declared that a Bond Forfeiture Warrant was to be issued for Thomas Sullivan, who had failed to appear in court for his arraignment. What this meant to Pat was that unless Tom showed up before the court within 30 days and had a good reason for why he wasn't there that morning, his bail, Pat's home, would be forfeited, and a judgment would be enforced against his house.

Bernie turned to Pat with a sorry and perplexed expression. He motioned for Pat to meet him outside the courtroom. When Pat attempted to leave, his legs felt like he wore lead boots. He shuffled out of the courtroom, feeling twenty years older.

"Where the hell is he?" asked Bernie.

"I don't know. I haven't seen him for a couple of days now."

"Have you talked with him at all?"

"No. As I said, it's been days. The last time I saw him, he was heading out the door to go to your office."

"Yeah, he was there. He showed up, and we talked. He seemed scared but up to it."

"Now what?"

"We need to find him, get his ass in here, and beg the judge not to throw him back into jail. Pat, I don't have to tell you what is at stake here."

"I know, I know. How much time do we have?"

"Thirty days from today and maybe another 30 after that, but that's it."

Pat took a deep breath, and it seemed to energize him. "I'll find him," he replied as he walked away. Pacing through the corridors to the main exit, his legs felt stronger and lighter. He moved at a swifter pace to the courthouse exit. He had a mission and a time frame in which to get it done, and he would start immediately.

Pat exited the revolving doors between the epic columns of the Criminal Courts building. He buttoned his coat as he walked down the stairs to the sidewalk on California Avenue, then pulled his collar over the nape of his neck as he crossed the street. He looked to his right and then to his left.

Where would he start?

CHAPTER ELEVEN

Mary Sullivan, nee Boykin, was raised in a solid Catholic environment. She was the last of nine children, five sisters and three brothers, the baby of the Boykin clan. She had to be, for her mother had died while giving birth to her.

She found this out at the age of nine when she overheard two of her aunts discussing it at a family picnic, and from then on, the guilt she carried burdened her like heavy, wet snow on a groaning roof. The fact that her father, consciously or not, developed a distant and cold relationship with her did not help to ease the load. To the day he died, he never mentioned Mary's mother's death in her presence. Every year on the anniversary of his wife's death, Mary's birthday, Mike Boykin would sit in his garage, drink beer and weep until he fell asleep.

Mary's brothers would put him to bed after he passed out, but Mike would not go easy. One year, he started swinging, so they decided to throw a blanket over him and let him sleep it off in the garage. The following day Mike would be awake before anyone else in the house and go about his business without a raspy word about the night before.

Mary turned more to the Catholic Church. By the time she was sixteen, she had become a daily communicant and would light a candle every morning after mass and pray for forgiveness for being the cause of her mother's death. Her siblings tried to convince her that her mother's death was not her fault, but she never could grasp that concept. *But for my existence, she would be alive.*

It was a clear black-and-white issue with Mary and was her cross to bear. She would seek forgiveness through the church. From her 16th year on, she missed Mass on only one occasion, in February of 1967, when the snow fell so long and deep that she could not get out of the house. Racked with guilt, she spent the entire day on her knees in prayer, asking for atonement for the sin of being snowed in. Pat tried to explain that God was forgiving and would let her slide on this one, but Mary did not want to hear it. Since that day, Pat never again tried to persuade or debate any theology with Mary. It was her way or the highway to Hell.

Pat acquiesced and accepted that she was a devout worshipper and that there was no questioning of any of the Church's tenets, at least in front of her. Her faith and belief were unchallenged, and the mystery of the Holy Trinity could be explained just as that: a mystery, a divine mystery that, maybe if you were pious enough while on the good Earth, would be revealed to you when you reach Heaven. Heaven was where Mary would get her forgiveness, and the weight she had carried around for almost her entire life would be lifted from her shoulders and allow her to breathe calmly and serenely. It was her only goal in life.

Of course, being the Irish woman that she was, she did have opinions and would let anyone know about them, especially if she felt it went against the grain of the Church teachings or if she thought it somehow disrespected the Church, like Masses said in English, hatless women in church, or those "damned guitars, God forgive me." She eventually capitulated like all the other traditionalists and eventually learned to enjoy some of the guitar songs.

A close second to her religion was her family. She toiled and strove to do the right things for them. Besides the washing, cooking, and cleaning, she also attended the school meetings and bake sales, tried to reason with the kids, and sent Pat off every morning with a kiss and a filling lunch. She wasn't the type to leave cute notes or pictures in the lunch bag, that certainly was not her style, but Pat ate well.

Occasionally she would socialize, but for the most part, any gatherings were family- or parish-based. Whether they were Altar & Rosary meetings or fund-raising spaghetti dinners, the same faces were usually present. Once a month, however, she did attend or host the "Club". The "Club" consisted of Mary and her four remaining friends from the old neighborhood, the Back of the Yards, getting together to play gin and gab. They called it "Club" for lack of anything else to call it. The ladies would meet at one of the member's homes on a rotating basis, giving Mary the meeting every five months. They skipped December because of the Holidays. When Mary's kids were young, they would look forward to her club night. She would buy candy and snacks for the club members and the kids would be the beneficiaries of the remnants of the sweet goodies. It was almost as good as Halloween. Pat also looked forward to club night, as he would have a legitimate reason to leave the house and go to McGurn's until well after the woman folk went home. Everyone liked club night in the Sullivan household.

But there would be no more club nights at the Sullivans.

The wake for Mary Sullivan was crowded and hot. Pat constantly felt flush and overheated as he stood at the head of the receiving line next to Mary's casket. The Flanagan Funeral Home was one of the largest on the southwest side, but it had trouble containing the crowd that arrived that night to say goodbye to Mary. The funeral home was a neighborhood institution as generations of southside Irish were waked there. Mary's father was waked there. Pat would be waked there. Claire would be waked there, and so would Tom.

It had been almost two weeks since Tom disappeared, and Pat had yet to get a chance to look for him as Mary's illness took up all his time. Still reeling from the news of Tom's disappearance, Mary finally disclosed her situation to Pat. She had no choice as Pat came home early one day from work and found her lying on the floor next to the bed, too weak to get up. At first, he was enraged at her that she had not told him of her sickness, but then settled down and was at her beck and call until the end.

After Mary died, Pat mentally wandered to areas he had never gone before. He became agitated. It was not supposed to be like this. He had been good and had done everything right. He had obeyed every one of the goddamned Commandments, and this is what he gets. He had so much thrown at him for the past few weeks that he wondered what was next.

Pat tried to make Mary's last days comfortable. He didn't need to explain Tom's absence from her bedside as she was in a deep sleep most of the time. He was sure that she wondered about him, but he sure wasn't going to tell her that their son was on the lam for murder and that their house would be taken from them in under two months if he didn't show up to face the music. No, she had too much on her plate right now.

Pat could not believe that Tom was guilty of the crime that he was accused of, but this latest development bothered him. Why would Tom do this? He had the best criminal defense attorney in town and would have beaten this thing. Now, he had forfeited the chance to see TJ every day and couldn't even attend his own mother's funeral.

Whether Bernie Tannenbaum thinks so or not, he must have scared the hell out of Tom for him to run like this. That had to be the reason; the alternative was unfathomable.

The line that formed to pay last respects to Mary Sullivan was long and patient. Each person kneeled before the open casket, silently said a prayer, did the sign of the cross, rose, and then turned to Pat and said, "I'm so sorry, Pat. How are you holding up?"

Pat understood the repetitive rite, yet he didn't have to like it. He turned to Claire, standing beside him, "I'm gonna get some coffee. Want some?"

"Maybe some water, but don't worry, you go and sit for a while; you've been standing here for a long time now."

Pat attempted to make his way through the crowd to the area reserved for family members when he encountered two uniformed police officers who had just entered. At first, he thought they were there for Tom, but the larger of the two took off his hat, and Pat recognized him as his childhood buddy, Danny Crotter. Catching Danny's eye, Pat walked over and shook his hand.

"Danny, glad you could make it."

"I'm so sorry, Pat. How are you holding up?" said Danny.

"I'm fine. I'm fine. Thanks for asking."

The officer with Danny was younger and shorter. He had a slightly reedy frame but was muscular nonetheless. He looked like a runner. His red hair was matted down with a severe case of hat head as it was rather long for a patrolman.

"Oh, Pat, this is my partner, Larry Wiggin."

Larry Wiggin extended his right hand to Pat and simultaneously expressed his condolences : "I'm sorry for your loss."

"Thank you. Wiggin is it? That's Irish, right?"

"Yeah, yeah. Third generation."

"That's good. Where you from?"

"Bridgeport. Born and raised."

"That's okay too. I knew I liked you."

Pat turned back to Danny. "New partner? What happened to Garvin?"

"He's filling in at Tach for a while. He'll be back."

Larry and Danny seemed like an odd pairing. Pat had met all of Danny's partners over the years, and somehow, they all seemed to "fit" with Danny. This new guy didn't seem to "fit." He was much younger but not baby-faced, cop-like but not frayed around the edges like most beat cops. He was too crisp, too starchy, too something.

"Excuse me, guys, I was on my way to get Claire some water."

"Yeah, yeah, Pat. We'll talk. I'm sticking around."

Walking away, Pat pulled out his handkerchief and patted his brow. Maybe he had too much coffee and needed to sit for a while. He was sweating and felt lightheaded again.

Joe Hinckley approached the open casket and knelt before it. He looked at Mary's sallow face. The effects of the disease and treatment visibly showed its impact on her, yet strength and dignity still reflected the Mary Sullivan he had come to know. He had known Mary since the early days when he started for the organization, and Pat took him under his wing. He remembered the hot coffee and food she used to bring to the whole crew on election days, and each time he would drop in at Pat's, she made sure he left with a full stomach. As a single guy, he appreciated that and would sometimes invent reasons to drop in on Pat. Pat knew this after a while but did not say anything to Mary.

He silently recited a "Hail Mary" and "Our Father," the only two prayers he could remember, did the sign of the cross, rose, turned to Claire, and said, "I'm so sorry, Claire; how are you holding up?"

"I'm fine, Joe. My mother was a strong woman, and I suppose it was a blessing that it occurred as quickly as it did."

"How is Pat?"

"Why don't you ask him?"

Joe turned as Pat approached with a bottle of water for Claire. He took his place next to her in the line.

"Hi Joe, thanks for coming."

"Oh yeah. I wouldn't miss this for the world." Joe wondered if he had said something stupid. Pat did not let on if it was. He patted his forehead with his handkerchief.

"Is it hot in here, or is it just me?" Pat asked no one in particular.

"Dad, please go and sit down."

"It's okay, really. Where are the kids?"

"They're downstairs in the sitting room. I brought some Legos for them to play with. Mrs. O'Toole is keeping an eye on them."

"Mrs. O'Toole. Jesus Christ, she's a lush. Couldn't you find anyone else?"

"Dad! Please. Someone will hear you."

Pat did not hear the last admonishment. The room was spinning; people and objects blended into streaks of light that circled the room at high speed like an evil ride at the parish carnival. The room's sounds turned into an ominous white noise that was sucked into the same nauseous vortex, followed by a loud shriek as if an el train was passing overhead, and then nothing: darkness and silence.

He woke up on the couch in the sitting room. His first sense of the space was the smell of old coffee and stale cookies. He opened his eyes and saw Claire, Joe, Danny, Larry, and a young man he did not know leaning over him as if they were peering into his grave.

"Dad," Claire softly said.

The young man patted his head with a damp towel.

"Pat, take it easy," explained Danny, "you passed out back there."

Larry stood beside Danny, saying nothing and looking into Pat's dazed eyes.

"I'm okay. I'm okay," said Pat, irritated by all the attention. He tried to get up.

"Pat, stay put," pleaded Danny. "Just rest a minute, okay?"

The young man put two fingers at the base of Pat's neck while looking at this watch.

Pat grabbed the young man's fingers and asked no one in particular, "Who the hell is this?"

"Pat calm down," said Danny. "This is Dennis O'Connor; he's an EMT with the fire department. He's here with Mrs. O'Conner; it's her son. He knows what he's doing."

Pat released the fingers while staring up at Dennis O'Conner.

Dennis smiled. "Just trying to see how fast your heart is going, Pat. That's all."

"My heart is fine, pal," said Pat as he tried to rise while fighting the hands that gently tried to keep him down. "I'm fine, everyone; I'm fine. Take it easy." He sat up, and Claire sat beside him and put her arm around him.

"Dad, take it slow. I can take you home if you like."

"No, no." He looked down at his bare feet. "Where the hell are my shoes and socks?"

"Right here, Pat," said Joe, sheepishly holding them up. "I thought it would help your circulation, so I took them off you."

"Did you check to see if I had clean underwear on too? Christ man! You're all making too much of this! Give me my goddamned shoes!"

Pat rose and took a step to take the shoes from Joe. Instantly he cried out in pain and collapsed back to the couch. "Jesus H. Christ!" he yelled.

"Dad!"

"My foot! My goddamned foot!"

Dennis grabbed Pat's ankle and searched for the source of the pain. Blood was flowing from the bottom of his left foot. Dennis grabbed some napkins from the cookie table and wiped the wound as he tried to look at it.

"Looks like you stepped on the kid's toys here. You have a piece of one of these Legos in your foot. Hold on."

Dennis tried to extract the sharp piece of toy from the foot but lacked the necessary implement.

"Jesus, this hurts," said Pat.

"Come with me," said Dennis. "We have to find a place to get this out."

Dennis assisted Pat to the bathroom. Pat sat on the vanity top and put his foot in the wash bowl. Dennis turned the water on and let it run over the wound to clean it. "This may sting a bit but let this run over your foot for a few minutes. I have to go out to my truck and get some tweezers. Be right back."

Dennis left the bathroom, and Pat was suddenly all alone, sitting on the vanity top with his left foot in the sink and cold water pouring over the bloody wound. Surveying his situation, he leaned against the mirror and wept, a soft and weary sobbing that echoed in the tiled bathroom like a ghost moaning late at night. The reality of the circumstances was hitting home and becoming overwhelming. His pain was undoubtedly physical, but it did not compare to the deeper inner pain that he was feeling. A pain that he had tried to hide for the past 27 hours and up until now had been successful. He grabbed some tissue and wiped his eyes. He could not recall the last time he had cried.

Dennis returned with a small medical bag. "All right, Pat, let's take a look at that foot. I have an emergency kit here with me now, and I should be able to get this thing out."

Pat obeyed while wiping the teary remnants from the corner of his eyes. Dennis focused on the bottom of Pat's foot.

"Hmmm."

"Hmmm. What does that mean?" Pat asked in a cracking voice.

"It's still bleeding. I think there's something still in there."

"You didn't get it all?"

"Hmmm."

"Is that a medical term?"

Dennis probed the wound with his tweezers. "I see it. I see it. Just hold on here."

"See what? Oww. Fuck, Man!"

"I see it. It's a ...it's a...face!. You have a face in your foot!"

"A what?"

"A face. Or actually, it's a head, but the face part is staring back at me through your skin."

"I got a fucking face in my foot?"

"Yeah, it's one of them Lego people or something. Yeah, it's a little head, all right." Dennis extracted the head from Pat's foot and held it before him.

"Look at that, huh? At least it's smiling. Look, Pat, this wound is deep. You're probably going to need some stitches. When was the last time you had a tetanus shot?"

"I have no idea."

"I'll take you to the hospital. You got to go."

"Can't it wait? I'm at my wife's wake, boyo."

"I wouldn't. Especially if you don't know when your last shot was."

"What if I don't? What if I waited a couple of hours? What then, Ben Casey?"

"You could lose your foot and maybe more if it gets infected. Pat, you may not have an infection, but you've had a head in your foot. A head that could have been anywhere."

Pat was silent as he mulled it over. An infection would be all he needed right now. "Let's go."

CHAPTER TWELVE

After he left the wake, Joe Hinckley went home to his now vacant third-floor apartment for a quick look around. The Andersons had moved out a week earlier, and Joe was painting and doing repairs needed in the apartment for showings to prospective new tenants. The flat reeked of fresh paint even though Joe had left the windows open to air it out.

He hoped he would find a good tenant quickly to put it behind him and focus on his precinct duties. It was getting near crunch time, and Joe would be out working the precinct every night. He worked as if his job and financial well-being were at stake, which was possibly true. He shuddered to think about what would happen if he lost his job or was transferred clear across the city. His incentive was genuine. Like clockwork, he would come home from his precinct work, walk upstairs, past the Patroski's door where he would hear their television blaring due to their hearing deficiencies, and up to the vacant apartment. He would take a quick tour to reassure himself that it was still there, ready to be rented to another perfect tenant.

That night Joe entered the flat and noticed the paint smell was somewhat different. He walked through the empty front room and to the bathroom. He let out a barely audible gasp. He stared at Tom Sullivan, who was leisurely sitting on the toilet doing his business.

Just as surprised, Tom looked back at him and held his palms in the air as if Joe was the intruder.

"Excuse me. Do you fucking mind?" Tom said impatiently.

"Oh, yeah. Sorry man," Joe replied, reaching in and closing the door. After a short wait, the toilet flushed, the sink ran, and the door opened.

Tom smiled at Joe and said, "Hi, Joe. Do you mind if I crash here for a day or two?"

Joe was speechless at Tom's presence and his cavalier approach to the whole situation. This wasn't a buddy crashing on your couch after too many beers.

"Joe? Can I?" Tom asked again.

"Uh, yeah. I guess. I, uh, may have some new tenants, you know; I might have to show the place."

"That's okay. Just let me know. Do you have anything to eat?"

"Yeah, yeah," said a dumbfounded Joe. He slowly realized the reality. "Hey Tommy, what the fuck? You're hiding out, aren't you? You're a fucking fugitive from the law. I can really get screwed."

"Relax. Only if you know that I am here."

"But I do."

"Do you? I've been up here for a week already. You don't know shit."

With that realization, Joe reverted to his dumbfound mode. "How did you get in?"

"You never lock the door, idiot. Listen, Joe, I'm outta here in a day or two. You don't have to come up here until then; everything will be cool. For you and me. Come on, Joey, give me a break."

"Tommy, man, if someone finds out you're here..."

"Nobody will find out," Tom cut in. "Nobody. Besides, my dad would appreciate it."

All Joe needed to hear was Tom to invoke his father. "All right, all right. I will leave here and not come back for three days. See you."

Joe turned to leave when Tom grabbed his arm and looked at him desperately, "Can you get me something to eat?"

Joe could not say no. "Be right back."

"And Joe, maybe a couple of beers?"

Twenty minutes later, Joe returned with a bag of White Castles and a twelve-pack of Old Style beer. As Joe walked through the front door, Tom eagerly grabbed the bag of wee hamburgers and tore at it like the hungry fugitive that he was. He quickly took one of the burgers from the bag and wolfed it down in a bite and a half.

"Come on this way," Joe said as he headed for one of the bedrooms, out of the way of any prying eyes that may be lurking outside. A small desk lamp sat on the bare hardwood floor in the middle of the room. It was the only piece of furniture and light present. They sat on the floor pow-wow style with the remainder of the fast-food meal in the middle. Tom started on another burger, and the two sat in an uncomfortable silence.

While he was out getting the burgers, it dawned on Joe that he had just come from the wake of Tom's mother. Did Tom know of this? Did he know that his mother was dead? Do I say anything? He began to feel sympathy for Tom and wished he knew what to say.

Tom finished his second burger and reached into the twelve-pack for a beer. He opened it, took a long sip, wiped his chin, and looked at Joe. "How was the wake?"

Relieved that he did not have to tell Tom that his mother had died, he felt a different form of awkwardness. Do you say that you had a good time? Or that it was a "great" wake?

"Okay."

"Okay?" Tom smiled and reached for another burger.

"Tom, I'm sorry about your mom. She was a good person," Joe said from the heart.

Tom held the boxed burger in his hand and dropped his head, not moving for a full minute before looking up at Joe.

"Thanks, man." His eyes glistened, but not a drop fell.

"The wake was full. Your mother had a lot of friends."

Again, Tom dropped his head, but the dam below his retina collapsed and sent tears cascading down his cheeks. Gathering himself, Tom wiped his face with the back of his hands and stared at the burger in his hand.

"You know, I hate these fucking pickles," he said as he reached between the small buns of the burger and extracted the pickles as a dentist would a tooth, and tossed them on the paper bag. He continued to eat.

Joe felt like a fly on the wall of another man's soul. It was uncomfortable. He had never felt this way before and pondered what to say or do next. He could feel Tom's pain.

"Don't worry," said Tom. "I don't know what to feel myself."

There was a brief pause as Tom finished the last burger, lit a cigarette, and finished his beer with a long swig. He reached into the twelve-pack, retrieved two more beers, and handed one to Joe.

"Two people who I was closest to the most have died within the past month, and I could not do anything for them. Couldn't help them, console them, couldn't...," Tom swallowed hard, "...couldn't tell them I loved them."

He took another sip of beer. "I feel powerless. I run a good crew for the ward, I run a good precinct for Eddie. All the clout a man could want. But there was nothing, not a fucking thing I could have done for Janis or my mom. And that's what hurts. It's a deep pain like someone just kicked me in the gut, and I can't get that first breath out after the kick. Gasping for air, like drowning without any water. Just trying to do a simple little thing like take a breath, and yet I can't. Something won't let me."

"But you will breathe again," blurted Joe.

Tom looked at Joe with an appreciative look and attempted to smile but could only manage a slight twitch of his lower cheeks.

"Yeah, I'll breathe again." He deposited his cigarette butt into the beer can. "Good night Joe. Thanks for the sliders." He stretched out on the floor and closed his eyes.

"Can I get you a blanket or something?"

Without opening his eyes, Tom softly replied, "No. I'm going to lay on this cold hard floor tonight."

CHAPTER THIRTEEN

Pat slowly made his way to the gravesite, limping and aided by a cane. It had lightly snowed the night before, and the morning sun turned the dusting into a treacherous muddy obstacle course. Claire was at his side, clutching his elbow and helping him to navigate the slippery terrain. Usually, Claire would be in the background during any family event, with Mary doing the planning and execution. Claire was now the feeder, planner, and general go-to person during this family crisis. To Pat's subtle amazement, she now cooked supper every evening.

He had trouble the night before. After three hours in the emergency room at the hospital, he welcomed the chance to get some sleep. Dennis had stayed with him during the entire time. He had not known Dennis before the evening but found him to be a good guy and hoped to thank him somehow in the future.

When he finally got into bed, he stared at the ceiling. He tried to close his eyes, but his lids did not respond. The last forty-eight hours flittered in his head like speedy fireflies darting from one dark corner to another, too fast to collect and too many to hold, should he even catch them. It made him restless, and he kicked the blankets off his right leg and exhaled..

What happened to his life?

Just a month ago, he was counting the days before he and Mary would sail to their Golden Years, happy and radiant, surrounded by grandchildren who go home at night, free to love and spoil them. An occasional trip to Vegas or somewhere nice in Florida, sleep-in a little bit longer, read a little bit more, or learn how to fish. Isn't that what you were supposed to do?

He had fished before, in the Marquette Park lagoon, and caught some blue gill and carp with the kids when they were young, but maybe he could have taken it further, saltwater or deep-sea fishing, who knows? Isn't that what retirement is all about? Weren't you entitled to some casual decisions after years of working, providing for your family, and being a good neighbor? He felt betrayed and sorry for himself as if something was waved in front of him as a prize at the finish line, only to be cruelly snatched away as he finished the race.

Why Mary?

Mary was the only one among them who was without sin. Of course, she had Original Sin, but everyone had that. Why was the devoted, practicing, and helpful daily communicant the first among them to go? The thought disturbed Pat and led his train of thought to the station from hell... Guiltville.

How could he not have noticed that Mary was ill? He thought of the signs, her weight loss, the wigs, and the general malaise in her that was not there before. Had he known her condition earlier, could he have made a difference? Probably not, he assured himself. But his hindsight gave him a troubled feeling. She was in a better place; that had to be it. Because of her piousness, she got to be the first to go; much like Pat's retirement, her work was done, and she was being rewarded, and she was up in Heaven now learning how to fish.

The sinners and assholes are left here on earth to deal with life; they remain in a living gray hell. Am I an asshole or a sinner?

There had to be a difference. He didn't consider himself a sinner. To him, a sinner was plain evil, like a murderer or a rapist, or a child molester. These acts were heinous and needed a deprived and sinful mind. Pat had always tried to do the right thing and behave himself.

Occasionally, he would have too much to drink, and he was not the most regular attendee at Sunday mass. But were these sins or just malfeasance? Did any of these actions ever hurt anyone else?

Did it hurt Mary? Did I hurt my family?

Maybe I'm just an asshole, thought Pat. He knew sinners went to hell; that was a given, but where do the assholes go? Is there some Purgatory where maybe assholes enter a conditional program to get to Heaven, like driving school for a minor traffic ticket? What did he ever do to deserve that? But Heaven seemed so distant and, for the moment, unreachable.

Mary is there, that's for sure. Maybe she would come to him and give him some coded message about how he can get in, like sneaking into a drive-in movie through a hole in the fence. Maybe that's why she went first. Mary was casing the joint for the rest of them, and when it was our time, if we could not get in through the front gate, we would sneak in through the rear.

But there had to be a gray area. Would you call it gray hell or gray Heaven? That has to be where the assholes go. What would it be like?

He accepted the fire and brimstone images of the ultimate hell just as Sister Concetta had drilled into him in grade school; pain and fire would befit the evil sinners, but she never mentioned anything about gray Heaven.

Then there was Limbo, which, if he remembered correctly, was filled with babies who died before they were baptized. No fault of their own, but a sin nonetheless in the eyes of the church, but they were given a break.

To him, the image of Limbo was of a large playroom with Little Tykes toys and Golden Books strewn about as the babies occupied themselves until Armageddon. He didn't believe that God would hurt or punish babies; babies should never feel human pain. That just wouldn't be right. But maybe in gray hell, he surmised, you feel internal pain. Not a physical pain but a feeling something like when you walk around all day knowing that you forgot to mail the mortgage on time or when your boss is pissed at you, or even that split second when you close your car door, and you realize that your keys are still in the ignition.

A ray of morning sun pierced through a slit between the curtains, and he realized what gray Hell was all about. He had hardly slept a wink all night, and now he had to get up and bury his wife. The living remain in Hell. Gray hell.

* * * * *

The gravesite stood in the middle of Section C of St. Mary's Cemetery. When Pat and Mary first looked at it ten years ago, it was a bright, warm July afternoon. The setting was pastoral. Mary liked it, so Pat immediately paid the asking price.

Today, the overcast clouds and the layer of dirty, melting snow cast the site as gray Hell. The bare trees, more significant now than when Pat first saw them, loomed overhead in stark contrast to the ashen sky as the attendees gathered around the grave. Wisps of vapor from the mourners quickly vanished into the cold air. Collars were up, noses were red, and each person was given a flower.

Pat was oblivious to the surroundings as he walked with his cane. Claire assisted him with every step. His foot hurt, but he sure as hell wasn't going to be pushed to the site in a wheelchair. There was plenty of time for that later in his life. As he approached the site, he looked up at the small crowd, seemingly all staring at him. He realized he was the last to arrive.

Father Martin stood at the end of the hole, prayer book in hand and heroically trying to act as if the weather did not affect him. When Pat settled in, Father Martin took it as his cue to start the service.

"Eternal rest grant unto Mary Sulivan, Oh Lord, and let perpetual light shine upon her…"

Pat glanced at the crowd gathered around in a semi-circle. Eddie Byrne was there, as were Mary's church lady friends and Pat's ward co-workers. Claire also had some friends in attendance, and he recognized some neighbors from the block. It made him feel a little better knowing that these people cared.

But then, an unmarked police car stopped about thirty yards behind the funeral procession. Two plainclothes got out of the vehicle and each watched the proceeding as they went in their separate directions, widely circling the solemn gathering in a conspicuous attempt to be inconspicuous. Pat recognized one of the cops as Larry Wiggin, Dan's "new partner" at the wake. *What the hell is this? Why are they here?*

"May the souls of the faithful departed through the mercy of God rest in peace…," continued Father Martin.

Tommy. They are looking for Tommy. What sort of man could not attend his mother's funeral, even if he was on the lam? Could Tommy be here? He looked around, wishing that he had taken the sunglasses that Claire offered him as they got out of the car. He slowly panned the entire cemetery, eyeing every bare tree and every oversized headstone that could conceal a six-foot figure.

A crow leaped from a branch causing it to bounce like a dreary diving board. He looked up and felt as if he caught the eye of Larry Wiggin. He glanced down to the hole but sensed Wiggin's stare on the side of his face like a hot lamp in an interrogation room. It was warm and unpleasant and, despite the cold, made him sweat. Claire looked at him and patted her father's brow with her handkerchief.

Wiggin and his partner had completed their lap around the crowd and met behind the edge of a small wooded area on the grounds. A wide berth was given. A few heads had bobbed up and glanced at Pat. Father Martin's words turned into background noise as Pat adjusted his cane as a diversion to his now rising tide of anger.

Wiggin lit a cigarette, watched the mourners for a couple of minutes, and then entered the wooded area with his partner, disappearing temporarily and coming out about fifty yards down from where they had entered. Again, they paused and watched the ritual.

Run, Tommy, run.

Pat looked about more noticeably now, his eyes darting to the source of any movement in the cemetery. Shadows, rustling leaves, moving autos, flying birds, and distant airplanes were all he saw.

Run, Tommy, run.

Claire sensed her father's tension and grabbed his hand in hers. He squeezed back, signaling to her that he was all right.

"Amen," said Father Martin, and the congregation replied in kind.

The casket was lowered into the hole, and one by one, the crowd tossed the flower they clutched into the hole. Pat's wrath had ebbed as he waited until only he and Claire remained, and each said a silent prayer. He bowed his head, made the sign of the cross, and whispered, "Goodnight, my dear. I'll be waiting for you to show me the back door."

Assisted by Claire and his cane, Pat composed himself and made the slow hike back to the limo provided by the funeral home. He was not in any hurry as he again scanned the cemetery, hoping for a glimpse or a sign of Tommy's presence.

Wiggin stood next to his car, and Pat's ire rose again. His angry thoughts returned to the funeral home where he first met Wiggins. You fucker. You son-of-a-bitch. This is a big fucking joke for you, Shamus. You weren't at the wake to mourn; you were there to spy. You fucker.

He tried to stare two painful holes into Wiggin's skull, but it didn't work. Wiggin still stood there, alive, and returned the stare with a terse business-as-usual manner.

"Come on, Dad," Claire pleaded.

Pat obeyed and let Claire take him to the car. The procession pulled away in a sad parade, each car displaying the bright orange "FUNERAL" sticker in the front window. After the last car left, Wiggins followed but turned opposite of the funeral cars at the cemetery's exit.

The mourners gathered at "Kirk's Family Inn" for the post-funeral luncheon. Clair had made the arrangements. Again, Pat admired Claire's new attitude and wondered how long it would last. He was glad that Claire was handling the whole thing because he felt like getting extremely drunk. To hell with it, he would get a snootful and go home to bed, his new life starting tomorrow. It was all becoming too much for him.

He headed straight for the bar and ordered an Old Style and a shot of Irish Times. The shot went down quickly, and the glass was immediately replenished. The bar started to fill up as the group arrived. Joe Hinkley, Ernie Diaz, and Stu Miller, all Pat's co-workers, gathered around Pat, ensuring his glass never saw the bottom and making small shoptalk.

A nervous edge hovered over the bar until a couple of rounds were finished, and the ambient volume increased to a level where conversation levels had to be upped. Sporadic bursts of laughter were heard above the din. Pat tried accommodating everyone he talked to, realizing how awkward the situation could be. His sorrow abated, and the rage at Wiggin now also ceased. Despite how tired he was, he felt pretty good. His foot throbbed while he was in the car on the way to Kirk's, but the pain lessened as he rested his foot on the bar rail.

Pat understood and approved that the gathering was standard after an Irish funeral. He thought that these post-mourning festivities were directly culled from the old country's three-day wakes. He had never been to one but recalled stories from his grandfather about the food, drink, music, and conversation. This was similar in a way. He turned to Joe Hinkley.

"Hey, Joe. Did I ever tell you about Father Danaher?"

"Who?"

"Father Danaher."

"Who's that?"

"My grandfather's parish priest."

"Yeah, sure. Hold on just a second." Joe turned to the bar, signaled the bartender for two more, and turned his attention back to Pat. "Now, who is this?"

"Father Danaher, jeez. I told you, my grandfather's parish priest."

Suddenly, Officer Danny Crotter, in civilian clothes, approached the bar.

"Pat. How are you holding out?"

Pat looked Danny straight in the eyes. "Fine, Danny, fine. Where's your new partner?"

"He was only temporary. Just for last night," Danny replied. Pat nodded and turned back to the bar. Realizing that Pat was now aware of who his partner was from the evening before, Danny left the restaurant.

The crowd was now streaming into the dining area as the food was served. Pat threw down another shot of Irish Times and ordered another beer to take to the table.

"I'll bring it to you, Pat. Go sit down," said Joe.

Pat nodded his approval and slowly headed for his table, where he found Claire and the kids seated.

"How many are coming?" he asked Claire as he sat beside her.

"I made reservations for 75."

"Jesus Christ, who's gonna pay for all this stuff?"

"Dad, stop it.

Pat turned to Jesse and Tommy Jr, each sitting across from him at the table.

"Hello, boys."

"Hello, Granpa," the boys answered.

The food was served, and so was the liquor. Pat slowed his Irish Times intake, and the luncheon helped him feel even better. The food was decent, and he was together with what was left of his family. Claire was cheerful and acting very adult-like, and the kids were behaving. It was a small moment, but Pat savored it and tried to etch the scene in his mind like a photograph for future reference.

The only drawback was Father Martin's presence at the table. He didn't care for Father Martin. He thought the priest was full of himself and looked down at the parish flock as if they were his sheep. He was about fifty-five years old and had a full head of hair with graying temples that hovered over a thin and toned body. He looked too healthy to Pat. The good father obviously worked out at the gym, and somehow that didn't jibe with Pat. A pastor should have a look of wisdom on his face, not a tan, but today it did not matter. Today Father Martin was being bearable, and Pat thought he would drink to that.

"I'm going to the bar," Pat announced. "Does anybody need anything?'

Getting no response but a tacit look of disapproval from Claire, he headed for the bar. The bar area was cleared out as everyone was now in the dining area. The bartender stood idle behind the bar when the day's best customer approached.

"Irish Times and an Old Style, please."

"Coming up. How about your friend?"

Pat turned and saw Father Martin standing behind him. "Father, I didn't see you there."

Father Martin smiled at the bartender and answered her, "Heineken, please."

The order arrived, and the priest paid for the round.

"So Pat, how are you feeling? Are you hanging in there?"

"Pretty good, Padre, pretty good. Better than I thought, to tell you the truth. I'm a little tired, did a bit of tossin' and turnin' last night, but I'll be all right."

He wondered if he should bring up the Gray Hell thing. No, he would let it slide; he was in no condition right now to get into a deep philosophical discussion with Father Martin.

"That's good, Pat, that's good. Tell me, how will everything work out at home?"

"What do you mean?"

"Home, with Claire and the kids. Are you going to need some help? Daycare or anything like that?"

Pat had no idea. He had hardly thought about it at all. Daycare? Claire would be home, but if she was at home during the day, she was not working and not bringing home any money. He already knew his retirement was long gone and he would have to continue working. He still had to pay off his equity loan and 401K loan, which he had used to pay Tommy's lawyers and bond. He suddenly felt lightheaded.

"We'll be okay, Father. We'll just have to tighten things up a little bit, that's all." His forehead became moist as he put one arm on the bar to steady himself. He was wobbly as he reached into his pocket, pulled out his handkerchief, and wiped his forehead and brow.

"Pat, are you feeling okay?"

"Yeah, I'm okay, Father. I just gotta go to the bathroom. Excuse me, Father."

Pat walked to the far end of the bar and entered the Men's room. It was empty. He rushed to the sink, ran the water, and splashed his face several times, hoping to get some blood rushing to his cheeks again. It seemed to help. He stood up from the sink, grabbed the towel machine, and stuck his face directly into the linen towel loop that hung from the device, wiping the water off his now circulating cheeks.

Suddenly, an arm reached over the top of his left shoulder, a hand covered his mouth and spun him around. It was Tom.

"Tommy, what the fuck are you doing?" Pat said with anger.

Tom held his index finger to his lips for Pat to keep it down. But he would have none of it.

"Don't shush me!" Pat continued, "My house and everything I own are at risk here!"

Tom grabbed Pat by the elbow, led him into the only stall in the bathroom, and closed the door behind them.

"I need some answers, boy." Pat was still livid but more constrained. The anger over another act of selfish recklessness by his only son rose in him through the regular channels. He had felt this way many times before. He waited for the usual shouting response from Tom, but there was none. Tom only peered up at his father with an expression and look Pat had not seen since he was a baby, helpless and fearful and making silent visual plea for reassurance and help. Instantly the fury in Pat drained and left him. His boy needed his help.

Recognizing the situation, Pat spoke in a hushed and severe manner. "What are you doing here? They are looking for you all over the place. They were at the wake and funeral."

"I figured as much. That's why I wasn't there, but I had to come, to apologize to you."

"But why, son? Why did you run? It makes you look guilty as hell."

"No, Dad. You've got to know that I didn't do anything. She was dead when I got there."

"I do, son. I do. I always did, and so did your mother. But you have to convince twelve people who never met you before that you are incapable of this. This running is not going to help."

"Dad, I'm scared. I won't be like those DNA guys who spent twenty years in the joint for something they never did."

The bathroom door opened, and another person entered. Tom quickly hopped onto the toilet, and Pat sat beneath him, allowing only one set of feet to be seen below the stall door.

"Pat, are you all right?" Father Martin on the other side of the door.

"Yeah, Father,' Pat answered, "this roast beef is going right through me."

"Thanks for the warning," Father Martin said as he exited the bathroom. "I'll see you at the table."

After Father Martin left the room, Tom climbed down from the toilet and continued his discussion with Pat.

"That was close."

"I'm assuming that this wasn't the first time you've hidden from a priest," said Pat.

"I'm not saying."

The attempt at levity broke the tense atmosphere just a bit.

"What are you going to do now?" asked Pat.

"I'm not sure. I've got to find out who was in that house before me. I saw someone; I'm not sure who it was. I can't hang around here, though, and I'm out of money."

Pat reached into his pocket and pulled out what money he had on him. "Here, here's forty-seven bucks. It's all I have on me. Can you wait? I can run over to the ATM across the street."

"Yeah. I guess, but I can't wait too long."

"Wait here. I'll be back in a minute. There's a Seven-Eleven down the street."

Pat unlocked the stall door and started to leave when Tom put his hand on his shoulder and turned him around.

"Dad, I love you."

"I love you too, son," Pat responded. "Wait here."

Pat walked as quickly as he could with the cane and exited Kirks. Outside, he tried to move as fast as he could, but the best he could do was a rapid limp.

Red–faced and out of breath, he entered the Seven-Eleven store, found the cash machine down the first aisle, and withdrew five-hundred dollars from his account, the most the machine would permit. He turned to leave; Larry Wiggin stood between him and the door.

"Hello Pat."

You fucker. "Hello, Larry."

"What are you doing? Is the luncheon over?"

Looking about the items on the shelves in the aisle, Pat grabbed a box of sanitary napkins and showed them to Wiggin.

"Emergency. You know how it goes sometimes. A real man isn't afraid to buy tampons." Pat walked around Wiggin, took the box to the cash register, paid for them, and turned back to Wiggin. "Gotta go. Urgent. See you later," and he exited the store leaving Wiggin standing in the aisle.

Pat hurried back to the restaurant and returned to the bathroom via the same route he used when leaving. As he passed through the bar, he found Joe Hinckley waiting for a drink. He gave Joe the bag as he passed by. "Here, these are for you."

Joe peered into the bag and dropped it as if Pat had handed him a bag of shit.

Pat entered the bathroom and knocked on the stall door.

"It's me open up."

The door opened, and Pat walked in, locking the door behind him.

"Damn, I've been sitting here making people think I have the worst case of diarrhea in the world. Where have you been?"

"I ran into Larry Wiggin. He's a cop."

"That fucker."

"Do you know him?"

"He interrogated me at the police station. He's a detective."

"Well, he was at the funeral and wake. And he's nosing around here. He followed me to Seven-Eleven. His only goal in life right now is to catch you, so watch yourself."

"I will. Did you get any money?"

"Yeah, here. There's a little under five hundred dollars here. I could only get five hundred a crack at the ATM. Will I see you again?"

"I don't know. I can't tell you anything right now because I don't know. Listen, Dad, you have to do me one other thing. You gotta tell Tommy that I didn't kill his mother. He's gotta know that."

"We told him that Mommy and Daddy are on vacation. He doesn't know anything. But whatever happens, he will know the right thing. Believe me."

Both men looked directly into each other's eyes and exchanged a lifetime of regret- regret for chances missed, moments passed as routine and should have been special, and many other lapsed opportunities.

"Goodbye, son."

"Goodbye, Dad."

And then Pat left. Outside the bathroom door, he stopped momentarily composing himself and went to the bar.

"More Irish Times, please."

CHAPTER FOURTEEN

Pat woke up the morning after the funeral on the couch, with a pillow beneath his head and blankets spread over his body. His shoes were off, and his shirt lay neatly over the back of the overstuffed chair in the corner of the room. It was early. He heard no other sound from the rest of the house. He sat up and looked around, trying to recall the last hours from the day before.

The limo had dropped them all off at the house, and Pat continued to drink. He had pulled out photos of Mary and gazed at them until Claire took them away and laid him down on the couch. Was he weeping then? He wondered if it all became too much for Claire, and she just took the pictures away, or if he just passed out and let them slip from his hands.

The luncheon. The friends and family, Tommy. Larry Wiggin. Four hundred ninety-six dollars. A box of sanitary napkins.

He stood up and went to the kitchen to find Claire quietly starting the morning procedures.

"Good morning, Dad. How are you feeling?"

"All right, I guess." It occurred to him that he should probably be feeling a lot worse than he felt.

"Want some coffee?"

"Please." He sat at the kitchen table.

Claire poured a cup from the steamy glass pot and placed it before Pat.

"Are you hungry? Do you want some eggs or something? I can make some toast if you like."

"Maybe a piece of toast," said Pat as he ran his hand through his hair. "Are the kids up?"

"No. Not yet. Any minute though."

Claire put two pieces of bread into the pop-up toaster and sat across from Pat at the kitchen table. "Are you going to be okay, Dad?"

"Yes, I'll be fine. I got a lot out of me yesterday. I apologize for being a pain in the ass."

"Stop it. I talked with Eddie Byrne at the wake, and he said to take as much time as needed before you return to work."

"Eddie was there? I didn't see him."

"You were at the hospital at the time with your foot."

"Well, I may take a day or two off, but we have less than four weeks until the election. I've got to get some stuff done."

"Don't overdo it. Dad, you've got to slow down now; there's no need to kill yourself over this election."

"Nobody's killing themselves. I said I'd take a couple of days off."

"I want you home for one week, at least. Besides, you can't do too much with your foot the way it is anyway. Stay home; I'll take care of everything around here. Keep your foot up, watch some TV, and take a break."

The far bedroom door opened, and two sleepy-eyed cousins walked out in their pajamas.

"Good morning, boys," said Claire.

"Morning, boys," said Pat.

The cousins returned the greeting in unison as they both took their seats around the table. Claire rose and prepared two bowls of cereal.

"I mean it, Dad, at least a week."

"Okay, okay. You got me."

Larry Wiggin sat at his cluttered desk. A few days of messages and papers had piled up on him. The stake-out at the funeral had not led to anything concrete. However, he didn't consider it a total waste, as something had happened, but he didn't know what.

When he met the "old man" Sullivan in the convenience store, by chance, as he went in there for a pack of cigarettes, Sullivan seemed to act like a fox caught in a hen house.

Wiggin saw him at the ATM but didn't think anything of it at first. But when Sullivan grabbed a package of sanitary napkins, Wiggin smelled mischief in the air. Even if there was an emergency of some sort, the aged and gimpy widower would not be the first choice to run to the convenience store. Sullivan needed cash for some reason, not sanitary napkins.

From the small mound of paper on his desk, he grabbed the forensic report on the Sullivan murder and started leafing through it like a dime store novel reader going to the last chapter first. His veteran eyes scanned the report at all the usual places until he found information that caused his heavy red brows to knit. Wiggin grabbed the desk phone.

"Felicia, Hi. It's Larry. I'm looking at the Sullivan report. I'm a little puzzled as to what was found at the scene. Can you confirm this?"

"Just what it says. We found human feces on the scene, next to the body."

"And it wasn't from the victims? Are you sure?"

"Positive. That was the easy part. Keep reading. Did you get to the clothing samples yet?"

"Come on, Felicia. Help me out here. What are we looking at?"

"I thought you were the detective!"

"Okay. If the information is good, it may be worth a nice dinner at Gibson's. How's that sound."

"Sounds nice, but I don't think my husband would care for it too much. But okay, here's the deal, we found fibers in the feces that indicate that the person probably shit in his pants, and it came down his pants legs to the floor."

"Like a sick calling card or something?"

"No, I don't think so. The calling card types are a little more symbolic and more artistic. This was just there, lying next to the body. Like maybe the person got scared or something."

"Can you compare it to Tommy Sullivan?"

"I'll have it for you by tomorrow."

"Felicia, couldn't you have given me a heads up on this a little earlier?"

"Have you checked your voicemail in the last couple of days?"

"No."

"You ought to try it sometimes. It's a new technology that helps the whole communication thing around here."

"Touche' Felicia. Thanks."

"Bye,' love."

Wiggins accessed his voicemail.

"You have twenty-three messages," spoke the auto voice.

"Damn." Larry started his messages.

"Larry, your son would like to see you sometime. His play was this weekend, and you missed it again, but what else is new? Call me."

He hung up the phone and sat back in his chair. He thought that he explained why Daddy couldn't make it last weekend. His son, Peter, seemed to understand. Daddy's job kept him busy. Apparently, his mother did not get the message. He felt a sudden twinge of guilt. He had not seen Peter in over ten days, as he had been working on this Sullivan thing almost 24/7. It had to stop. He would make it up to the boy when this was all over, even though he promised the same intentions last month and probably the month before.

Wiggin again reached for the phone and listened to his voicemail. This time he wrote down phone numbers and other important information before deleting the voicemail. Most of the calls were old news.

The last message was from Sheila Perkins.

"Detective Wiggin? This is Sheila Perkins. I'm Janice Sullivan's neighbor. You had talked to me at the scene. I just wanted to tell you that I seemed to remember something else. There was a door slam. I don't know why I forgot to tell you about this, all the excitement, but I heard a door slam when I was freeing little Tommy. I hope this helps; please call me if you want. Thank you."

A door slam? What door? He reached for the reports and pulled Perkin's statement. She hadn't mentioned anything about a door slam. The defense attorney will have a field day with this little tidbit. She said that she heard it when she was freeing the kid. He again reviewed her statement and tried to place the door slam in the time-line of her statement. She had seen Tom leave the house before she entered. She went in and found the boy tied up in the bed. She went into the kitchen and got a knife to untie the kid. She runs back into the kid's room and cuts his bonds.

A door slams. Someone is left in the house. This probably is an amateur. Tom walks through the house yelling and screaming and in a violent rage, and this amateur is literally scared shitless as he stands over the bodies.

Wiggins arose from the desk and left for Sheila Perkins's house.

CHAPTER FIFTEEN

Joe Hinckley worked his precinct furiously. If Eddie Byrne was going to lose this election, it would not be for lack of votes from Joe's precinct. Eddie would survive. He always did. He had a knack for surviving.

Joe had hoped to hitch his employment future to Eddie's wagon. Eddie had many connections and would certainly look out for Joe if Joe was a good soldier. Something maybe even out of the ward. Something city-wide with more money, or even, God forbid, a county job where he could move out to the suburbs. That would work. He could even get closer to the gambling boats in Joliet. However, these scenarios would not be possible if Eddie didn't take his ward. That was imperative. Eddie would see the effort and results from Joe's precinct and appreciate his efforts even more; good precinct captains are like gold, that's what Eddie always said.

Joe's commitment had not left him any time to seek new tenants for his apartment. Much to Joe's relief, Tom left after a few days. Joe had brought some food for Tom after the first night's meeting. A couple of days later, he went up with another meal and found Tom gone without a trace.

Joe breathed a sigh of relief. He had done what he could for Tom, who disappeared as quickly and silently as he had arrived, and Joe had no idea where. Tom was on his own now as far as Joe was concerned. They had never hit it off. Tom was a couple of years older than Joe, and both ran with different crowds, but they had seen each other enough at the ward office to at least acknowledge each other's existence; plus, Joe worked with Pat on several occasions, so he had some insights on Tom.

Joe looked up to Pat, not just for his ward instincts, but also as a mentor. Joe's parents were gone. Pat was his chief advisor when he first bought his apartment building. Pat explained the procedure and the financial aspects of the whole thing to Joe in a manner that he could grasp and understand. From then on, Joe held a special place for Pat and would do anything for him. Even shield his fugitive son in his building.

He would have to get the ball rolling again on the apartment.

"Got to get it done today," he thought; the main thing was to get the ad in the paper and some paying tenants.

* * * * *

The week crawled for Pat. On Monday, he sat on the couch and let Claire wait on him. It was easy to be waited on, but he started to feel worse as the day went on. He rarely got as drunk as he did the night before, and the day off helped him to recuperate. He felt better on Tuesday, and by Wednesday, he was ready to stroll to McGurns and watch some animal TV. Thursday, he went with Claire to do the food shopping, his foot feeling better enough to walk the aisles while leaning on the cart, and by Friday, he was almost restless.

Each night, however, he dreamed of Mary or, better yet, had visions of her. Her smiling image appeared not surreal-like but realistic, black and white, grainy, moving images like an aged and silent 8mm film, with scratches appearing and disappearing as she waved to him. The images soothed Pat and made him feel better. Her presence was still with him when he dreamed of her. It made him feel like she was lying beside him in his bed as she had for forty-six years.

He would endure this spell of tragedy and pain, and be strong. Mary was rooting him on with her waves and smiles. He no longer felt like an asshole.

His Gray Hell would end, that he knew, and what lay ahead would be good and just. Things would be right again.

* * * * *

On the following Monday evening, the ward office was packed. The precinct workers filled the meeting hall until it overflowed with bodies, each bundled in heavy winter clothing. After Eddie addressed them, they would leave and spread throughout the ward.

Pat stood at the rear of the hall and scanned the room. It was a multicultural gathering. The Hispanics stood next to him; they would work the north side of the ward. The African-Americans would work the east end, and the white would take care of the south and west sides of the ward. This was a real source of pride in this ward. Every time Eddie spoke to them, he would bring up the various ethnicities in his office; indeed, it was rare.

The city of Chicago had been traditionally divided into ethnic neighborhoods. The boundaries tended to reflect the actual ward map, but not this ward, thought Pat. He had listened to numerous testimonials of ward residents claiming they would not move even if the neighborhood started to change. Most of them stayed true to their word, so the ethnic turnover in the ward slowed and caused a stability. The turnout this evening was proof of that.

Eddie took his place before the podium in the front of the hall.

"Okay, okay! As you all know, this race is going to be close, real close, and the difference in this election will depend on you," Eddie hollered as he pointed to the crowd. "You and your hard work are going to be the difference-makers. Our people tell us we are neck and neck right now, but we've got an advantage, a sizable advantage. Our organization has the city's best and most hard-working workers!"

The crowd responded with cheers and shouts.

"Yeah, yeah, you guys know what I'm talking about here. We've always had the hardest working crew in the city. We knew that. Just look at our numbers. Just look at them!"

The scene was starting to resemble a lively sermon. "Pastor Eddie" was bringing in the flock.

"But I hate to say it," continued Eddie as he held up his hand to be heard. "I hate to say it, but it's not enough. We have to do more, work harder, and reach out to every registered voter in this ward. We have to make contact, face-to-face, person-to-person contact! When you feel like you want to get home to your family at the end of the night, you have to do one more block! Just one more, that extra effort show, believe me!"

"For you, Eddie!" came a shout from the crowd.

Pat glanced over to the side of the hall and watched an excited Joe Hinckley clap and hoot like he was at a high school football game.

"Knock on those doors and tell them we represent the 51st Ward. Tell them why our business district is booming, tell them why we have more jobs now than four years ago, and tell them about the new library!"

"We tell them, Eddie! We tell them! We tell them all that!" came various shouts from the crowd.

"As you know, no organization is worth more than its people. I feel good about our people. I feel confident. We're facing a whole new set of issues today, issues that my challengers will bring up constantly. Believe me; I know that I'm not black or Hispanic. I'm very aware of that."

A slight murmur of laughter rose from the crowd.

"And while I'm proud of my Irish heritage, it doesn't matter. It's a non-issue for me; I can be black, brown, white, red, or purple, just like this room here," Eddie continued as he made a sweeping gesture over the room.

"But let me tell you something. I will serve every resident of the 51st Ward and serve them competently and to use the best of my ability, to serve every person fairly and evenly, no matter where you live, no matter who you are, no matter what color that person is, they will be served with equal treatment!" The volume of Eddie's voice rose to the apex of the speech.

"That's just the way it is here in the 51st Ward! That's always the way it is in the 51st Ward!"

The crowd reacted boisterously as Eddie clasped his hands over his head.

Pat had seen it all through the years, and he had to admit that Eddie was pretty good at working the crowd up to a rabid Knute Rockne-type lather.

The energized crowd started to file out of the hall, milling about in front, most holding literature and flyers to be passed out during the evening to each house in the ward. It was brisk outside; an inch or two of snow still lay about the city, but the workers didn't seem to mind. Still warm from the coffee, hot chocolate, and Eddie's rah-rah speech, they were genuinely enthused about the task that lay before them. They slowly dissipated into the ward.

Pat was among the last to leave the hall. He ensured everyone had enough of the correct material to distribute. There was indeed a timetable for the various pieces to be dealt out, and tonight's batch, the first batch, was a four-color piece with Eddie's official city hall portrait, the city's flag, and the city seal behind him. This was a photo that no other challenger could produce; thus, it immediately separated Eddie from the rest of the candidates. This would have to be established first and foremost, which was why this expensive and eye-catching color portrait would be distributed first. It was fluff with few words, but the visual impact was the goal. The black and white pieces and county-provided pieces would be sent out later. The last pieces, which had yet to be put together, would address any last-second issue that may arise and be sent out a night or two before the election. This was the standard time frame. Pat was generally responsible for getting the pieces out in the proper, timely order.

"Pat. Hey Pat."

Pat turned to the voice. He was bundled up and about to leave the hall. It was Glen Barker, one of Eddie's campaign chiefs.

"Hey Pat, how ya' doin'?"

"Okay, Glen, I'm doing okay."

"That's good, that's good. Listen, Eddie and I talked, and we think it's a good idea to give you some help."

Two young Hispanic men appeared behind Glen.

"Pat, we'd like you to take these two gentlemen with you. Meet Octavio and Juan."

"It's not Juan, it's John," said John, not Juan.

"Sorry, it said Juan on the form," Glen said as he returned to Pat. "Both speak good Spanish and English."

"Spanish? I don't have any Hispanic in my precinct."

"Yeah, we know, but we need you to go to the 18th Precinct tonight."

"The 18th? What's this all about? I've got work to do in my precinct," Pat protested.

"I know Pat, but Eddie's not worried about the west side of your precinct; he knows you have your precinct under control. We need help north, so we're shuffling our resources a bit." Glen crept closer to Pat's ear and softly said, "You know we have to keep our eyes on these fuckers. That's why Eddie asked for you."

"Oh, and I suppose I should feel honored?"

"Come on, big guy, just a couple of days."

"Days? He wants me to do this after tonight? What the fuck?"

"Well, yes. Actually, until election day. You would still work your precinct on election day."

"And who's going to watch my precinct?"

"Well, you have a handle on that already."

Son of a bitch, Pat thought, my workload just doubled.

"Thanks, Pat. Eddie's not going to forget this," finished Glen as he walked away, leaving Octavio and Juan with Pat.

Pat turned and walked outside to the sidewalk with the two new aides dutifully following him like obedient puppies.

"Where's your car at? You guys will have to follow me."

They looked at each other and then back to Pat.

"We have no car," said Octavio. "We took the bus."

"So I have to drive you guys? Is that it?"

"Si," said Octavio.

"Yes," said John.

"Did you guys get any material to hand out?"

"No."

"We'll go back in, get some from the back room, and bring it out here."

They looked at each other again.

"Inside!" Pat spoke louder as if volume would somehow transcend the perceived language barrier. "Material. Literature. To pass out." He mimicked the act of passing out material but realized he looked as if he were dealing a deck of cards. "Never mind. Come on."

The trio returned inside the hall to retrieve that material. Pat grabbed neatly bundled stacks of flyers and handing them to his two new assistants.

"Here. Take this stuff."

They dutifully obeyed. When their arms were full and could not carry anymore, Pat led them to his car, which was parked behind the building, where they deposited their load into his trunk and got in the car's back seat.

Pat slid into the driver's seat and stated the plan of attack.

"We'll start at 71st Street from Kedzie to Sawyer and then work south to 75th Street. You guys got that?"

"Si," said Octavio.

"Yes," said Juan.

"Then, if we still have time, we'll go over to the next block and do what we can. We only have one piece tonight, but we have to make sure that each house with a registered voter gets at least one. I'll give you guys a list. You got that?"

"Si," said Octavio.

"Yes," said John.

"We don't want to waste this stuff on people who don't vote. Any house with two or more voters, we knock on the door and give them the stuff personally and, if possible, talk to them a little bit. If they seem bored or uncomfortable, bail on 'em and leave. We don't want to be a pain in the ass. Do you guys live in this precinct?"

"Si," said Octavio.

"Yes,' said John.

"But if they seem interested, I suggest getting to know them. A good captain knows every person and family in his precinct. He knows the family member's names, where they go to school, and their ages. When they get to be 18 years old, he registers them right away. When they go to college or the military, he gets them absentee ballots. This is essential, especially with big families. If you kept on top of it, you used to be able to get maybe ten or twelve votes from a single address. Not anymore; families just aren't that big anymore. Now a good address might get you five or seven votes; you know what I mean?"

"Si," said Octavio.

"Yes," said John.

Pat stopped at a red light and turned to his kept audience in the back seat. "Who are you guys?"

Both passengers had jet black hair, Octavio's was cropped close to his skull like a good old-fashioned crew cut, and Johns's was longer and parted down the middle. John's build was lean, and although he was roughly the same height as Octavio, he looked taller. Octavio had a round face and wore wire-rimmed spectacles with a faint line of hair below his nose and above his lip. It could not be called a mustache.

"I'm Octavio; he's Juan."

"Fuck you," John said to Octavio. He turned to Pat, "It's John." He turned back to Octavio and said, "Don't make me kick your ass."

"Whoa, whoa. Calm down back there now," Pat said to his rear-view mirror as his light turned green, and he continued driving.

"His real name is Juan, but he wants to be called John because he's Mister Americano," explained Octavio.

"No, man, I'm American; I was born here. My legal name is Juan, but only until I get some money to get a lawyer to change it to John. He wants fifteen hundred bucks, and I'm working on it. When I get the dinero together, I'm gonna have it done."

"Why? What's the big deal?" said Pat to his rear-view mirror.

"Because I want to live on your block. Your block is full of Mikes and Daves and Steves and Johns; there are no Juans, no Pedros," he turned to his co-passenger, "no Octavios."

Octavio shook his head in mock pity.

"You can live anywhere you want. This is America," Pat explained.

"Come on, Mr. Sullivan, do you really believe that?" countered John.

"Yes, I do. You can live on my block, but my question is, why? Why would you not want to live with your own kind? Why do you want to live with a bunch of boring old white guys?"

"Because you boring old white guys have everything better. Better schools, better stores, better neighborhoods."

"Well, whose fault is that? Look, don't get me wrong, the folks who I really feel sorry for are the hard-working middle-class guys who want to go to work, raise a family, and have a decent place to live, but when they go to another neighborhood, the rats follow. Like a sinking ship,"

"So, I couldn't live on your block?"

"Yeah, I said you could. But when you start killing chickens in the backyard for dinner, I have a problem with that."

"Killing chickens?" Octavio incredulously retorted, "Come on, man, is that what you really think we do?"

"Don't you?"

"No, man, I get my fucking chicken at the Jewels, just like you, man."

Pat chuckled. "Do you guys go to school or work?"

"I do both," said John. "I work at the auto warehouse on Kedzie during the day, and I'm taking some classes at Daley College at night."

"How about you, Octavio?'

"I work for the Park District."

"Did they tell you to come out here and help?"

"No, not really, but I know how the game is played."

"Smart kid."

Having reached their destination, Pat parked the car at the beginning of 71st Street. They all got out of the car and loaded up on the literature.

"Okay, we'll work the same side of the street, using the leap-frog method. I start, you take the next one, and you take the next one, and so on. That way, we do every three houses and stay together; there's safety in numbers," explained Pat as he closed the trunk.

The two rookie campaign workers grasped the concept well, and their hustle and enthusiasm pleased Pat. They were energetic and acted like no one was making them be there, an attitude often displayed by fresh city workers. They would be all right, thought Pat; they didn't seem to need to have anyone watch over them. A couple of nights with them, and they would be able to handle this section of the precinct by themselves.

When the evening's work ended, John and Octavio walked home. Pat stopped at McGurns to see who was around. There was no reason to hurry home; no one was waiting for him.

Entering the musty tavern, Pat surveyed the room and didn't see anyone he knew, so he pulled up a stool in the corner of the bar. McGurn came by with a full glass of Old Style.

"Evening Pat."

"Evening Mike. How are things?"

"Pretty slow tonight."

"Well, I'll help you out. Cheers. Can I get you one?"

"Maybe I will."

Pat always offered to buy McGurn a drink and was usually turned down, but the slow night allowed him to imbibe this evening. He pulled out a bottle of Irish Times from the speed rack below the bar and poured himself and Pat each a shot. They both grabbed their glasses and held them up to each other.

"God bless you, Pat."

"And you also," and the drinks disappeared.

"So, how are you holding up, Patrick?"

"It's tough," conceded Pat, "but I'll survive. Everything will get back to as normal as it can. This too shall pass as they say."

Another patron called for McGurn. "I'll be right back."

Pat sat and sipped his beer as he watched the television above the bar. A cobra and a mongoose were squaring off in what looked like a fight to the finish. They circled, jabbed, exposed their teeth, and finally started to tussle. McGurn appeared in Pat's line of vision.

"Wait, move," Pat said as he gestured McGurn out of the way.

McGurn stepped aside and turned to the television. The mongoose had the snake by the back of its head, with the rest of its body writhing and coiling, trying to wrap itself around any portion of the mongoose's body. Finally, all the writhing slowed and then stopped, becoming a lifeless snake. The mongoose was declared the winner by the off-camera narrator.

"Okay," said Pat, "just wanted to see the end of that one. It was pretty good."

McGurn turned back to the bar. "Those mongooses are bad mother fuckers." He grabbed Pat's glass to refill it from the tap as the last of the bar patrons filed out, waving to McGurn as they passed.

"Good night now," said McGurn. Only he and Pat remained.

"Where's Pete?" asked Pat.

"He's in the back, whacking off. No, I sent him home early. No business tonight."

Pat sipped the fresh beer placed in front of him. "That's good. Hey Mike, how old are you now?"

"Fifty-nine."

"Fifty-nine. Jeez. What's your game plan? I mean, are you sticking around here or what?"

Mike let out a sigh.

"I dunno. I'll tell you, I never planned on leaving. I thought I could have done this forever, but now, everything is changing, the neighborhood, the people, the businesses. Is it good or bad?

"People around here still work and still try to raise a family. That's good, but they're different, not like you or me. Their customs, their ways, their ethnic habits. That's bad for me; I don't want to come off like a bigot or anything like that; I'm not. I respect those people and their customs. Show me a race that doesn't respect their own customs and ways, and I'll show you a race that doesn't exist anymore because it just dies out, but those customs and ways are foreign to me; I'm not used to them or their meaning or what they represent. I'm Irish; I'm comfortable with Irish customs and ways.

"Does that make me a bad guy? Am I a bad guy if I feel more comfortable living among people who practice the customs and ways I'm more familiar with?"

"No, no, Mike. You have a little old school in you. Neighborhoods will never be like that anymore, at least the middle-class neighborhoods. They take this melting pot shit a little too seriously sometimes. This melting pot, this hot pot of old crayons that you melt down and stir up until it becomes an ugly maroon color, which is dull, bland, and stagnant."

"Melting crayons?"

"But if you take the same crayons and just stir them once or twice, blend them, it becomes a swirl with the colors clearly identified, yet woven together into a large and beautiful mass."

"I'm going to cut you off in a minute."

Pat gave out a small laugh. He knew he pushed that one as far as he could.

"Okay, silly analogy, but my point is that you have to preserve your identity and culture while at the same time blending in with the American identity and culture."

McGurn cocked his head to the side and looked at the ceiling before posing his response to Pat. "But just what is American culture?"

Pat paused and thought. "That's a good fuckin' question. English language, for one, you gotta speak English here. We've been speaking it here for over five-hundred years; that's gotta count for something. Freedom also, free to make a living, give your opinion, and raise a family without too much shit from the government."

"Yeah, that's the usual bullshit," countered McGurn, "but we want immigrants to accept our ways. They want freedom just like we do; I don't think that's an issue with them. And language, most of them learn at least a little English. Let me ask you something: how many Americans speak two languages?"

"What do you mean?"

"Everywhere else in the world, they speak at least two different languages, but here, if you speak two languages, you are either majoring in it at college or an immigrant. I mean, is that good in your culture?"

"It's the language we speak here. What do you want me to do? Learn some African dialect?"

"No, but what about Spanish? Half the fuckin' city is going to be Hispanic. If I were a businessman, I'd be taking Spanish lessons right now."

"But you are a businessman."

"Yeah, but if I were to speak Spanish around here, I'd start to get that clientele, and before you know it, it's welcome to Mike's Casa de Cerveza, and that ain't gonna happen. Cinco de May my ass."

Pat laughed aloud and pushed his empty glass to McGurn for a refill. McGurn obliged and came back with two more shots of Irish Times. He continued to speak as he poured.

"I think they want everyone on the same page, everyone to be the same, identical. They ask for tolerance, but what they really want is androgyny."

"What's that?"

"Everyone is the same, just what I said. It's a-racial, a-sexual; they want everyone to blend in, like your maroon crayons, but to the point where no one can tell if you are female or male, white or black, young or old."

"I get you; they want everyone to look like Michael Jackson. They want a country full of Michael Jacksons."

"Yeah, sort of. Boy, that's a creepy thought. Can you come up with anything else?" replied McGurn, obviously disturbed.

"But that's not right either. God put us here, each of us, with our own faults and warts. I don't think that was by accident. I gotta disagree with you, Jack; I don't think they want a nation of pasty white robots." Pat chuckled and raised his glass. "To American culture."

McGurn countered, "To Michael Jackson."

Pat paused and raised his glass again. "To parking lots and strip malls."

McGurn accepted the challenge and raised his glass as they swapped toasts to American culture. "To baseball."

"To the automobile."

"To the Fourth of July."

"To Thanksgiving."

"To Jazz."

"Ooh, Jazz. Good one. To cable TV."

"To fireworks."

"I think the Chinese discovered fireworks."

"To American fireworks."

"Yes! Here's to cherry bombs!"

Together they clinked their glasses in mid-air, took long sips, and put them back on the bar.

"You know," continued Pat, "it had to come down to this sooner or later. We begged for immigrants a hundred years ago. My grandfather got off the boat from Ireland in New York in 1888. He saw how crowded it was and hopped on the train to Chicago. He got off at 14th and Wabash found a job at the stockyards within five days. He never left and retired from there 45 years later. He wasn't alone. His wave of immigration came and set up the neighborhood we know. Then the blacks came up from the south and, granted not by choice, set up their area in Bronzeville. There's Chinatown. Greektown. Little Italy. Kiss 'em all goodbye."

"Maybe not," McGurn said. "See, right now is a whole new wave of immigration, but it's not European. It's Hispanic; it's the new wave. See, America's like a beach, wave after wave pounding the American beach, changing the coastline and features of the beach, dragging little pebbles of sand, back and forth, back and forth. And baby turtles too. The waves sweep the baby turtles from the beach to the ocean, where fish and other weird shit try to eat them. Maybe one in a hundred makes it out to the open ocean, where their chances are a little bit better. Did you know that?"

"Baby turtles? You have to turn the station on your TV set once in a while. What the hell are you talking about?"

"Sand, baby turtles, the point is, the waves change everything. Like this country, the beach constantly moves, changes, and reshapes itself forever."

"I liked my melted crayons better. More visual, less esoteric. Less stupid."

"Okay, maybe I went too far with the baby turtles."

"I got to go anyway," said Pat.

Pat got up from his bar stool and put on his hat and coat as he headed for the door. While he threw his scarf around his neck, McGurn said, "Keep your head up; it could always be worse."

"How so?" asked Pat.

"You could be a baby turtle."

"At least I'd be where it's fucking warm," finished Pat as he tied his scarf and walked out the door into the frigid night.

CHAPTER SIXTEEN

The workload was constant. The election was still three weeks away, but the campaign's intensity seemed to increase tenfold each day. Pat continued to work both his precinct and the 18th with Octavio and John. The evenings were tiring and cold, especially after he had worked his day job. With little time to spare and the fast food intake increasing, the walking never seemed to stop, and thanks to the dull omnipresent pain in his foot, Pat developed a limp in his gait that contributed to the general miserable feeling. The good news was that Octavio and John seemed to be getting the hang of it.

Despite their differences, Pat had taken a liking to both young volunteers. John strived to be liked and was a bit of a pest to Pat sometimes, but the hustle and ability to grasp directions were well worth his annoyance. He worked the field well, talking to the voters and trying to answer any questions regarding the voting procedure. His knowledge needed to run deeper on the issues, which usually were union or financially related. Still, he could dance around any direct answer, and sometimes Pat wondered if the kid didn't have a future in politics.

On the other hand, Octavio was a tough nut to crack. He was just as efficient and a go-getter, but this kid had a side that Pat couldn't quite make out. Even though John was a college student, Octavio was the thinker of the two. He was curious and seemed to have deep thoughts. Pat wasn't sure if that was a good or bad thing.

In addition, Octavio didn't seem to care much about assimilating as John took the whole thing to an extreme.

Octavio was proud of his heritage, and rightfully so. He talked about his family and their Mexican heritage at length. Pat appreciated it as he had his familial lore from the old country. Bottom line, the kid worked his ass off, so he was OK in Pat's book.

However, Pat was annoyed by Octavio's tendency to jump from Spanish to English and back again in the same sentence. Pat would shout, "Speak English, you dumb fuck!"

Octavio would laugh and say, "Oops. That's right, my *malo*, I'm the bilingual one here, and I'm the dumb fuck," but he would always oblige and return the conversation to English. John spoke fluent Spanish also, but rarely around Pat. Occasionally, he and Octavio would speak in Spanish between themselves.

The temperature was stuck at twenty-five degrees and was not expected to warm up for another three days. The dry and bitter cold infiltrated both buildings and bodies no matter what precautions were taken. Pat wore his wool cap, with the ear flaps out and tied around his chin. John wore a Bears knit cap and an overstuffed down ski jacket, making him look like one of the inflated characters floating down Broadway in the Thanksgiving parade. In contrast, Octavio wore a green army jacket and no hat, just a wide headband that covered his ears.

"How come you don't have a hat on?" asked Pat.

"I don't wear hats, man."

"When it's cold out, you shouldn't care how you look. Look at this guy." Pat gestured towards John. "He looks stupid as shit right now, but I bet he's warm."

John offered up a weak defense. "Hey, I don't care, man. Ain't no good-looking chicas out tonight anyway."

Octavio seemed blasé about the subject. "I just don't wear hats, man. No big deal."

It was almost too cold to be out, but Pat thought staying ahead of the game would be a good idea, even if they were not to finish the entire night's work. They would catch up when the weather broke. Working the leapfrog method, they worked Komensky two blocks up to 79th Street and then back down the same block, but on the opposite side to the back to where they started, where Pat gave instructions for the rest of the night.

"Real cold out tonight, guys. I'll tell you what, let's work Keeler to 79th, and we'll call it a night. It'll be my treat tonight at McGurns when we're done."

* * * * *

Pat and his "posse" walked into a lively crowd at McGurns. The jukebox was on, and the conversation level was high. Quarters lined the side of the pool table to mark who would play winners. A hazy veil of smoke hovered above the table below the faux Tiffany drop light.

The television was on without sound. An old lion was trying to escape a pack of hyenas. One of the hyenas jumped on its back and bit deeply into the lion's neck. It held on for dear life like an urban cowboy on a bucking bull machine. The lion tried to shake it off. Finally, the lion slowed, stopped, and finally fell. The remainder of the hyena pack quickly pounced on their new prize, and soon the area was reduced to a limp mound of hair, bone, entrails, and bloody, sated hyenas.

Sinatra sang "The Lady is a Tramp" in the background.

Mike McGurn was in his 33rd year as owner of McGurn's Tavern and was the main bartender for 35 years. He bought the place in 1973 from an ex-cop named Walter Borzofski, who owned the place when McGurn first started to tend bar there.

Walter suddenly had to disappear. McGurn paid what he thought was a fire sale price at the time. Walter's career with the CPD ended abruptly when he tried to shake down what he thought was a local drug deal. It turned out it was an FBI sting set up for an entirely different suspect.

Walter had a silent interest in the bar before his exit from the police department, as police personnel could not legally have an interest in a liquor license. After he was fired, his interest became loud, and a steady parade of shady characters would drop in for quick visits with Walter in the back room.

Mike was never involved in any of Walter's antics, but he occasionally heard more about Walter's business than he wanted. Walter would tease him. "Getting nervous, Mike?"

Mike McGurn was a straight arrow. After he bought the bar, he wanted to clean it up, make it a respectable place where a guy could go and prop his kid up at the bar with a bag of potato chips and a soda while Dad sat with a cold one and watched the Bears. A genuine honest-to-goodness neighborhood tavern like the ones Mike remembered that his father took him to when he was a kid.

It never turned out the way McGurn wanted. He did his best, but it dawned on him about a year or two into his ownership that this was what it would be. He cleaned out the real riffraff, the pseudo-made guys, and the heavy lifters for the well-connected. But there was still an element that he didn't care for, an undercurrent of arrangements and deals and midnight bargains that was ingrained in the plaster walls, tin ceiling and the clientele. It was just the karma of the bar, the mojo of the building. The way it was.

McGurn was behind the bar, just below the television set, watching the old lion's demise. He didn't see Pat and his friends as they found three seats in the corner.

"Hey Mike!" yelled Pat.

McGurn turned around and recognized Pat as the source of his beckoning and smiled.

"You're a real sicko; you know that? Showing this crap on TV," said Pat.

"I love this animal channel; you know that. Something gets slaughtered every day. Who are your buddies?"

"Mike McGurn, meet Octavio and John; they work with me in the 18th precinct," said Pat as he gestured to his companions.

"Hello, guys. What'll you have?"

"Miller Lite," said John.

"Bohemia," said Octavio.

"Don't have that," said McGurn.

"Dos Equus," continued Octavio.

"Nope. Don't have that either."

"Corona?"

"Sorry."

"Okay, give me a Bud."

"That I can do. Pat? Old Style?"

"Yeah, Mike, and I do assume that you have tequila? You're not a total redneck, are you?" answered Pat.

"You're a funny guy; you know that, Pat?" Mike said as he turned to fill the order.

"What's the tequila for?" asked Octavio.

"I figured we would do a shot."

"I don't drink tequila, man."

"I'm sorry. I just thought, oh, never mind," Pat said.

Stutterin' Dave came by the bar where the trio sat, dutifully grabbed the ashtrays and dumped their contents into a plastic garbage bag he was holding.

"Hi, Dave."

"Hello Pat."

"Dave, these are some friends of mine. Octavio and John, this is Dave."

"H-h-h-hello," said Dave to Octavio and John. They both nodded in response as Dave walked away to find the next ashtray.

"What's his story?" asked Octavio.

"He's okay," said Pat. "He works here at the bar. McGurn adopted him years ago. I don't mean really adopted but took him under his wing. As you can tell, he's also a bit slow. Mike gave him a job and the apartment above the bar. One day he was just around, taking orders from McGurn, and that was that.

"His stuttering has gotten better through the years. God, you should have heard him when he first started. It took him ten minutes to ask us what we wanted. I was surprised when he said 'hi' to you guys. He doesn't talk with many people. There's a lot of hurtful assholes in here at times, but once he knows you and knows that you won't fuck with him, he'll chat with you. He's a good kid, you know? So is Mike. They're both good people."

"So this is where Pat Sullivan spends his leisure time," said Octavio as he looked around the establishment.

Pat smiled and said, "I might have been here a couple of times."

McGurn came back with the three beers, a bottle of tequila, and three shot glasses.

"Just two tequilas," Pat said to McGurn. "Seems like we found the only Mexican in the world who doesn't drink tequila."

"Make that one," said John through a sheepish grin. "I don't drink tequila either."

"Jesus, what are the odds of this?" Pat said. "Well, make that one tequila for the Irishman."

"Coming up, boss," said McGurn as he poured.

Pat took his one-ounce prize and held it up. "Here's to you, lads." He clinked his shot glass with the beers of Octavio and John and drank it down with a quick backward jerk of the head. "That was good. It's been a while since I've drank any tequila. Shouldn't I be chewing on a piece of lime or something?"

"Only if you're a girl," cracked Octavio.

"Were you guys working tonight? Tough night to be outside if you ask me," asked McGurn as he refilled Pat's shot glass.

"Yeah. Didn't stay out that long. That's why we're in here," said Pat.

"Nice place you have here," said John to McGurn.

No one had ever said that to McGurn, so he temporarily froze and tried to respond graciously. "Uh, thanks. I take it you don't get out to a lot of classy joints," was all he could muster up.

"It's a bar," said Octavio.

"You're right. A joint is a joint," said Pat, "the only difference between this place and where you guys hang out is that I can read the beer signs in here."

"And no soccer on the television," added McGurn.

Everyone chuckled as no offense was taken, and none was intended.

"Nice meeting you guys," said McGurn. He turned to attend to the rest of the bar.

"So, Pat, how is this stuff going to work out? Is Eddie going to win this thing?" asked John.

"Yeah, he'll win, but we may have a runoff this time; this thing is closer than normal. Your guy, Lopez, will get a strong showing with the Hispanics, but he's too young. If he keeps his nose clean and gets his name out there a bit, he could be a player the next time."

"Why did you say,' your guy'? We work for Eddie, man," said Octavio.

"Hey, sorry. I just meant that he was a Hispanic, you know? Believe me, I know who you work for," explained Pat.

"Sorry, I just get a little nervous in Anglo bars."

"Oh, yeah? Why?"

"Oh, just some bad experiences. Bad vibes."

"Are you getting bad vibes here?"

"No, not at all. This is all right. I'm having a good time."

"Good, you have nothing to worry about here. Not in this place. It's just full of old drunks watching animal snuff films."

"Yeah, lighten up," chimed in John. "I'm getting good vibes here. Lopez is a punk; he doesn't know shit."

"He's no punk," responded Octavio. "He's educated and a neighborhood dude. Nothing wrong with that."

"Look, I have no idea if the guy is a punk or not," interjected Pat. "The point is, we work for Eddie Byrne and his organization. They're the ones who help us make a living. He could be an Adolph fucking Hitler, but as long as people are working, they don't care."

"Don't issues matter to you?" asked Octavio.

"What issues? The city isn't bankrupt, and the people are working. What other issues are there?" responded Pat.

"Issues, man. You know, fucking issues," continued Octavio.

"I'm telling you, there aren't any big issues. Pollution? I'm against it. Nuclear war? Bad shit, I'm definitely against it. I think all the candidates are against those things. The only issue here in the streets is, are you working?"

"But there's got to be more."

"In a national election, maybe, but realistically every alderman, to me, has two basic duties. First, work for the people and make sure that we get more than our share of city services, and second, find work for your people. That's it. End of story. Eddie's followed through on both counts, so I'm happy and know I'm backing the right guy." Pat was starting to get a head of steam going.

"I don't know, man, it just doesn't seem right," replied Octavio shaking his head.

"Look, Octavio, you're still a young guy. You still have your idealistic streak, which is nice, but you'll find out over time that this streak will be beaten out of you by life itself and the people you love." Pat's intensity was turning up a notch as he spoke.

"Just when you think you got things licked, you get kicked in the face. With no warning, just a big boot with steel toes from out of nowhere. Maybe undeserved."

He reached for the second shot of tequila on the bar and quickly downed it. "And maybe not."

Pat's gaze turned stony and astray as if he were the only one present and talking to himself. "But what are you going to do about it? "

There was an awkward silence before Pat turned his attention back to Octavio. "The older you get, the more practical your issues become. Trust me on this one."

On the television, a giant snake was on the bank of a small water-hole, its body wrapped around the stem of a bush, with a pair of small mammals' legs dangling lifelessly from its mouth.

"Hey Pat, you a Sox fan?" asked John in an attempt to alter the conversation.

"Yeah, of course."

"What about Hispanic issues?" continue Octavio.

"What issues are those?" responded Pat.

"Immigration."

"That's a federal thing. What's an alderman going to do with that?"

"Do you think they'll catch the Twins this year?" continued John.

"Oh, please," said Octavio. "They can't do anything to help people who risk everything to get a job cutting your lawn or making your French Fries?"

"I cut my own lawn."

John tried one more time to steer the conversation another way. "So do you think big Frank is going to have a good year or what?"

The snake finished swallowing the small mammal, and through the magic of time-lapse videotape, a large ovular shape made its way down the length of the snake's body, slowly being digested along the way.

Pat glanced at the TV and took a drink of his beer. It seemed to calm him down. "Octavio, pretty soon you guys, the Hispanics, will run this ward. I'm sure of it. This Lopez kid could very well be the one who runs it; I don't know. But for now, it benefits me to have Eddie Byrne running the show.

Four, eight, twelve years from now, who knows. I could be retired or dead or both, and you could be sitting here, with all these beer signs," he gestured around the bar, "written in Spanish, talking to a new precinct worker and explaining the ropes. That's the way this shit goes. You support who best protects your interest. That's American Democracy one-oh-one."

Octavio took a sip of his beer. "Then why am I working for Eddie Byrne?"

"You're asking me? Didn't you tell me you knew how it worked? Isn't that what you said?"

"I thought I did. Now I'm not so sure."

Suddenly, a group of six or seven hyenas tossed the gorged snake about like a plaything. They stretched, pulled, and nipped at it until it finally snapped like a thick Italian sausage, with all the meat falling out of the casing.

"You know, I think I'll take that tequila now," said John.

"Yeah, so will I," said Octavio. "How about you, Pat?"

"You lying bastards. I knew you guys drank tequila."

"Like you said, I might have been here a couple of times," explained John.

Pat motioned to McGurn to bring another round. McGurn obliged and even got a shot glass for himself. He would have a drink with Pat, one of his most loyal customers.

McGurn realized that Pat was a good guy, and McGurn hated to see good guys kicked around. He had known Pat for almost as long as he owned the bar. He was the local precinct captain for as long as McGurn could remember. Pat was on top of it if he ever had a problem with the city.

Of course, this special attention would cost him. He would buy the fundraising and raffle tickets and make the ward golf outing on occasion. That was the cost of doing business here, part of the overhead just like the gas and light bills.

Pat Sullivan was all right in his book, but his kid was another matter. McGurn, for the life of him, could not see any connection between Pat and Tommy. Tommy was the total inverse of his father, like a photograph negative, where white was black and black was white. There was a physical resemblance, to be sure; the jaws of both men were square and similar and matched to a tee, and as Tommy got older, his hairline started to recede much like the old man's, but the personalities of the two was what stumped McGurn.

Pat was pliant, agreeable, and friendly, while Tommy was stubborn, argumentative, and a prick. Pat and Tommy would often be in the tavern at the same time but not together, each within a circle of their acquaintances, barely acknowledging each other's presence. They never came in or left together, and McGurn sensed a barrier between the two, even though they would never bad mouth each other.

"Cheers," said Pat, and the final shot of the evening was down the hatch. Looking at his watch, he proclaimed, "I've gotta get going. Ten o'clock news and then to bed. You guys need a ride?"

"No, I can walk from here," said John.

"No, I'm good," said Octavio. "I've still got to meet a friend of mine."

"At this hour?" said Pat. "Getting kinda late. Don't you have to work tomorrow?"

"It won't be long."
"Ah, to be young again. Okay, gotta go. See you guys tomorrow."

CHAPTER SEVENTEEN

The next evening Pat sat in his big living room chair; a box of tissues next to him. Claire grounded him again due to the cold making his head feel like an overloaded box of sand. He felt miserable and wished he could go to bed, but he was waiting for the evening voter lists that John and Octavio would drop off. The lads were on their own that evening, and the checked-off voter lists would let Pat know which homes were contacted, either face-to-face or with literature.

Claire was rounding up toys strewn about in the living room. She had just finished washing the evening's dishes, and the kids were now in the bath, so she made a general sweep of the house, picking up and straightening as she did every evening now. It was almost three weeks since Mary was buried, and Claire was now comfortably assuming her role as the matriarch of the Sullivan family.

Pat, however, had yet to learn how Tom was dealing with everything. He had not seen or heard from him since the Kirk's Family Inn bathroom. Each night, he watched as an unmarked car rolled slowly down his street, pausing in front of Pat's house, presumably looking for Tom or just checking on Pat himself. He was uncomfortable being a target. He assumed it was police work, but it made him feel that he was a criminal now.

He had not seen Larry Wiggin since the convenience store encounter, but that certainly didn't mean Wiggin had stopped searching. "Oh, no," thought Pat. This Wiggin guy had a hard-on for Tom that Pat thought was disturbing. He assumed that Wiggin was the nightly visitor in the unmarked car even though he could not see into the vehicle as it crawled by the house, but he sensed it.

The doorbell rang. Claire answered. It was John. He took off his knitted Bears cap as he entered the house. He still wore his down-filled jacket.

"Hello, come in," Claire said.

"Hello. My name is John. I work with your father, Mr. Sullivan."

"Yes, that's my dad. He's right over there." Claire pointed to Pat in the corner.

"Hello, Mr. Sullivan. I have the lists with me."

"Come on over, John, and have a seat on the couch. Do you want a beer or something?"

"No thanks. I want to get home. I have some homework yet to do tonight," John replied as he sat on the couch.

"Are you a student?" asked Claire.

"Yes, second year at Daley College. I hope to transfer somewhere next year."

"That's great. So you'll get your Associates this year, huh?"

"Yeah, at least I hope so anyway."

Claire pressed on. "So, where do you want to go?"

"I don't know. The whole thing is kind of strange to me, living away and all that. No one in my family has ever gone to college, so I'm still doing my homework on these schools."

"Well, good for you."

Curtis called from the bathroom, "Mommy, we're done now!"

"Okay, be right in," Claire responded. "I have to get the kids out of the bath. It was nice meeting you."

"Yes, me too."

John stood and shook Claire's hand, and then she left the room. John turned back to Pat.

"So, how did it go tonight?" asked Pat.

"Well, we covered everything that you told us to. Everything is on the lists."

"Where's Octavio?"

"He left a little early tonight. He said he had some running around to do."

"That's okay. You guys got the stuff done. You're catching on well."

"Thanks."

Suddenly, a still-wet Curtis burst into the room and posed like a bodybuilder wearing nothing but a big grin. "I am the Hulk!" he announced.

Curtis!" yelled Claire from the bathroom.

"Oops. Hulk must go," Curtis said and turned back to where he came from, disappearing as quickly as he arrived.

"She's got her hands full," said Pat.

"How many does she have?"

"Just one, but she's taking care of two right now. Tommy's kid is with us."

"Is his Dad at work or something?"

"No. I have no idea where he's at. He left years ago."

"Oh," John said. "Uh, is she seeing anybody?"

Pat's eyes furrowed. "What are you getting at?"

Embarrassed at his lack of subtlety, John went into full denial. "Nothing, nothing. Just curious, that's all."

Claire returned to the room with two pajama-clad boys, each with combed hair and freshly scrubbed faces.

"Say goodnight to Grandpa."

The two boys ran to Pat and attempted hugs around his ample girth.

"Good night, boys. No kisses tonight. You guys don't need to catch my cold."

"Now say goodnight to Mr. uh, I didn't catch the last name."

"Munoz. John Munoz."

"You gonna change that one too?" teased Pat.

"Say goodnight to Mr. Munoz, boys."

In unison, the boys said, "Good night," and ran from the room.

"I'll have to get them tucked in later," said Claire. "Can I get you something to drink? A beer or soda?"

"I'll have a beer," John said. Claire headed for the kitchen.

"I thought you said you had homework?" said Pat.

"I do, but this will put me in the mood."

"For what? Hitting on my …"

Claire reentered the room, handed John a bottle of Old Style, and sat opposite the couch.

"I've never seen you with my father before, have I?" Claire asked.

"I just started a couple of weeks ago; this is my first election."

"Oh, an election virgin!"

"I guess," John sheepishly replied.

"Well, you're in good hands. My father wraps up every voting-age individual in the entire precinct. He'll give you the ins and outs."

"Oh, you're right about that. He already has."

Just then, loud shouts of juvenile boys were heard from the back room, arguing over a toy.

Perturbed, Claire stood up. "Excuse me; I have to see what that is all about. It was nice meeting you, John."

"Yes, likewise."

Claire left the room, and John turned to Pat, who returned an incredulous look.

"You gotta go, right? Homework waiting for you."

Getting the hint, John agreed. "Yeah, yeah. It's getting late." He looked at his watch, took a long final sip from his beer, and stood up from the couch. "My, look at the time."

"You know your way out, right?"

"Yes, of course." John put his Bears cap on. "Good night Mr. Sullivan."

"Good night John. Be a good boy now."

"I will, sir."

"You better."

* * * * *

Later that night, Claire watched late-night TV which provided the only light in the room. Using the remote to switch back and forth between the talk shows and bad teenage movies, she found nothing to her liking. She turned it off and lay back on the couch in the darkness.

She found herself thinking about John.

She had not enjoyed much social life since returning to her parents' house. Before her mother's passing, she felt sorry for herself, thinking about her past actions and consequences. She had never returned to school as intended and had been living with her parents since Curtis was born. He was old enough now to be left with a sitter. Claire felt as if she had to make a move, something to get her back into the game. Find a job, go back to school, something to get out of the house and back into her life.

Her brief attempt at rebellion had backfired. She accepted that, and now her sights were lowered. She loved Curtis with all her heart, and her family had accepted him with theirs, but she had to do something for herself now.

She now wondered what she had seen in Adam. What's done is done. She started thinking long and hard about what qualities she had seen in him. He was mysterious and seemed financially able to allow them a fun and carefree life. Plus, he would piss off her parents. This last quality now seemed like the one that stood out as she recalled the father of her son.

She had not heard from him since shortly after Curtis was born, which made him an afterthought in the Sullivan household. Claire had a couple of photos of Adam, and occasionally she would bring them out for Curtis's benefit. He would point to them and say, "Da da."

That was the nature and extent of Adam's presence in Curtis's life. A few photos and a child were all that remained of the brief relationship between Adam and Claire.

They had met while Claire lived in the Lake View neighborhood on the city's North Side. She was attending Loyola University as a second-year undergrad. She never did find out what he did during that time.

Claire softly shook her head. She knew nothing about him then and still didn't.

He wandered in and out of the campus parties and events, catching her eye each time. They finally spoke to each other. Several dates followed before she would permit him to sleep with her. Adam then stayed at Claire's regularly, bringing in groceries and his toothbrush.

As far as Claire was concerned, they were living together, this Irish South Sider and her Black man, in this culturally enlightened North Side neighborhood. The plan was simple. She would continue to take classes, get her degree, and keep taking classes throughout her adult life. That is how they do it up here, she thought. Being raised in an Irish Catholic household, she was hell-bent on making some noise when she left for college.

Growing up, she liked to compare how her parents treated her to how she perceived Tom was treated. Although Tom was an adult when Claire started to see the difference, it did not matter to her. She was always treated as if she was a child. She would make her own decisions on how and where to live and with whom she lived, with no input from the family peanut gallery.

While maintaining a 'C' average in college, she partied hard and snubbed her nose at her roots. She was never confrontational, but her parents were well aware of her restlessness and social awakening. They thought they were prepared to deal with it-her mother by rationalizing and discussing the issues with Claire. Her father left it to her mother. Despite her mother's best efforts, Claire wanted something else.

Claire's new life and intentions were grand. The hardest part was how to tell the family about Adam. She was going through her rebellious phase, but an inherent sensibility etched in her Irish Catholic soul would not let her burn any bridges. She would have to slowly pave the way for her to bring Adam home. They knew that she and Adam had been seeing each other but were unaware of their living together or that he was black.

They had been together for four months when she mentioned the idea to Adam. He was open to it, so he would not be the problem. Her parents would probably accept it after some initial handwringing. Her big concern was how Tom would react.

Tom had an undercurrent that always made Claire uncomfortable. He had a temper and a half and a nasty habit of flying off the handle. She would have to play him and gradually ease the news to him. As she was growing up, he played the big brother role, but she always doubted his sincerity. There was an eleven-year gap between them, so he wasn't living at home during her teen years. It was brief and rare if he paid any interest in anyone she would date. Of course, she always dated white boys; that's all there was in the neighborhood, but now, cut loose in the big city, she was going to bring Adam home. A large black man. As her boyfriend. Her lover.

However, her concern was all for naught, as Adam never met the family. Meetings were tentatively scheduled several times, but Adam had to be at work, or some other conflict arose. Claire didn't mind the first couple of times but grew suspicious and leery after each subsequent postponement.

The issue came to a head when Adam could no longer get out of the dates. He said he was not ready to meet her family. Claire then told Adam that she was pregnant. He stormed out of the apartment. It was the last time she saw him.

They talked on the phone during her pregnancy as he tried to convince her into getting an abortion. With her tail between her legs, she dropped out of school and moved back home to have her child. After Curtis was born, she talked with Adam once more to tell him he was her son's father. That was the last she had heard from him.

She had more mature thoughts now. She was now the single mother and caretaker of two children and a fast-aging father who needed her, especially now.

Could she afford to fall in love again?

CHAPTER EIGHTEEN

Pat was laid up for two nights. He could neither shake the cold nor Claire's constant TLC. He stayed buried beneath the blankets while resting and recuperating. By the third night he felt better. His tossing and turning had stopped. Mary still waved to him on most nights, causing Pat to look forward to going to bed. When he woke up, he remembered the dream, which helped him carry through the day.

When he reconnected with Octavio and John, Pat felt like a new man. Much ground was covered and re-covered between his new-found energy and the efficient ways of two young bucks. The three went up and down the porches, made their spiel, converged at the end of the block, and started again on the next one.

Darkly clad in layered winter wear and in perfect sync, they moved like precinct ninjas in perfect sync, bounding up the steps in short hops and back down even quicker. The young bucks were hard to keep up with for Pat, and the leapfrog pattern was customized to accommodate his slower pace.

The rows of bungalows and raised ranch houses tended to look alike. They usually met at the end of each block and checked the precinct map to see if they had not already completed the next block.

Octavio and John saw Pat standing motionless, staring at the front of a home as if waiting for something to happen. Puzzled, they walked back to Pat.

The address was 7818. The house was dark, and the shades were all drawn, giving the impression that it had somehow closed its eyes and fallen asleep. A tragic sadness hovered over the house. It was Janice and Tom's house.

Pat could only think of the cheerful events that had taken place there. He thought of Janice, Tom and TJ in better times - TJ's christening, his first birthday party, and the other family gatherings - the way it was supposed to be. The memories warmed him, and despite the grim site before him, he felt no sadness. He indeed sensed the hope that maybe this thing would work out, that Tom would come home, Janice would rise from the dead, and everyone would live happily ever after.

"Bad shit happened here," said Octavio as he and John approached Pat.

"What?" asked John.

"Bad shit, man. I heard a dude and his old lady were popped here, man. Drug deal or something," said Octavio.

"Shut up, man. You don't know shit," said John.

"That's what I hear."

"Who told you that shit, man? Who would tell you anything about that stuff."

"My amigo, Tony Petro. He would know."

"Tony Petro don't know shit. He's a punk. When did you start running with him? He's trouble, man."

"I don't run with him; I just ...I just see him once in a while."

Pat's interest was piqued. "Who's this Tony Petro?" he asked.

"He's trouble," said John. "He's a gangster wannabe, a punk."

"Hey, he's not so bad if you get to know him," said Octavio.

"Well, what the hell have you heard about this place?" asked Pat.

"Well, this house was dealing. I know that. Small shit, quarter, half-ounce of reefer, that type of shit. Housewife money. Quick stop, run in, get what you need, run out," explained John.

"How did you know that?"

"He's right," said Octavio. "Everyone knew. No big deal."

Pat was stunned. He had no idea and never saw any indication of any of that stuff going on here. This must have been what Tannenbaum was talking about. He had to find out more.

"What did that have to do with the murders?"

"I heard that she was short some money to her dealer. Zuko's guys," said John.

"Is that what you heard? No, no. That's not right. You don't know shit," scolded Octavio.

"Well, what did you hear?"

"I heard the chick's old man came home and found her with some dude. Zuko had nothing to do with it. Do you think Zuko would get involved with petty shit like this? Over less than a grand? Anyway, I heard he's straight now."

John shook his head. "I don't know, man. I don't know Zuko. I only know what I hear."

"Who is Zuko?" asked Pat.

"You never heard of Zuko? The Reverend Zuko?"

Pat then recalled his meeting with the good Reverend behind the ward office.

"Big guy? Dressed in black?"

"That's Zuko," answered Octavio.

"Why would he be involved?" responded Pat. "After all, he's a reverend, right?"

By now, John was shaking his head at Pat's naivete, and Octavio started to chuckle and explain to Pat about the Reverend Zuko. "Mr. Sullivan, you need to get to the other side of the tracks more often. Have you ever heard of the Rosados?"

"No."

"The Rosado family controls the drug scene around here. They're *muy grande*. Come on Mr. Sullivan, someone from that family gets busted at least once a year for something, and then they usually walk out. It's in the papers. Don't you read the papers?"

"Yeah I do. Must have missed it."

Octavio continued. "Well, Zuko is a cousin, rumor has it. Even though he looks Puerto Rican if you ask me. Anyway, he was involved in the family business but turned over a new leaf after finding Jesus in prison. Now he's got a church on Halsted. He preaches against any violence or drug use and feeds a lot of people at his church. His sermons from the pulpit talk of the evil ways of the drug dealer and the gangbanger all the time."

"Well, what's wrong with that?"

"Not everyone believes him. Not around here anyway."

"Why don't they throw him in jail if it's such common knowledge around here that he deals in drugs?"

"Who's gonna snitch? You heard what happened here. Ain't nobody gonna drop dime on them. Not if you want to live."

Pat was still trying to grasp what he was hearing. "Did you guys hear anything else about this?"

"Just what I told you. She was dealing and that ain't good, man. Eventually you're going to cross somebody, just a matter of time."

* * * * *

That night, Pat lay awake, fully dressed on the bed for almost the entire night. His eyeballs almost dried out from the blank stare he gave the ceiling. The drug dealing revelations were new and from out of right field.

What was all this about? Tom liked to have a good time and probably drank more than he should, but dealing drugs? Was he using? Was Janice? Was there a difference between selling and using? And probably most importantly, why? What would cause a seemingly normal family to start dealing drugs in the neighborhood unless it was the money? Was Tom taking care of his family? He knew how much Tom was making and did not see any signs of extravagance on Tom's part. He drove a used car and was still renting an apartment, for crying out loud.

Why?

Pat's eyelids slowly dimmed as he finally dozed off. Questions made him sleepy, and he was now dog-tired.

CHAPTER NINETEEN

Pat woke up and looked at the alarm clock. It was past ten. He hadn't fallen asleep until the crack of dawn. The same thoughts he had the night before raced in his mind like a movie that started from pause. The questions came to him quickly.

What does Wiggin know? He doesn't know where Tom is, but he must think that he can get to Tom through Pat, and Pat doesn't know anything, so Wiggin doesn't know shit. And this drug thing? What the hell was this all about? Zuko?

He rolled out of bed, changed the clothes he slept in, and left the house to go downtown. If he wanted answers, he would have to get them himself.

He called in sick at work, his first sick day in 23 years, drove to Midway Airport, and parked in the commuter lot for the Orange Line to head downtown, a thirty-minute ride to the Loop. It was still cold, so Pat appreciated the working heat in the new El cars. The Orange Line was the newest of the CTA's train routes, and thus, its cars still retained the creature comforts like heating and air conditioning that tended to get ruined by time and rowdy train riders.

He had not been to the Loop in over a year, as the crowds and distance turned him off. Regardless, he had no bona fide business downtown anyway. The shopping was now done at the regional malls, and city business could be tended to at the local ward office, so it was rare if Pat had any reason to go downtown. But today, he had business to attend to there.

The elevated train headed northeast, over the airport street traffic, and above the city's southwest side neighborhoods. The single-family homes and the two and three flats of Brighton and McKinley Park spread out below like a patchwork of structured fabric hastily put together without regard to any esthetics until it created an esthetic of its own.

When the sun peaked out through the dark and somber clouds, it gave the city a gray overtone and a hard, steely edge that almost dared anyone to get off the train and sample the area's day-to-day existence. The train followed the tracks that ran in a narrow corridor between Archer Avenue and the south branch of the Chicago River, heading towards the shining towers and high-rise buildings ahead.

Pat gazed through the windows at the flat, endless plain of neighborhoods. Overlaid on the plain was a geometric pattern, which was the product of the city's grid street layout. Like the castles of feudal lords, church spires broke the urban canopy to oversee their neighborhood domains and cast a spiritual net over the entire Southside.

Ask someone on the Southside where they are from, and they will tell you their parish. Southsiders don't live in neighborhoods; they live in parishes.

The train wove its way through Chinatown and entered the fringes of the South Loop, now an extreme example of gentrification. He smiled as he recalled some of the X-rated establishments that once existed on the sight of the current Chicago Public Library.

As the train came to his stop on Clark Street, he realized that he had enjoyed the ride. He had not been on the El in... probably God knows how many years. It allowed a temporary diversion from his destination, the Circuit Court of Cook County, 8th floor. He had called earlier to find out if he could check if a person was involved in a lawsuit. They said "yes," and he could even look at the file.

He wanted information. He had never pried into Tom and Janice's affairs; even during their divorce, he kept his mouth shut. He knew how Tom could be and how hard he was to live with. His temper could be a problem at times, a big problem.

Pat liked Jan; he always did. She was a good mother, and he knew she tried to be a good wife. Tom would tell Pat how Janice was always trying to change him and his lifestyle, and yet, despite Pat knowing that the changes Jan wanted would benefit Tom, he tried to keep neutral. He never did, however, hear about money problems. Tom made good wages with the city and more than enough to support his family.

Pat passed security screening and took the elevator to the 8th floor, where he found the computer terminals to begin his search. The posted instructions seemed simple enough. He got to the appropriate screen and typed in the word "Sullivan." The screen went blank as it retrieved the information and displayed information for 147 cases in columns with "Sullivan" in the title. Narrowing his search by including the first names, he reduced the load to three cases.

He took the case numbers to the clerk behind the counter, who returned with the three files, each varying in thickness. Pat signed for the files, took them to the opposite counter, and sat and read the file jackets for specifics as to the parties of the cases. The thickest file was marked HOMEGROWN LENDING V. THOMAS SULLIVAN, JANICE SULLIVAN, AND 7818 S. KOMENSKY, CHICAGO. It was a foreclosure case. After reading the file's contents, Pat discovered that the lawsuit had been filed six months earlier, and a foreclosure judgment had been entered against Tom and Janice two months later. He found that it had been nearly a year since Tom paid the mortgage. This was not good.

He looked at the attached list of the people who had previously checked the file out. The last entry was for "Wiggin, L. CPD."

That fucker.

*****

"Eddie? You got a minute?" asked Pat as he peeked into the alderman's office.

Looking up from his desk, Eddie Byrnes gestured to Pat to sit down. Pat entered and sat in front of Byrne's desk.

"How are you doing, partner?" asked Eddie.

"Okay, I guess. Moving on with my life," responded Pat.

"Have you heard anything new about Tom? I'm sorry, I've been so busy with this shit that I haven't heard any news."

"No, even though Wiggin has been following me around."

"Who?"

"Wiggin. The undercover dick. He thinks I will somehow lead him to Tom."

"Is he hassling you?"

"No. No hassle. He's just there, you know. It's gotta be him. The slow passes in the car at night, hanging out at the funeral and wake. It can get kind of creepy."

"I'll take care of him. He won't bother you anymore. I'll see to that."

"That's okay. He's a pain in the ass, but he seems to be trying to do the right thing. I'm just not sure he's on the right path, the right lead."

"He's still a pain in the ass. I'll see that he has something else to do," continued Eddie.

"Really, Ed. He doesn't bother me. That's not why I came in." He paused and asked the question that was the purpose of his trip.

"Who is Zuko?"

Eddie got up from his desk, walked over to the half-open door, shut it, and then turned the volume up on the radio that had previously supplied low background music. This was a constant in Eddie's office as he feared eavesdropping. He went back and seated himself behind his desk. "The Reverend? Is that who you are talking about?"

Pat nodded. "Yeah, I guess. If he is a Reverend."

"He runs a soup kitchen on Halstead. He also runs a couple of precincts for me in the area. Why do you ask?"

"Just curious, I guess. It helps to know who is on your side."

"Yeah, he's on our side. Look at the numbers over there since he's taken over. More registered voters. More registered voters." Eddie chuckled. "He won't feed the motherfuckers unless they show him a voter's receipt on Election Day, and he puts out quite a spread. He even gives a little wine to the guys who work the streets for him. He calls it his own 'Jesus Juice'. He's good for us."

Pat's bravado gathered as he listened to Eddie extol the virtues of the good Reverend. Usually, he wouldn't think of questioning a sitting alderman on anything, but now for the first time in his adult life, politics be damned, he wanted answers. "Were you aware of his past?"

"Listen, Pat, everyone has a past. Everyone has a base of who they are and what they do. He's doing the right thing now. I'm not worried about the Reverend's rumored history. It's exactly that, history."

"But there are rumors. Can't this association hurt us?"

"Pat, listen, I appreciate your concern, I really fucking do. You're a great soldier

and a friend of the 51st Ward for longer than I've been alive, but believe me, we've looked at that. His benefits outweigh his minuses. I understand he was involved with some bad people, but he saw the light. He's walking the straight and narrow and has benefited his community. He feeds a lot of people and preaches the importance of self-accountability. They love him over there. His story is that of the prodigal son. He was on the dark side, and now he's back with new wisdom and a vision, which he shares now. It's a hope thing. There are a lot more potential prodigal sons over there, and his story goes over well. Real well."

"Do you know what prompted his conversion?"

"Jesus. What else? He was doing time from his bad days; I think he did three years and found the good Lord in prison." Eddie was getting uncomfortable with the conversation. He wished it would end. "Anything else, partner?"

"No, no. I guess that's it."

"How are the streets going? We're getting down to crunch time. What, two days to the election? Do you have enough help?"

"Yeah, I'm good," said Pat. "Those two kids you gave me seem to be working out well."

"That's good. If you need anything else, you come right to me, okay?"

"Yeah, Eddie, and thanks."
"Anytime, Pat, you know that."

Pat left the room and closed the door behind him. Eddie turned the radio down and picked up the phone. "Get me, Commander Sheridan, in the fifth district, now."

With the election two days away, Eddie wanted to make sure that any news about this case gets run by him first. He could not take a chance on any crime stories coming from his ward this close to the election. And most of all, he could not take a chance on the Reverend Zuko being involved.

CHAPTER TWENTY

A car pulled into the Christ Hospital parking garage the night before the election, just before visiting hours ended. One person exited the vehicle while the driver found a parking spot to wait. Twenty minutes later, the loud tone of the monitors attached to the body of the barely breathing Charlie Bedrun suddenly went off like a jailbreak. Lights blinked, lines flattened out, and nurses scrambled. They did what they could to keep Charlie alive. During the confusion, a person slipped out of the room from behind a curtain that separated the beds and walked down the hallway to the exit at the end of the hall.

After making a phone call, the car met him at the hospital's main entrance. He entered the vehicle on the passenger side.

"Well?" asked the driver.

"Got him, man," answered the passenger.

The car left the garage and turned east on 95th Street.

"You sure, man?" asked the driver again.

"Fuck yeah, I'm sure, man. Lights were going off and shit. That fucker is dead, man."

"How did you do it?" continued the driver.

"How did I do it?"

"Yeah, asshole. How did you do it?"

"You sure you want to know the gory details? You sure you got the stomach for it?"

The driver's irritation was increasing. "Yeah, asshole, I can handle it. How did you do it?"

"I'm not sure you can handle it."

"I can handle it. Tell me now, or I'll pull this car over and kick your ass."

"Fuck you. Go ahead and pull over, then."

"You really want me to pull over? Are you daring me to pull over?"

"Yeah, I fuckin' dare you," the passenger responded.

"You dare me?"

"Did I stutter?"

The driver quickly turned into the vast K-Mart parking lot that was on their right and sped to a distant area of the lot where they would be alone. Hitting the brakes with as much intensity as he had hit the gas pedal, the driver got out of the car, walked around to the passenger's door, opened it, dragged the passenger from the front seat, and threw him to the ground. He pounced on him with his left knee and drew back his fist in the air.

"Now motherfucker, how did you off this guy?"

The passenger started to laugh. "I pinched his nose hose."

"You what?"

"I pinched his nose hose. You know, those two hoses that they stick up your nose to get you air? I pinched them."

Still with his fist in the air, the driver continued. "That'll kill him?"

"Hell, yes! You try breathing without air. See how you do," the passenger said through his laughter.

The driver relented and let the passenger up. "You better be sure, man," he said as he wiped his hands. "This ain't no fucking around now."

"I'm sure, I'm sure he's dead. You should have seen all the lights and beeps and shit that came from the machines that he was hooked up to. It looked like fuckin' Christmas."

They got back into the car.

"You just pinched his hose and that was it?"

"Yeah, man."

The driver smiled, "That's wild, man."

They left the parking lot and continued heading east on 95th Street.

CHAPTER TWENTY-ONE

Election day arrived. At the 4:30 a.m. mark, Pat's alarm went off. He showered, dressed, and left home in the early morning darkness. It would be a long day, and the morning air indicated it would also be chilly. At least it wasn't supposed to rain.

Election days for a precinct captain are the longest of the year. Pat arrived at his precinct polling place, Murray Park, at 5 a.m. He set up John and Octavio with the necessary literature and palm cards and then went to work measuring for the lawn signs. The local ordinance required all signs to be at least 75 feet from a voting station entrance. Pat learned long ago to bring a measuring tape to answer questions regarding the distance of the signs. It was a quick and objective way to settle disputes with the opposing candidate's workers.

It was hard enough jostling for position by the front doors to hand out your palm cards, and sometimes, these things got physical to the point where fights broke out, and the police would be there. Pat had never gotten into a fight and never would; it just wasn't worth it. It usually involved the young guys, the newbies who bought into the political meanderings of the candidates. At times, alcohol would be involved.

In his early days, Tom sometimes got involved in these scrapes, but even he learned that the tussles would not do anyone any good. Today would not be any different. Pat's signs would be exactly seventy -five feet and one inch from the entrance.

With his crew and signs in position, Pat entered the park's gymnasium, where the voting booths were set up, and grabbed a cup of coffee from the urn in a makeshift kitchen. Doughnuts were laid out in paper boxes from the local bakery, courtesy of Eddie Byrne, and a small coffee bar was set up next to the boxes. Looking out through the kitchen window, he saw 40 voting booths set up and situated about the gym. The booths were delivered to the park in their self-packing carrying cases. When opened, each popped out like a bureaucratic jack-in-the-box, ready to perform its only expected task, the process of democracy.

The election judges still hovered in the kitchen area, waiting for the polls to open in another ten minutes. Pat was familiar with most of them because he would see them at most elections. He kept his distance, however, and would only occasionally make small talk over coffee before heading out for the day. He knew the routine, as did the judges. Election day was long and tedious, with flurries of activity at the beginning and end, the commuter times. Most people voted either on their way to work or coming home that evening, so during the day, most of your voters would be housewives or retired people who would sporadically trickle in.

Pat would keep an eye on the voter lists to see who voted and who didn't. He knew his precinct like the back of his hand, who voted in the evening or morning, who he had to arrange a ride for, and who would need a quick phone call as a friendly reminder. As of now, he would send John to pick up Mrs. Durkin and Mrs. Dolan, probably at about 11 a.m., because he knew that each liked their tea and watched Oprah in the morning.

He went outside and surveyed the front of the park fieldhouse. John and Octavio were ready, each bundled up for the long, cold day. Of course, Octavio was not wearing a hat. Pat was surprised at the number of workers there for Dale Robbins. Six were present, ready, and armed with their literature and palm cards to help influence the voters. That's okay, thought Pat, we'll see what the numbers are at the end of the day.

The morning rush was heavy. The workers for both Byrne and Robbins formed a gauntlet to the fieldhouse entrance as they passed the palm cards out fast and furious. Each voter dutifully accepted the card as a regular procedure of the process. The morning commuters were faster and in more of a hurry than the evening commuters, as they had train and bus schedules to keep. Therefore, the morning rush went quickly and had tailed off considerably by nine o'clock.

The slow part of the day was upon them.

"John, I want you to pick up Mrs. Dolan and Mrs. Durkin this morning. You can use my car. You know how to drive, right?"

"Yes, of course," answered John.

"Octavio, I won't know what I'll need from you until I get a peek at the voter lists, so hang around, okay?"

"Si, si. I may have to pick up my sister from school this afternoon. Is that okay?"

"Yeah, sure," said Pat, "If there's someone you need to pick up, we'll time it for then. Cool?"

"Yeah, sure."

"Are you guys going to the party tonight?" asked Pat. "You both should go; I'll introduce you to Eddie. We'll have some fun."

"Sounds good to me," said John.

"Count me in," replied Octavio.

The morning dragged on. Pat and his crew stayed on one side of the fieldhouse entrance while the Robins crew was on the other, with nothing but an occasional glance being transferred between them. They all tried the usual methods to keep themselves warm: running in place, jumping up and down, blowing into their gloveless hands. A fire was burning on each side in a 55-gallon metal garbage can with holes punched in the sides to allow air to feed the fire. It kept you warm, but at the end of the day, your clothing smelled as if you were on a long camping trip.

Pat's method of keeping warm. involved layers of clothing, going in and out of the fieldhouse for coffee, and peeking at the voter lists. Usually, he would slip away and go home for lunch, where a hot meal was ready for him courtesy of Mary, but that would not be the case today. He would probably go to McDonalds instead.

Eddie Byrne's Lexus pulled into the parking lot in full view of everyone. He exited the car and walked towards the entrance of the fieldhouse when a Robins worker, apparently on a dare, approached him with a palm card. Entirely in on the joke, Eddie took the card from the worker and ripped it up in front of him.

"Your guy is a loser," Eddie said. The worker sulked back to his group amid nervous laughter and whispers. Eddie approached Pat and his crew.

"Hey, guys. How we doing?" said Eddie.

"Good Eddie," said Pat. "We're at about sixty percent right now and haven't gone out for anyone yet."

"That's good. You fella's need anything? You got coffee. I can have some sandwiches sent over a little later."

For the first time in his captain's career, Pat thought about Eddie's offer, which was made every prior election day but turned down by Pat, who normally anticipated getting fed by Mary.

"That would be good. We can use some chow later," Pat replied.

"Okay, you got it. Who are your friends, Pat?"

"This is Octavio, and this is," Pat paused, "John."

"Yes, sir, it's John. Pleased to meet you, Mr. Alderman,' John said as he extended his hand to Eddie.

Eddie grasped the outstretched hand. "Nice to meet you, John." He turned to Octavio and held his hand out. "Names Eddie Byrne, nice to meet you, Octavio. Thanks for your help."

Octavio slowly accepted the offer and shook Eddie's hand. "Nice to meet you also."

Eddie raised the collar of his jacket and turned to the opposition crew across the entrance. "How many do they have there? Ten, eleven?"

"They've been in and out all day, Ed. It looks like a lot of part-timers. Two or three hours at a time," replied Pat.

"That's still a lot of bodies."

"You don't have to worry about this precinct. You have a winner here, Ed."

"I know that partner, I know that. If every precinct ran like yours, Pat, we'd all be better off. Well, I got to go to the next one. Thank you, guys, and I'll see you all tonight, right guys?"

"Of course, Ed. We'll be there."

Eddie waved and walked toward his car. Pat called after him. "Hey, Eddie, don't forget about those sandwiches, okay?"

Without turning, Eddie waved in acknowledgment and continued to his car as the crew watched him drive away while holding their hands out over the fire.

"John, go and get Mrs. Durkin and Mrs. Dolan," mumbled Pat.

* * * * *

The day dragged on, and the weather got progressively colder. The temperatures were in the mid-30s in the afternoon and slipped into the 20s the minute the sun dipped below the horizon. It had been four hours since Eddie had promised lunch, and now Pat was feeling hungry and tired. He had never gone this long on election day without eating, and now it was almost three o'clock, his day only half over, and he had yet to eat anything other than some doughnuts that morning. He felt crummy. Suddenly, he felt worse.

Detective Larry Wiggin approached Pat and his crew. Pat had not seen Wiggin since Mary's funeral, but he sensed Wiggin had been watching him.

"Hey, Pat. How are you doing?" asked Wiggin.

"I'm okay," Pat coldly responded.

"Listen, can we talk for a minute?"

"About what?"

"Look, let's just talk. Believe it or not, I'm on your side."

The two walked away towards the parking lot. Octavio and John watched suspiciously.

"Well, what can I do for you, Officer?" asked Pat.

"Nothing, Pat, nothing. I want you to know that we may have a new theory on the case, some new evidence may have come up. Some good evidence for Tom. I feel that Tom may not have been involved in the murder."

Wiggins's declaration hit Pat like a blow to the side of the head. What was this weasel trying to pull? He better be careful.

"Then who did?" asked Pat.

"We don't know yet. There's still some things we're trying to figure out."

"Then why the doubt about Tom now?"

"I can't tell you anything else now. Let's just say we think someone else was at the scene. I think that Tom can help himself if he talks to us."

"That's it, you're still after me to give Tom up. Well, let me tell you, I don't know where he's at. I have no idea. I couldn't help you if I wanted to."

"I believe you, but look, you also have a lot to lose in this. You've got about a month left, and if Tom doesn't show up, you lose your home. Are you aware of that?"

"Yeah, I'm very fucking aware of that." A knot developed in the pit of Pat's gut.

"Then you have to believe me when I tell you that I have doubts about Tom's guilt. I need some information to put it all together, and Tom can supply that information."

Wiggin took a long breath. "Pat, someone tried to kill Charlie Bedrun last night, and it doesn't help Tom if he's still out there somewhere. He's a natural suspect."

"And I'm telling you, I don't know anything about where Tom is."

Wiggin paused and ran his fingers through his thick, red, wavy hair. He then reached into his coat pocket and pulled out a pack of Marlboro Lights, took one from the pack, and lit it with a disposable lighter. He sucked on the filter and exhaled a combination of smoke and cold breath vapor into the air creating a large cloud that disappeared instantly.

"Until this case, I've been pretty good about quitting this shit," he said. He kicked a stone on the ground, took another drag from the smoke, and continued.

"I promised my kid I'd quit. I'm trying hard. I really am. I've had this pack for almost a week now, and every time I take one out, I think about him. That's pretty fucked up, don't you think? It's embarrassing that I only think of my boy when I do something I promised him I wouldn't do. Sometimes I feel bad about that."

"Then why do you do it?"

Wiggin looked Pat in the eye and said, "I don't know."

"How old is your boy?"

"He turned nine last week."

"Did he have a party?"

"Yeah, sure, of course. They had clowns and balloons and all that shit."

"Were you there?"

Wiggin shook his head and looked at the ground. "No. I was out looking for your son."

A silent and awkward truce swept between the two like the chilling late afternoon wind that rolled down the sidewalks of the precinct. Pat didn't press the issue. He felt he was hardly the paragon of fatherhood,

Wiggin took a final drag from the cigarette, dropped it ceremoniously from his thumb and index finger, and ground it into the blacktop of the parking lot with his shoe.

"Anyway, I've told you what I wanted to tell you. It's up to you to believe me or not."

"But I've got to know more," said Pat.

"That's all I have right now. You have to trust me on this."

"I don't know who to trust right now."

"Trust yourself," said Wiggin as he turned and walked towards his car. After a few steps, he turned back to Pat and said, "And me."

Wiggin pulled out of the lot when another vehicle pulled in. It was Claire. She pulled into a spot and hurriedly popped out with a large shopping bag filled with assorted sandwiches, chips, cans of soda, and a thermos of coffee.

"I'm sorry, Dad. I wanted to get here over an hour ago, but Curtis had a doctor's appointment, which I completely forgot about. The kids got a hold of the refrigerator calendar, and I'm having a hard time keeping track of everything."

Pat took the bag from Claire, and his spirits were instantly lifted.

"That's quite all right, dearie." He turned to John and Octavio. "C'mon boys, soups on."

They gathered around the car. Claire laid the food on a small collapsible table that she took out of the trunk. The presence of Claire and the food made Pat feel much better. Claire was taking the reins of the family and doing well. He could tell that she worked hard on the spread, and everyone appreciated it as they were all cold and hungry and apparently forgotten by Eddie Byrne.

Claire poured Pat a cup of coffee, and he took a long sip. The coffee and watching Claire break out the well-planned lunch warmed his insides. He felt like he could make it through the rest of the day.

"Claire, this here is Octavio," Pat said as he gestured.

"Hello, Octavio," said Claire.

"Hello, Claire. Thank you for this food. These sandwiches look great."

"You're welcome. It's your basic ham and turkey sandwiches; I put some mayo and mustard on the side. They're in the Tupperware containers."

Pat continued the introductions. "And this is John. I believe you met before."

Claire smiled. "Yes, we did. Hello John. Nice to see you again."

"Hello, Claire," said John. "Thank you for all of this. You're more than kind."

"Oh, it's just a little food and coffee. They'll feed you again tonight at the party. Are you going?"

"Of course. A victory must be celebrated. Will you be there?"

"I will be there to either celebrate a victory or mourn a loss."

"Who's going to watch the kids tonight?" asked Pat."

"I've got Ms. O'Toole for tonight."

"Ms. O'Toole?" replied Pat. "You know how I feel about her. She's a lush. Probably already started drinking."

"Oh, Dad, stop it. She's very good with the kids, and they love her. I'll stay for a few hours and get home before she gets smashed."

"Well, all right, but I see a long night right now. This election may be closer than most people think."

"I'll be home no later than nine. Now I have to go pick Curtis up. When you guys are done, just put everything in the bag and put it in the fieldhouse entranceway; I'll pick it up later. Most of the stuff you can toss anyway."

"Thanks again, Claire," said Octavio through a mouthful of ham, turkey, and white bread.

"Yes, thanks again," said John. "And we'll see you tonight, at least for a few hours?"

"Yes, you will," replied Claire as she entered the car.

Pat watched John as he stared at the leaving vehicle. A small smile crept over John's face.

CHAPTER TWENTY-TWO

The Eddie Byrne campaign party was held at Kirk's Family Inn. The thick window coverings, plush carpeting, and faux ornate furnishings of the room stood in contrast to the attire of most of the crowd as precinct workers arrived directly from the poll sites, looking tired and haggard and smelling like campfires. Most headed straight for the bar, each with a war story from the long day. Despite the chill in their bones, the cold beer tasted good.

The captains arrived later as they had waited at the polling places for the punch tape from the voting machines that would give them the official tally of the day's vote. Then they delivered them to the campaign office, where the harried campaign directors totaled the tapes amid empty Styrofoam coffee cups and soda cans.

Pat entered the campaign headquarters and gave his tapes to Warney Richmond, who sat behind a battered desk in the corner of the small room.

"How we doing, Warney?" asked Pat.

"I don't know Pat. It's pretty tight. We lost a lot on the east side of the ward. Thank God for Zuko and his crew, or it would have been a total loss."

"Could be a run-off then? Well, I'll let you geniuses be, and I'll go watch the results on the TV right from the bar at the party."

"You go ahead, Pat. Hopefully, I can join you soon with some good news."

"Okay, Warney, I'm off."

Pat left the headquarters and walked out into the chilly night air. He would have to walk to Kirks as he left his car at home for Claire, who would meet him later. He didn't mind. It was clear and dry, and he was still bundled up enough that the cold air didn't bother him. Of course, he was tired, but it was a tiredness that he felt after many an election. He felt he had laid it all out on the table, worked hard, and the fruits of his labor would be enjoyed and rewarded. His numbers were good from the tapes he brought to Warney. He had an eighty-six percent turnout, and Eddie carried his precinct almost three to one. If Eddie found himself in a runoff, it certainly wouldn't be because Pat hadn't held up his end.

"Hey Pat, wait up."

Pat turned and saw Joe Hinckley trying to catch up.

"My car's over at Kirk's. I left it there this morning. I'll walk with you,'" said Joe. "How'd you do?"

"I was just thinking about that. I did all right. Eighty-six per-cent turnout, and we took it by three times the Robin vote. How about you?"

"Okay, I guess. I'm a little disappointed by what Robins got, but I hear that's pretty much the talk around the whole ward."

"I know. Warney's not optimistic. He thinks we may be in for a runoff."

"Boy, that would suck. We'd have to do this shit all over again. I've never been involved in a run-off before. Have you?"

"Eddie's first campaign was a run-off. Of course, I was working for the other guy. But it was still the same. We just had to do the same shit all over again. Yeah, it did suck."

They walked together in the cold, exhaling a vapor trail like a steam locomotive on concrete tracks.

"Have you heard any word about Tom?"

"No, nothing," said Pat. "Not a word from him or about him."

"Are you okay with that?"

"If he shows up, fine. If not, I'll deal with it. What can I do?"

"Nothing, I guess."

They walked in silence for another half block. Joe seemed to be struggling with something. As he walked, he fidgeted. He took his cap off and put it back on. He put his hands in his coat pockets and then took them out.

Finally, he blurted to Pat, "You know, he showed up at my place a couple of weeks ago."

"What? Tom? You're just telling me this now? What the fuck, Joe?"

"He was staying at the vacant apartment in my building for a couple of days. I was scared. He told me not to say anything, not even to you."

"Boyo, he certainly did not mean me," an agitated Pat said.

"I don't know Pat. He was pretty scared about the whole deal."

Pat stopped and turned to Joe. "Where is he now?"

"I don't know. I thought that maybe you would know; he said he met you at the funeral lunch."

"Yeah, that's the last time I saw or talked to him. Did you tell the cops anything about this?"

"No, they've never questioned me or asked me about anything."

"Good. Let's keep it that way. Did he tell you anything about where he was going?"

"No, nothing. I came home one day, and he was gone. It was the last I saw of him."

"Is the apartment still vacant?"

"Yes, but not for long. I have a couple of calls on it, and I'll probably be showing it in the next couple of days."

"Have you been there recently?"

"Yeah, every day. I've been painting the kitchen. He hasn't returned. I would know."

"Listen to me, Joe. If you ever see him again, I have to know. I have to get to him and talk some goddamn sense into him. They think that maybe somebody else did these things."

"I will, I will," promised Joe.

"You must do this, Joe."

"I will. I swear it."

They walked in silence until they arrived at Kirks Family Inn. Just before entering the doorway, Pat turned to Joe again. "You can't tell anyone about this, Joe. No one. Do you understand me?"

"Yeah, yeah, Pat, no problem."

They entered the hall to find the party in full swing. Volunteers and ward personnel surrounded the bar or the television sets around the room, which displayed the vote counts, colorful graphics, and commentary courtesy of the local television stations.

By now, winners were declared in most of the city ward races, but a handful were still too close to call. The 51st ward race was in that handful. The last graphic displayed by Channel 5, the local NBC affiliate, showed Byrne leading with 46 percent of the vote and Dale Robins with 26 percent. The remaining votes were strewn among the also-rans who were on the ballot. About 75 percent of the vote was counted as of then.

Pat and Joe found a niche at the bar and soon were joined by John and Octavio, who had gotten there earlier.

"How we looking, Mr. Sullivan?" asked John.

"I don't know yet, but it's close. We need at least fifty percent of the vote to avoid a run-off, and right now, we're not there yet."

A round of beers was set before the group.

"Have you seen Claire?" asked Pat.

"No. Not yet," answered John.

"She should be here soon unless Ms. O'Toole got snockered early."

The lead story of the evening on each of the news shows was the clear and decisive victory by the mayor, who was shown with his family sitting on a long couch in a hotel suite. He smiled and discussed the mandate he was given by the people. It was the same speech as the last four terms.

* * * * *

Back at his office, Eddie Byrne sat behind his desk, feet up and a tumbler of scotch in his hand. His desk was littered with adding machine tapes that reflected numbers that concerned him. He was looking at a run-off. Three more weeks of campaigning. Three more weeks of campaign funds to be spent.

In his first race, he was a challenger, which resulted in a run-off, but this was the first time since then that he would face one as an incumbent, which concerned him. His numbers were down by 15 percent from the previous election. He mulled over the potential reasons. He thought his record on ward improvement was stellar, and while he did have some factory closings in the ward, these jobs were replaced with retail development on 83rd Street and some on Pulaski.

That boiled it down to race. Eddie's numbers seemed down on the east side of the ward, indicating that it had become Dale Robin's voter base. Only the Reverend Zuko's precincts saved Eddie from a total crash. The whole Zuko thing was weighing on him. He was hearing the ugly rumors that Zuko had some sort of involvement in the Sullivan murder deal. Eddie's ears were still on the street. He would have to deal with the good Reverend, but only after the runoff. He still needed the good Reverend's numbers.

Gulping down the remainder of his drink, Eddie stood and pulled his tie knot up to his neck. "Warney!"

Instantly, Warney's face appeared in the doorway.

"Yeah?"

"Let's go."

The two departed out the back door and headed to Kirks Family Inn.

* * * * *

"We are now ready to announce a result in the 51st ward. Mike, what do you have?" asked the female anchor on the TV.

The bearded and gray-tinged political reporter's face appeared on the television screen. "Channel Two now projects a run-off in the 51st ward." Announced Mike, the political reporter.

"Incumbent Alderman Eddie Byrne has garnered just 46 percent of the vote, and challenger Dale Robins has just over one-third. Quite a showing by the south side activist. Byrne has never had a run-off in four prior terms, and this could be a statement by the voters there that they want a change."

"Byrne has quite an organization with ties to the Mayor. Does this send a signal to the Mayor?" the veteran anchorwoman asked.

"Well, not yet, Carol. The main message will be in just over three weeks when we get a winner. Robins and Byrne will go head-to-head then, and maybe, just maybe, a little message will be sent."

"Thank you, Mike. We'll be back with the other results after this," said the anchorwoman.

The television cut to a commercial for an erectile dysfunction remedy.

Watching the monitor from the bar, Pat and almost everyone around him shook their head- three more weeks of this shit. Pat gazed about the room, sensing the mood of the crowd was sagging like burning wax on a candle. Some put on a brave front and crowed about how they would double their numbers for the next vote, but their declarations failed to convince anyone. Pat sensed a grim atmosphere in the room.

Pat saw Claire and John sitting at one table. They were laughing and seemed to be having a good time. It seemed that they were the only ones in the room smiling and enjoying the evening. Pat had inklings that Claire and John were getting chummy. This confirmed it. He was bothered that it may be too soon after her mother's death.

Even though Claire pulled the whole family through the ordeal, Pat wondered if she was putting on a front for his benefit. She was almost too sensible and level-headed, at least for his daughter. Her history of irresponsibility and carefree ways made him question whether she could keep up this brave front. And now a relationship? With John?

Pat liked John. He was a good kid, seemed to be drug-free, and was enthusiastic and hard working, but couldn't Claire just find a local Irish kid from a good family? Couldn't one of his kid's relationships be just a plain normal affair? He'd even settle for a local Italian boy.

Pat stared at his beer. Nothing in his life would ever be normal again. Not now, not in the future. In the last month, he had watched as his life was grabbed by the ankles, turned upside down, and shaken violently until all the contents of its pockets lay scattered on the broken sidewalk.

The PA system suddenly came alive with a loud burst of feedback as Warney adjusted the microphone at the podium.

"Okay, Okay," Warney tested into the microphone.

The crowd gathered around the podium, anticipating the emergence of Eddie Byrne. The sound from the television monitors was turned down, and the bar area cleared. Pat stayed at the bar. "Another Old Style," he told the bartender.

From his vantage point, he had a straight view of the speaker and watched as Eddie entered the room and approached the podium. The crowd noise went up, cheering his arrival.

"All right, all right, everyone," Eddie said as he held up his hands at the podium for quiet. "Listen, everyone. Listen up."

The crowd dutifully obeyed.

"First off, I want to thank everyone who helped us out. Give yourself a big hand."

Waiting for the noise to die down, Eddie continued.

"Okay. Now, as you know by now, we have to roll up our sleeves one more time. One more time, we have to get the message out."

Shouts called back to Eddie from the crowd.

"No problem, Eddie!"

"We'll get the job done, Eddie!"

Eddie acknowledged the shouts. "I know, I know you'll get the job done. I have faith in you folks, and I appreciate everyone's effort, but you know what? You know what?" He paused for the response.

"What, Eddie?"

"Tell us, Eddie!"

"You know what? We have to double our effort, double our work."

Eddie's voice was rising. He approached the patented crescendo rah-rah part of his speech. "And I know you all can do it! Look about you; look around the room. Take a look at the faces of your peers and your neighbors. This is the 51st ward! White, Black, Hispanic, this very room has the fabric of what we are and what we strive to be!"

The excited crowd played to his comments.

"You see," continued Eddie, "I'm real confident about this run-off. I just look over the faces of this crowd. There's Warney and Leonard and Joe! I see all of you, the people who have taken care of me for over sixteen years! You are the people I want to go to war with. Yeah, I'm really confident about this runoff. We've got the best organization in this city." He paused. "Now, Mr. Robins may be feeling a bit confident tonight, I'm sure!"

The name of his opponent set off some catcalls.

"But that's all right, every dog has its day, and Mr. Robins, enjoy yours because you will feel the results of the efforts of this organization in all its glory!"

Eddie played the crowd like a veteran entertainer at a dinner theater.

"Now, everyone, have a good time tonight. God knows you've earned it, but we're going to have to go back to the well one more time! Everyone has to reach back and pull out what they're made of. We will need it because the people of the 51st ward deserve it!"

With that, Eddie waved, walked away from the podium and immediately left Kirks through the back door, with Warney dutifully behind him. Before getting into his car, he turned to Warney. "Tell the captains, mandatory meeting tomorrow night."

"Tomorrow? Don't you think we should give them one day off?"

"Fuck 'em. Winners get the day off; losers go to work. Tomorrow, six o'clock."

Eddies got into his car and drove off.

Pat left the bar and circled the room until he stood behind the seated Claire and John at their table. "Hello, kids."

Claire turned and looked up. "Oh, hello, Dad. Have a seat. John was just telling me about Mrs. Dolan."

Ah, Mrs. Dolan. John had gone to her house to pick her up to vote, but she wouldn't let him in despite John's telling her he wasn't a gangbanger and really worked for the organization. Pat had to go to her house and convince her that John wasn't there to hit her over the head and take her money. Pat must have convinced her because she allowed John to take her home; she even invited him in for tea afterward.

"Nice old lady," said John.

Pat laughed. "Yeah, nice old lady, just a little touched in the head."

"Dad! Don't say that. She's just a little confused sometimes."

Pat sat between the two and tried to participate in the conversation but felt like a fifth wheel. Suddenly, he felt tired. The room was starting to thin out, and after a long day, he was considering going home to bed.

"What time did you tell Mrs. O'Toole you would pick the kids up?"

"About ten o'clock."

Pat looked at his watch; it was just past nine-thirty. "I think I'm going to go. I'll pick the kids up if you want to stay. I'll have Joe give you a ride home."

"Thanks, Dad. If you don't mind, I'd like to stay for a little while longer."

"Okay, call me if you need anything. I'm going home."

"Goodbye, Mr. Sullivan. I'll wait to hear from you," said John.

"Where's Octavio?" asked Pat.

John looked about the room also. "I don't know. He must have left."

"All right," said Pat, "I'll give him a call also."

Pat left the hall and walked into the parking lot, where he saw Warney standing alone, finishing a cigarette and looking like a guy who had just finished a twenty-hour day.

"We've got a mandatory meeting tomorrow night," Warney said to Pat.

"Tomorrow? Jesus Christ, Warney, no day off to rest?"

"Sorry, Pat. He's pretty hot about everything."

"Well, okay, but there's going to be some pissed-off people there."

"Including Eddie."

"Yeah, whatever."

CHAPTER TWENTY-THREE

Eddie Byrne pulled his car into a spot behind the rear entrance of the East Side Mission House and entered through the heavy security door, walking past two black-clad sentries who assented to his entry with a nod of their heads. He descended a dimly lit flight of stairs that led to another door, which allowed him access to the Reverend Zuko's private lounge area.

It looked like any commercial establishment with booths that lined the walls. A plush multi-colored carpet offset a twenty-foot bar with stools. This was Zuko's retreat where he entertained guests and business associates. He had held a fundraiser for Eddie there two months earlier. Eddie had attended several other functions there.

Zuko sat at the bar, his rock glass in front of him having just been refilled by the tuxedo-clad bartender. The lights were dimmed except for the recessed overhead lights of the bar, which highlighted two bar stools, the one Zuko sat on and the one Eddie was about to.

"Mr. Alderman, welcome."

"Reverend."

The bartender poured scotch over ice into a glass and placed it before Eddie, who took a long drink and placed the almost empty glass down on the bar. It was immediately topped off.

"Well, my friend, it seems our work is not done just yet," said Zuko.

"Yes, that seems to be the case."

"Do not worry; we will have numbers for you again, but you may have to help us with the surrounding precincts. Robin's people are strong there, stronger than I thought. We'll take care of that this time around."

"I'll get you some people; the city organization can help me there," said Eddie. "What do you plan to do about Robin's people?"

"Don't worry. Their numbers will drop considerably."

"Okay, but go easy on the violence, only if needed."

"You've never had any concern about my methods before? Why now?"

"I'm not concerned now; you know what you can and can't do. I've got no problem with that; you know my only parameter of our relationship is no drugs."

"I've kept my end of the bargain. You will never hear my name mentioned with drugs."

"How about murder?"

Zuko's brow furled. "Come again?"

"One of my captains has been asking questions about you. His kid is on the lam from a murder charge. Names Sullivan, Pat Sullivan. His kid's name is Tom. You know anything about that?"

"Like what?"

"His daughter-in-law was found murdered in her basement. There was another victim who's still alive, but barely. They filed murder charges against her ex, Sullivan's son; a witness put him in the house at the time of the murder."

"So what's the problem?"

"I know his family, and it doesn't seem right. The kid may have been an asshole at times, but he could not have done this. This was almost execution style like someone planned it. Plus, he's jumped bail; he's still on the loose. The old man could lose his house if the kid doesn't show up."

Zuko shifted his heavy torso on the bar stool and turned closer to Eddie. "So why are you telling me this?"

"The other victim may have had a prior relationship with you in your bad old days. He wasn't even a month out of the joint when this happened. He was just released after doing five years. His name is Charlie Bedrun. Know him?"

"Charlie had a past with me. He's been cut loose for years now."

"Well, apparently, Charlie never got the message. I heard he'd been aligning himself with you even when he was still in the joint."

"Yeah, I heard Charlie had a big mouth; he could yak a lot, but there's nothing to it. He was a small-time soldier with big ambitions. I warned him once about his chatter, and that was the last I heard of it, but he's done with us since we gave up that line of business. Upon your demand."

Eddie drained his tumbler and put it back on the bar, where it was refilled.

"That's good, but there's something here. Why is Sullivan asking questions about you?"

"I have no idea."

"Plus, there was a visit to Bedrun at the hospital. Someone tried to finish him off. I think somebody wants this kid dead."

"Well? Did they finish the job?"

"No, he's still alive."

Eddie thought he saw a quick wave of displeasure on Zuko's face, but it instantly disappeared when he took a drink and motioned for the bartender to top him off.

"Look, Mr. Alderman, what are you asking me? And, more importantly, are you sure you want to ask me anything about this?"

Eddie paused. It had been a long day, and it now showed on the typically dapper politician. He loosened his tie and passed his long fingers through his hair while the lines on his face ran longer and deeper.

Zuko continued, carefully trying to craft his words with caution. "Let me just say, Mr. Alderman, this is, as the man once said, a 'city on the make', and certain things must be done to keep the status quo. You know what I mean?"

Certain people say certain words that, whether true or not, give a perception that other groups of people would believe despite it being bullshit. It doesn't matter to them. It's the perception. I deal with perception every day. I do not 'keep it real' because my world would fall apart if I did."

Reality in my part of town has a habit of sucking, so I cannot offer these people 'reality'. This is a refuge from reality. And your world would come down, too. As a politician, you also have to deal with perception every day. Am I right? And ask yourself if you can afford to 'keep it real'? Can you? I mean, can you?"

"We're talking about two entirely different things here."

"Are we?"

Eddie's silence was answer enough for Zuko.

"Now listen to me, Mr. Alderman. This issue with Sullivan will be resolved, but not until after the run-off election. We cannot afford any publicity involving me with this situation; if I'm involved, you're involved, whether you like it or not. I've got legitimate business concerns that could not tolerate anyone spreading a bad perception of me; this is bigger than the two of us. The ball is rolling on this, Mr. Alderman and neither one of us can stop it."

"And, of course, you will get your share."

"Of course. That's the way this shit works in Hustlertown. I'm surprised that you would even bring it up."

"What's going to happen after the election?" inquired Eddie.

"A resolution. A quiet resolution."

Daring an answer, Eddie pushed it. "What kind of resolution?"

"Look, it's too bad about the Sullivan kid. He and his wife had a knack for being in the wrong place at the wrong time, but I can't help that; that's not my fault; we had to do what we had to do. Bedrun had to be shut up. He didn't listen to us, and we had to make sure that he never opened his mouth again. The police had their killer; he just slipped out of their hands." Zuko paused as if he were debating his following words.

"We need to find this Sullivan kid. He saw one of our guys and needs to be silenced."

"The cops can't find this kid. What makes you think you can?" "Look, the old man is looking, the cops are looking, we just need to keep an eye on them. We just keep our own eyes in the right places."

"You've got eyes on Sullivan?"

"We keep tabs on him."

"In my organization? You have eyes in my organization?"

"Hey, Mr. Alderman, we have eyes everywhere. It's part of the game, you know that?"

Suddenly, Eddie felt overwhelming betrayal. How could this be? The spy being spied on, the snake killing the mongoose. He felt like he was now the prey, the hunted. He was suddenly uncomfortable.

"I got to go," said Eddie as he rose from the bar stool and retraced his entrance route. As he got to the door, Zuko called out to him.

"Mr. Alderman, remember we deal in perception."

As he continued walking, Eddie mumbled to himself, "And deception."

* * * * *

The drive home through the dark, empty streets allowed Eddie to reflect on the entire evening. He made his deal with the devil, and now it had come back to bite him in the ass. Zuko wanted to wait until after the election. Then, a chilling thought shot through his head. Zuko wanted Tom dead. If that happens and Bedrun dies, case closed. No more murder investigation, and Zuko carries on.

And those spies. Red-hot anger replaced his chilling thoughts. That mother fucker has eyes in my organization. Eddie then realized that his relationship with Zuko would have to end or be reined in and controlled.

It was good that he was wired to record the conversation that evening.

CHAPTER TWENTY-FOUR

The day after the election, Joe got a call from prospective tenants for the apartment, a young Hispanic couple who wanted a clean place near the wife's mother. Joe's apartment qualified, but they wanted to see it that evening, their only night off together. Joe had taken a quick application over the phone, and they seemed to qualify; both had jobs and good credit scores.

Joe needed to lease the apartment. He had taken a financial hit when his previous tenants moved out, and his last few trips to the Joliet gambling boats were certainly not kind. As his losses mounted, he took cash advances on his credit cards for the first time. He would rebound, he thought; he always did.

His problem this evening was the mandatory meeting that Eddie had called for. He couldn't miss it. Joe knew that Eddie was mad about the results, and expected more of a tongue-lashing than any rah-rah speech tonight. He would tell the prospective tenants that Mrs. Patroski would have the key, and if they had any questions, they could certainly reach him on his phone.

Joe walked up to the second floor and knocked on the door. Mrs. Patroski answered, loosely clad in her bathrobe.

"I've got a new tenant coming tonight to look at the upstairs apartment, and I have to be at the ward office. Would you mind if they picked the key up from you? They'll knock on your door."

"No problem, Joe. I'll give anyone you want the key."

Joe wondered if he had made a mistake by leaving Mrs. Patroskis the key, but at this point, he had no other solutions as the new tenants needed to see the place tonight. He then called them and explained how to get the key and to call him if they had any questions. Yes, this should go well, thought Joe.

For a final check, Joe walked through the vacant apartment. Everything was freshly painted, and the floors were cleaned and buffed. He was proud of how he kept up the building. The flat was ready to move into. This would start his rebound, paying tenants and a clean slate with the boats. Hopeful and satisfied, he left the building and headed for the ward office.

* * * * *

The 51st Ward Hall was crowded with captains and workers, all wishing they were somewhere else. They milled about while sipping coffee from white Styrofoam cups and waiting for Eddie to appear.

Finally, Eddie entered from a door behind the podium, dressed casually but with a severe and stern look. He approached the podium on the platform and started reading out loud from a list of voting numbers he held in front of him. His reading glasses slid down to the end of his nose, reflecting a scholarly man when he looked up, but no one in the room wanted to incur the teacher's wrath.

"Precinct 13, down twenty-two percent. Precinct 24 down thirteen percent. Precinct 16 down nineteen percent. And get this: Precinct 32 down twenty-nine percent. Who's running the show in 32?"

Sheepishly, Larry Simmons raised his hand. "It's me, Eddie."

"What happened, partner?"

"I don't know what to tell you, Eddie. We did our groundwork."

Eddie looked back up at the rest of the room.

"This is what I mean, guys and gals. We have to find the problem and then address it. I know the city's numbers are down, but we have to be better than that. We must get our message out to anyone who even thinks of voting for that asshole, Robins. So here's what we're going to do. I want every one of you to meet every voter in your precinct, fact-to-face, man-to-man or man-to-woman, Everyone."

A subtle groan arose from the crowd.

Eddie continued. "Hey, hey, I know it's a pain in the ass, but you guys know what's riding on this thing. For one, a lot of your jobs are at stake. If he wins, you're all fucked. You know that, right? He'll start whacking you guys off left and right and replace you all with his guys. You all know that, right?"

Suddenly, the crowd grew silent.

"That's right, folks. I'm not the only one with something to lose on this thing. I also want you to know I will be available for any group who wants to chat. Any group. Teas with old ladies, social/athletic clubs, churches, block parties, anything. Just make sure you check with Warney on the schedule. And finally....... '

The volume on Joe's cellphone was set on high. That was how he liked it. "You Shook Me" by AC/DC, Joe's ringtone, went off. Joe quickly grabbed the phone and left the room. Eddie's piercing eyes followed him to the door.

"That better be a death in the family, Hinckley!" shouted Eddie.

Joe walked out into the alley and answered his phone.

"Hello, this is Joe."

"Joe, this is Mrs. Patroski. There seems to be a bit of confusion here."

"How so, Mrs. Patroski?"

"Well, the nice Gonzalez couple came by, and I gave them the keys to the apartment, like you said, and they went up there. Well, I go back to watch my television program, *Everybody Loves Raymond*, and I get another knock on the door. It's the Gonzalez's, and they say someone is in the apartment with a signed lease."

"Wait. What? Who? A signed lease?" Joe was utterly confused. "Are the Gonzalez's still there? Let me talk to them."

Instantly, Gonzalez got on the phone.

"Hey man, this is bullshit. We come out here, and you've already rented it out? It would have been nice for a phone call, man."

"But I didn't. I didn't rent out anything."

Gonzalez continued. "Well, this black dude is standing right here with a signed lease with your name on it."

"What? Put him on, whoever he is."

The phone is switched again. A familiar voice comes on the line.

"Hello? Fat Joe Hinckley? This is Orvin Rodrick, your new tenant, man. Don't you remember signing this lease last night? Man, you must have been fucked up! We signed it down in your basement, you know, where you make the crystal meth."

Joe furiously shouted in his cell phone. "You son of a bitch! I ain't signed nothing with you, Orvin! And you know that! Now get the hell out of there and put Gonzalez back on!"

"Too late, man, they heard about your meth lab and bolted, but this nice Mrs. Patroski is still here. Talk to her, man."

Mrs. Patroski gets back on the phone.

"Joseph, I am so surprised about you. This nice gentleman says you do illegal things in your spare time and make a lot of money; you could at least give us a break on the rent."

"Mrs. Patroski, please put Mr. Rodrick back on the phone, will you?"

"Hello, it's me again, Fat Joe. How you been doin'? It's been a spell. Looks like a big old run-off, too, should be fun."

"Listen. Fine, you stay there, Orvin. Yeah, you stay there; I'll be right over!"

"Okay, Homes, I'll be here. By the way, the kitchen sink leaks; bring your tools, man."

"Be right there, asshole." Joe bolted from the meeting, speeding off in his car, tires screeching angrily, and arrived at the apartment in ten minutes. He stormed up the three flights of stairs and tried to open the door to the apartment; it was locked. He pounded on the door.

"Orvin! Orvin open up!"

"Orvin aint here, man." Said Orvin from behind the door in his best stoner voice.

"Orvin, I ain't kiddin'. Open this fucking door!"

Mrs. Patroski called up from the second floor. "Hey, we're trying to watch 'Raymond' down here."

"I'm sorry, Mrs. Patroski."

Calmer and now trying to reason with Orvin, Joe continued his plea.

"Orvin, would you open this door."

"I didn't hear the magic word," said Orvin.

"Orvin, would you PLEASE open this door?"

After a short pause, Joe heard the door unlocked. Joe turned the handle and stepped into the bare apartment. Tom Sullivan stood before him. The look on Joe's face was one of shock.

"Relax," said Tom.

Orvin appeared from the hallway.

"Sorry about the noise, bro, but we had to get you here. That Mrs. Patroski is a nice old lady."

"Relax," Tom repeated. "I need your help just one more time. I need you to set up a meeting with my old man. Here. Tomorrow. Just one more night, Joe."

"You don't want to meet here. This ain't a good place."

"Joe, the cops are watching my old man. His coming here wouldn't raise any suspicion. Maybe he could help you paint or something."

"What about after tomorrow?"

"You will never see my ass again. I promise."

"What the hell, you break in here, scare my tenants away, and where's this lease anyway?"

Orvin pulled a standard-form apartment lease filled out with all the proper information from his back pocket and handed it to Joe.

"Got it at Walgreens. Real cheap."

"Alright, alright. After all this shit, you need to tell me where you have been for the past couple of weeks. They've been looking all over for you."

"Maybe you don't want to know," Tom said.

"Just curious, I guess." Joe looked down and shuffled his feet.

Orvin blurted out, "He's been staying with me. At my crib on 58th and Indiana. Who would look for a white-ass Irish guy over there."

Joe turned to Tom. "How the hell could you stand to live with this asshole?"

"It wasn't easy, man. I'll tell you that."

"Okay, okay, that's enough now." stepped in Orvin.

"Alright," said Joe. "Tomorrow, seven o'clock, but this is it, guys, no more."

"Agreed. No more," said Tom.

Joe attempted to lay down the ground rules. "You guys have to turn off the lights. Everyone can see right in here from the street."

Tom reached over to the light switch panel on the wall near the door, and the lights were off.

"And you have to be quiet, no music or noise."

"Man, I brought my guitar and bongos and everything," said Orvin.

"Okay, I'll talk to Pat tomorrow. I try to get him here at about seven."

Joe turned to leave the room.

"Hey Joe," said Orvin.

"What?"

"Can you get us some beer?"

"You guys are fuckin' amazing," said Joe as he shook his head and left the apartment.

As Joe Hinckley drove to the liquor store, the electric boxes and video monitors hooked up to Charlie Bedrun went off with an alarm akin to a 727 going down. A team of doctors and nurses entered the room, assessed the situation, called out directions and started taking action.

The chaos ceased after ten minutes of desperation. Charlie was dead.

CHAPTER TWENTY-FIVE

Hoping to catch Pat at the ward headquarters the next day, Joe went in earlier than usual. He knew Pat was an early riser who took care of his ward business before he went to work. Joe hoped to run into Pat casually and explain his mock dilemma; he needed a second hand on a repair at the apartment.

Joe knew Pat was sometimes crusty and short but always offered his hand when he could. He had helped Joe when he first bought the place, going with him to inspect the building before he made his offer to purchase it. Pat knew his way around a furnace and foundation, and when he pronounced the structure solid, Joe made his offer.

Several times afterward, Pat had come by to help Joe with some other home projects. They had installed new kitchen cabinets in Patroski's apartment. They put new toilets in Joe's and the third-floor apartment, so for Joe to ask for assistance on a home project would be nothing new to Pat.

When Joe got to the ward headquarters, Pat was sitting at the communal desk with Juan and Octavio, working on their voting sheets, laying out plans for the next couple of weeks.

"Hey, Pat."

Looking up, Pat's brows arched with curiosity.

"Where the hell did you go last night? Eddie got hot when you left; he even asked about you."

"I had an emergency at the house; a water line to the toilet broke on the third floor, and I had to run and shut it off."

"Ouch. A lot of damage?"

"No, not really. Some water leaked through the Patroski's ceiling, but it could have been worse. Nothing a quart of Kilz wound cure."

"Well, that's good. Water will wreck a house, that's for sure."

"I have to replace the toilet, though. The ceramic cracked on the old one. Could you give me a hand, you know, guide me? I'll do the labor."

"Sure. When did you have in mind?"

"Would tonight work for you?"

"Tonight? Short notice, boyo. Why so quick?"

"I've got new tenants coming in tomorrow to check out the place, and I want to have it in before they get here."

"Okay, well." Pat turned to Octavio and Juan. "Looks like no work tonight, but we'll make it up." He turned back to Joe. "What time?"

"About seven or so."

"Okay, should be alright. I'll see you at seven, provided Claire has nothing going on. Not that she would; she seems never to go out anymore." He turned to John.

"Okay, I've gotta run and these two guys have to get wherever they're going. See you at seven tonight."

"Thanks, Pat. See you then."

That night, Pat approached Joe's building and noticed the third-floor lights were on, illuminating the bare apartment for the world to see. Thinking Joe was there, he walked straight up to the apartment and knocked on the door. There was no answer.

"Joe, are you in there?"

He knocked again, and the door slowly swung open, but now the lights were off, except the night light in the bathroom. Pat entered the apartment.

"Joe?"

Orvin appeared from the kitchen and held out an open flip phone for Pat.

"Hello, Mr. Sullivan. I have a phone call for you."

Orvin quickly left the apartment through the rear door and was gone. Pat was suddenly alone. He put the phone up to his ear.

"Hello."

"Dad, this is Tom." said a voice in response.

A charge went through Pat's body, weakening his grip on the phone. He quickly recovered and grasped the phone with all his remaining strength.

"Dad, are you there?"

"Yeah, Tom, I'm here."

"Dad, I need to meet you and talk with you."

"And I need to talk with you, son. I've got some questions myself."

"I'm sure you do. I hope to answer all of them for you someday."

"They now doubt that you did it. They have some evidence that maybe someone else was there."

"Who told you that? Have you been talking with the cops?"

"Yeah, Tom, I have to. They have questions, too. All they know from me is that I have no answers for any of this."

"How's TJ?" Tom's voice cracked.

"He's fine. He's fine. He asks when his Daddy is going to be home. We tell him you're on the job and will be home soon."

Tom slowly replied. "Tell him... tell him I'll be home soon."

"I will, son, I will."

The conversation slowed considerably, but suddenly, Pat was determined to get some information.

"Son, who was this guy Janice was with?"

"Charlie Bedrun was a low life. A real low life. He had gotten out of the joint about a year ago and went straight back to dealing. I knew him from high school.

"Well, what was Janice doing with this guy?"

"I think she was dealing small bags of pot. He was probably there dropping some off. I told her not to do that shit, but she was always complaining about money. I was behind on my support, and she had to make ends meet."

"Did you know that the house was in foreclosure?"

Tom sighed. "No, but I'm not surprised."

"Was this Bedrun guy a friend of the Reverend Zuko?"

"Reverend Zuko? I thought he had gone straight. I don't know, Dad. It was possible at one time, but Zuko found religion or something, and Janice was small-time. She wouldn't have had any relationship with that guy. Plus, this guy Bedrun, like I said, was just out of the joint. Zuko's been straight for a couple of years now, I guess. I knew Janice wasn't boinking this guy; I had more respect for her than that. I didn't want her to get involved with jags like that."

Pat glanced out the front window and saw Wiggin's unmarked vehicle pull up to the curb in front of the building.

"Tom, I have to go. I've got company now. Where can I meet you? And what do I do with this phone?"

"Ditch the phone, Dad. Wipe your prints off and throw it away; it's hot. Meet me on election night at the place where you wondered why they didn't take the monument with them."

"Where?"

Tom was gone. The phone was silent. Pat frantically wiped it off on his shirt. He looked around the bare apartment for a place to hide it. He raced into the bathroom, tossed the phone in the toilet, and closed the lid.

Suddenly, there was a knock at the front door.

"Pat, open up. It's Wiggin. I know you're in there."

Pat took a deep breath, and opened the door.

"Hello Pat," said Wiggin as he entered and switched on the light switch.

"What are you doing here?" responded Pat.

"Oh, I was just in the neighborhood. I usually drive by here and check for lights up here. I know this apartment is for rent, so you never know."

"Well, I'm done here now. Joe asked me to check the light switches before showing the apartment. They all seem to work just fine."

"That a fact."

"Yeah, it's a fact. The lights all work. See."

Pat then went through the apartment, flicking on and off all the light switches as some offer of proof of his real purpose for being in the apartment.

"Is there anything else I can help you with, officer?"

"Yeah, there is."

"And what might that be, officer?"

"I have to take a leak. Can I use your bathroom?"

"It's not mine, but go right ahead."

Wiggin walked to the bathroom. He left the door open, giving him enough light to aim and fire as he continued his conversation with Pat.

"So, have you heard from your boy lately?" He said over the sound of streaming water.

To keep Wiggin's eyes from looking into the bowl and seeing the disposed cell phone, Pat stood in the doorway, uncomfortably watching Wiggin do his business, and spoke directly to him, eye to eye.

"No, nothing. What can you tell me?"

"I've got nothing new."

Wiggins finished and looked down as he tucked his member and zipped his pants. He flushed the toilet and walked immediately out of the bathroom. To Pat's relief, Wiggin had not seen anything.

"Can I give you a ride somewhere?"

"No, thanks. It's a nice night for a walk."

They walked out of the apartment to the sidewalk. Pat's nerves relaxed. Wiggin noticed he was more at ease.

"Pat, I talked with Joe earlier today, and he told me you were going to help him install a ceiling fan." started Wiggin.

"Yeah, we did that too. All part of the electrical, you know."

"There isn't one fucking ceiling fan in the place, Pat. Plus, I never talked with Joe."

Busted, Pat just stared at Wiggin.

"Listen, Pat, again, for what it's worth, I don't think Tom did this. You know that, right? We know that drugs were involved, but this looks like a hit. The drugs, to me, were incidental, but Tom has to help himself. He's not doing that. He's making it harder on himself. Think about that."

"Look, Officer Wiggin, I keep telling you the same thing. I don't know where the kid is. I know what I have at stake here, believe me, but I can't help you. And following me home every night isn't going to do you any good either."

"Pat, I don't follow you home. I never have."

"Well, somebody has been."

"That's what I'm talking about here. There's more here than meets the eye; this is more than a lover's quarrel. I know he's your son, and that is what may have you a bit confused about what the right thing to do is."

"Stop right there. Where do you get off lecturing me about father and son relations?"

"No, don't get me wrong."

"Did you go to your kid's party?"

"What?"

"Your kid's birthday party. You told me he had a bunch of clowns and horses."

Wiggins looks down at his shoes. "No.

"Did you do anything? Have you seen him since?"

"Not yet."

"Too busy? Is that it? Too busy chasing around my innocent kid to pay attention to your own? Listen, boyo, don't make the same mistake I did. I'm trying to right things now, but don't wait until you have to risk everything you've ever had; it could be too late."

Wiggin bowed his head as he gathered himself.

"This isn't about me or my kid. Other people are looking for Tom. I'm not sure who yet, but that would explain the car going by your house. Be careful, Pat. I'm on your side."

Pat watched as Wiggin walked around to the driver's side of the car and got in. As he began to pull away, Pat bent over and called to Wiggin through the open passenger window.

"Hey Wiggin. I have a question."

The car stopped.

"Who is Zuko?" Pat calmly asked.

Wiggin pulled the car back and turned it off.

"Why?"

"I need to know."

"You don't want to mess with those people; you don't need to."

"I may have to."

Wiggin sighed and gave in.

"He's a big shot, but he's smart. He insulates himself well. He's been dealing on the streets for years."

"Still?"

"I think so. He's been laying low for a while now. He started a soup kitchen on Halsted, and some think he may have turned over a new leaf."

"Do you?"

"No fucking way. Once a shitbag, always a shitbag. Where are you going with this anyway?"

"I have no idea. I hear his name every once in a while. I just know that Tom is innocent."

"Did he tell you that?"

Pat smiled at Wiggin's attempt to trap him.

"Once a shitbag, always a shitbag."

Wiggin chuckled but moved to a somber tone.

"Pat, if you know anything, you have to tell me. These people are downright mean. Don't get in over your head."

"I don't know anything. Not yet, anyway."

"Watch yourself." Wiggin took out his card and scribbled his phone number. "This is my cell phone number. Don't hesitate to call if you need anything or have something for me."

Pat took the card and slipped it into his pocket.

"Don't be a hero," continued Wiggin. "I think we're on the same side. Call me if you hear or know anything, and don't be stupid, okay?"

"You'll be the first to know, Office Wiggin."

After watching Wiggin take off down the street, Pat began his four-block walk home.

Across the street from Hinckleys building, two sets of eyes peaked from behind a large bush.

"I didn't see his kid, did you?"

"No, all I saw from the alley was Orvin Rodrick leaving the building."

"Orvin Rodrick? What does he have to do with anything?"

"I don't know, man. I'm just telling you what I saw."

"That's it? That's all you saw?"

"Yeah, that's all I saw. What are you? A cop?"

"Don't get pissed at me. Hinckley said he was supposed to be here tonight. If we missed him, you know what he will do to us. We aren't exactly on his good side right now."

"I know, jagoff, but that's all I saw. What did you see?"

"Just the old man and the cop. I think he is looking for the same person as we are."

"Ya think so? You moron, of course he is. The kid is an escaped felon."

"Let's get out of here and report. I've got to make my rounds and get rid of a lot of literature yet."

"What are you crazy? Just dump that shit in the garbage."

"Don't tell me what to do, alright?"

"Okay, whatever, man."

* * * * *

That night, Joe went to bed and was almost asleep when there was a frantic knock at his front door.

"Joe! Joe! Wake up!" screamed Mrs. Patroski through the front door. "The ceiling is leaking right on my bed! Wake up!"

Jos scrambled out of bed and answered the front door.

"Mrs. Patroski, what's wrong?"

"Water! Through my ceiling! It's dripping right on my bed!"

Joe rushed up the stairs into the Patroski apartment and their bedroom. On the bed, Mr. Patroski smiled and waved. The area next to him, where Mrs. Patroski slept, was soaked with water that was dripping from the ceiling. Joe bolted from the apartment and up the stairs to the third floor, where he found the living room soaked in water. Its source was an overflowing toilet. Quickly, Joe lifted the back lid of the toilet, raised the toilet's ballcock to stop the flow, and glanced into the bowl, where he could see a blockage.

Under other circumstances, Joe would never reach into a toilet bowl, but he saw that the blockage was metallic, not of human origin. clogging the bowl. He pulled out a cell phone.

CHAPTER TWENTY-SIX

The time passed quickly. It was less than a week before Election Day. Pat and his aides worked the precinct tirelessly. A break in the weather made going up and down porch steps easier to get Byrne's message out. Joe Hinckley even stopped by on a couple of evenings to help out. Pat thought it strange since Joe had never before offered to help, but Pat willingly accepted. Pat had been feeling tired lately and seemed to be shaking off the effects of a cold. He also let John and Octavio carry more of the load as he now felt confident in them to do and say the right things.

John and Claire were now openly dating. Pat liked the kid. He was Catholic and had a good head on his shoulder. But sometimes, he wondered if it was just a continuation of his plan to eventually move into the neighborhood, like illegal aliens marrying a local girl for citizenship. The kid scored some points when he came to Pat first to ask him for permission to take Claire out. He was chivalrous in his request, a trait that Pat had thought had been long gone from today's youth. He was also worried that it was an attempt by Claire to irritate him as she did with Adam. Claire was now more mature, and she realized that her decisions in life affected more than just her. She had shed her selfishness like a snake that molts its skin, leaving behind a crusty shell of the past that would soon rot into nothing. He believed she liked John and seemed happy. Hell, if the kid plays his cards right, he could get hired by the city and make a decent living. He had a future.

He also looked forward to his meeting with Tom. It took him a while to figure out Tom's cryptic instructions as to where the meeting would take place, but he recalled the conversation they had on the way home from Cook County Jail as they passed Marquette Park. He would be there on election night.

His main concern was that he expected to be followed to their rendezvous. Someone was still following him; he could sense it. He knew Wiggin kept an eye on him, and he at least admitted it, but there was someone else who also wanted to know where Tom was, and Pat wasn't sure why. It made him feel uncomfortable.

But he had a plan. He would attend the party at Kirk's Family Inn on election night. When Eddie got up to make his speech, he would slip out the back. At the previous "victory party", he recalled being the sole person remaining at the bar while everyone else's attention focused on the politician at the microphone.

No one would miss him until the end of the speech. Eddie, being the blow-hard that he is, would probably go on for more than twenty minutes, long enough for Pat to get a good head start on anyone who would try to follow him.

Wiggin would be another matter. If he were watching Pat on election night, he would be outside, watching Pat's car. Pat would need assistance to evade Wiggin. Marquette Park was too far to walk. He would need a second car or a driver to pick him up. But who could he trust?

He came home that evening, tired yet comfortable with his plan and hopeful for results from his meeting with Tom. He would tell Tom to turn himself in. He had a shot now at beating this thing, and Pat hoped to convince Tom of this. Tom would be a free man, and Pat would get to keep his home; they would start over, father and son, father, son and daughter, a family. This was Pat's deepest hope. He had looked forward to his retirement but never felt the longing he currently felt towards putting his family back together and getting a new start with his son. This was his mission.

He felt Wiggin was being straight with him. He had cursed Wiggins months ago, but now he felt Wiggin was an ally. Of course, Pat could not let Wiggin know about his meeting with Tom. It would scare Tom off if he detected a cop nearby.

No, Pat would have to convince Tom to come home by himself.

Claire entered the front room and sat on the couch. The kids were still in the bath, so she had a minute.

"How did it go tonight?"

"Alright. Both those guys worked their asses off. We got a lot covered."

"Good. John's coming over again tonight. Is that okay?"

"Yeah, sure. I'm beat; I'll go to bed early tonight anyway."

"I'm going to the election party with John. Is that okay with you?"

"Yeah, fine. Mrs. O'Toole going to watch the kids again?"

"Yes, and I'll be home early enough."

"Good. You never know what's early with her, though."

"Dad, please."

"Okay. Okay. It went well the last time."

"Yes, it did, she's sweet with the kids." Claire paused and shifted gears. "Dad, what will we do if we have to leave the house?"

"What do you mean?"

"What if we lose the bond if Tommy doesn't show up to court?"

"Let me worry about that."

"But what will we do? Should I start looking for a place for us to live? Should I start looking for a job? I want to help."

"We're not going to lose the house, I'm telling you."

"How do you know? It's been months since anyone has seen Tommy."

"We won't lose the house; Tom will be back."

"How can you be so sure?"

Claire detected an air of confidence in Pat, similar to when she was a kid, and she would ask him what Santa Claus was to bring her.

"You've talked to him, haven't you?"

"Who?"

"Tommy. You know damn well who. Dad, tell me, did you meet him?"

Pat paused and debated himself on whether to tell Claire anything.

"I didn't meet him, but I talked with him."

"When?"

"About ten days ago."

"Why didn't you tell me? How is he? Where has he been?"

"I don't know. That's not important. I'm going to meet him on election night. At the park, at the Lithuanian monument."

"Dad! What are you going to tell him?"

"I'm going to tell him to give himself up. It's not as bad as he thinks it is."

"How do you know that?"

"I know, I just know. Let's leave it at that."

"I'll take some pictures of TJ. You can give them to him."

"Sure, I'll take them to him, but listen to me, you must not tell anyone, not even the cops. I promised Tom, only me."

"Okay, how about John?"

"No. No one. Understand? Not a peep to anyone. I think I'm being followed."

"By who?"

"I don't know yet."

"The police?"

"Yeah, probably, but there's someone else, I'm not sure who."

"Why would anyone else follow you? I don't get it."

"I don't get it yet either, but we'll fix this. I know that."

"Dad, are you sure about this? I mean the meeting, this could be dangerous."

"Don't worry, nothing will happen."

Pat tried to convince his daughter that the risk of danger was minimal. He only wished he could convince himself.

CHAPTER TWENTY-SEVEN

Pat rose early on Election Day, as was his custom. The TV weatherman said it would be dry and sunny today, with a high in the low fifties. He could deal with that. He dressed accordingly. Claire had a cup of coffee waiting for him. She placed a plate of eggs and bacon in front of Pat.

"Morning, Dad."

"Morning, Claire. I certainly wasn't expecting this."

"Well, you know it'll be a long day. You might as well start with something in your gut."

Pat started to eat his breakfast.

"I'll bring lunch also. What time would be best? I can do it any time before three o'clock."

"Oh, bring it well before three. How about somewhere between twelve-thirty and one?"

"Fine. Between twelve-thirty and one. Is it going to the three of you again?"

"Yeah, just the Three Amigos."

"The what?"

"The Three Amigos. That's what John calls us now."

"That's pretty funny."

"I suggested the Three Enchiladas, but that didn't go over well."

"I can see why."

Pat finished his bacon and eggs with several quick scoops of his fork and arose from the table.

"Well, gotta go. Thanks again."

"No problem. I'll see you later."

"Okay."

"And Dad, take it easy. Don't keel over on your last election day. Please."

Pat walked over to Claire and kissed her on the forehead.

"I'll try not to. I can't promise anything, but I'll give it my best shot."

He walked out of the house into a sunny morning, wishing this would be his last election day. His retirement plans were shot now and would have to be revised, his finances were in shambles, and the thought of losing his home hovered over him like Damocles' Sword, ready to fall like the quick hammer of a judge's gavel. There was time ahead, however, to figure out what he would do, and nothing could be determined until he met with Tom that evening.

The sun came up earlier and set later in the evening. Pat loved a good spring morning. It beamed optimism and of coming good things. The daffodils and hyacinths were peaking, their little bud-head through the damp soil, soon to be followed by the tulips and other late spring bloomers. They all reached up like a person who went to bed early the night before and woke up in the morning with a stretch and an enormous yawn. The walk to the park energized him.

When he arrived at the park, John and Octavio were already putting the signs out and starting the day. No one from Robins's camp had yet shown up.

"Morning, guys."

"Morning, Mr. Sullivan."

"Well, are you ready for this shit one more time?"

"As ready as we can be," said Octavio.

"Good, one more time, guys, and we can take a long break from this crap. Just hang in there."

Pat paused and looked around.

"No one from Robins yet, huh?"

"No," said John. "I haven't seen anyone yet."

"We'll see how many show up this time. They may be using them somewhere else where they may have a chance. That's okay. It makes it much easier for us. John, I want you to pick up Mrs. Dolan and Mrs. Durkin again today."

"Got it."

"Octavio, can you make sure the signs are exactly seventy-five feet away. Here, use this."

He gave Octavio his tape measure.

"Will do, chief. I did pace them off, though."

"Yeah, they look good, but I don't want any trouble. Double-check it with the tape measure."

"Okay."

Pat went into the field house to look for some coffee. It would be another half hour before the morning commuter rush started.

* * * * *

The day continued uneventfully. The turnout was constant and consistent with Pat's regular numbers. He had estimated an 85 to 90 percent voter turnout. His prognosis was correct. He would carry his precinct again by big numbers.

No one from Robin's camp appeared. Pat guessed that he had conceded this precinct and reassigned his people to focus on certain precincts where he barely lost to Eddie last time. Probably a good idea, thought Pat. Robins wouldn't want to waste any manpower. He would get his ass kicked here no matter how many workers he had dealing his palm cards. Pat would see to that.

John took a little longer to get Mrs. Dolan. She expected him this time and had a spread of cold cuts and cheese waiting for him when he arrived to pick her up. John didn't want to offend her by refusing her offer, so he sat down and made a sandwich when she placed a cup of tea before him. He never had tea before.

"What is this?"

"It's tea."

"How do you drink it? Like coffee?"

"It's up to you. Some people drink it with milk and sugar. I like mine black, but only this is green tea, so I guess I like mine green."

John tried it green.

"This is good, but it needs something. A little kick. Do you have any Tabasco?"

"Any what?"

"Tabasco. Hot sauce."

"Oh lord, no! In this house? Nobody would eat it."

"Maybe I'll try it at home."

Mrs. Dolan grabbed a handful of teabags from the kitchen counter and handed them to John.

"Here, take these home. Heat some water and dunk this in there for a minute or two. It depends on your taste."

"Thank you very much. I will, Mrs. Dolan."

He put the teabags into his coat pocket, finished the cup before him, and, looking at his watch, rose from the chair.

"We should be going. I also have to pick up Mrs. Durkin. Thank you for everything."

"The hell with Mrs. Durkin. Sit and have another cup of tea."

John obliged and had another cup before Mrs. Dolan finally agreed to be taken to the polls. Of course, Mrs. Durkin was a bit upset when John arrived 20 minutes late, but her anger did not last long, as John told her a story about his 'flat tire' on the way to pick her up. Feeling bad about getting mad at such a nice boy, she insisted he come for a sandwich and homemade potato salad afterward. And a cup of tea.

When John got back to the polls with Mrs. Dolan and Mrs. Durkin, he found Claire waiting in the parking lot with another tray of sandwich makings, as she did at the prior election, but this time, there were extra fixings and real plates and a tablecloth and small vase of flowers.

"I'm going to put on ten pounds working today," John mentioned.

"You better not. I like that body just the way it is." teased Claire.

"Alright, stop it, you two," said Pat while chewing on his sandwich.

"Hey, Mr. Sullivan, I had tea for the first time today," said John.

"You've never had tea?"

"No, never."

"Well?"

"It's good, I like it. I may have to have some more later on."

"Try it with a shot of tequila. I do it all the time."

"Really?"

"Dad, cut the bullshit."

"Okay, okay."

"Mrs. Durkin invited me for sandwiches when I take her home. I don't think I'll be able to eat a single bite."

"Don't turn Mrs. Durkin down. She's got family all over this ward. If she invites you in for a bite, you fucking eat. Do you hear me?"

"Even if I'm not hungry?"

"I don't care if you have food coming out of your ears; you eat."

"Okay, take one for the team, I guess."

John looked over Claire's spread. She had gone to great lengths to prepare and display everything.

"This is great, Claire. You sure went all out."

"Thank you." Claire beamed.

At that point, John realized this extravaganza was mainly for his benefit. He would have to partake, eat, and look like he relished every bite in appreciation of Claire's thinking of him, as the politics of love also existed. He loaded his plate and ate.

Soon, Mrs. Dolan and Mrs. Durkin emerged from the park house, fulfilling their civic duty, and John quickly finished the once-high mountain of food on his plate.

"Gotta go."

"Remember, you eat!" warned Pat.

"I will. I will."

John ran off to get the elderly duo into his car.

Claire turned to her father.

"Dad, I didn't know Mrs. Durkin had such a large family?"

"She doesn't. She's the only one here."

"Oh, you are so mean."

* * * * *

The evening voter rush kept the Three Amigos busy for the rest of the day, passing out palm cards and other campaign literature. A new wave of commuters arrived every 15 minutes as Metra trains unloaded their passengers on schedule at the nearby station.

When the polls closed at 8 p.m., Pat told his crew, "Okay, get the signs up, and let's get the hell out of here."

"Mr. Sullivan, is it alright if I bring a buddy to the party?" asked Octavio. "He may want to get involved.:

"Sure, no problem. We can use all the help we can get."

* * * * *

Pat waited alone for the voting tapes to be completed before returning to headquarters. John and Octavio had left for Kirk's Family Inn for what Pat assumed would be a victory party. He was feeling confident. He had been hearing good news throughout the day via the grapevine and had always felt that Byrnes would get a simple majority.

The tapes would take a few minutes, so he stood outside to bask in the last minutes of the sun, still peeking through the trees. He was glad he had kept busy during the day. He rarely found himself thinking about the meeting with Tom for that evening. But now that the election was over, it was all he thought about.

His emotions ran a gut-wrenching spectrum. He would meet his son face-to-face, and he certainly was looking forward to that, but he knew that either Wiggin or the unknown tail would try to follow him, and he could not allow that to happen. Everything was in motion for the meeting. Hopefully his plan would work.

Pat dropped his tapes off at the headquarters to an optimistic Warney. Then he left for the party at Kirk's, picking up Claire along the way.

"Claire, you're going to be driving this car home tonight. I'll get a ride from someone else."

"Who?"

"Don't you worry. I'll take the bus if I have to."

"Dad, I'm kind of concerned about this whole thing. Are you going to be safe meeting Tommy tonight?"

Pat turned to Claire with a sincere, straight face.

"Sure. What could go wrong?"

"Everything?"

"Claire, don't worry. This will work out; you just remember to stay at the party until at least ten-thirty. That's all I ask."

"Sure, Dad. Ten-thirty."

CHAPTER TWENTY-EIGHT

Pat and Claire arrived at Kirk's Family Inn under the watchful eye of Officer Larry Wiggin as he sat in his car across the street. The party was in full swing, with the talking heads on the TV sets speculating on the early returns.

Pat went straight to the bar as Claire went to find John, who had promised to save her a seat at his table.

"Hey Pat, how'd it go?" Joe Hinckley asked.

"Like clockwork. I'll probably get a ninety percent turnout, good numbers."

"Yeah, I think I had some better numbers too. Pretty much everyone I've talked to had good numbers. This party definitely has a better vibe than the last one."

"That's good., I'm getting better vibes myself. You good?"

Joe looked into his cup.

"Yeah, I'm good."

Pat ordered a beer as Warney joined them.

"Hey, Warney, you're leaving your foxhole early tonight."

"Yeah, it's all good, Pat. I think this one is in the bag. The numbers were all coming in great. We might get 60, 65 percent."

"Well, that's a big relief. Have you talked with Eddie yet? Does he know?"

"Yeah, I just left him. He's gonna make his speech in about another hour."

Perfect amount of time thought Pat. He would work the room, showing his face around so that everyone would know he was there, and when blowhard Eddie came out to speak, poof! He would be gone. He bounced back and forth along the bar, glad-handing and back-slapping everyone.

"Hey, Dave!" Pat yelled to Dave Majewski, a precinct worker. "We did it, huh, buddy!"

Dave hugged Pat, his right hand still clutching his beer.

"Yeah, buddy, it looks good."

"These run-offs are a bitch, huh?"

"Oh man, you got that right."

"We did it!"

"Good job!"

"Great numbers!"

"I am so glad this shit is over!"

The feeling of winning was nice, but it was no match for the relief that the aldermanic election work was over for the next four years. Now, everyone could return to regular jobs, a normal home life, and business as usual without worrying about numbers, palm cards, or mandatory meetings.

Pat made his way to the table where Claire and the other two amigos sat. Octavio was seated next to someone that Pat had never seen before.

"Hello, folks. How are we doing?" said Pat.

"Hello, Mr. Sullivan," said John.

Pat turned to Octavio. "Octavio, who's your friend?"

Octavio motioned to his friend, and both stood up from the table and made their way around it to greet Pat,

"Mr. Sullivan, this is my buddy, Tony. He wants to help us out in the future."

"Well, hello there, Tony," Pat said as he reached out. "Where have you been? We sure could have used you the past couple of months."

"Octavio just told me about the fun he was having last week."

"Fun?" Pat turned to Octavio. "You've been telling him that this is fun? Are you fucking crazy?"

"I don't think I used the word 'fun'. I'm sure of it."

"Well, Tony, we'll talk later. Right now, I'm going to enjoy the moment. My work is done for tonight."

"Sure, I understand."

"It was nice to meet you, Tony."

"Yes, sir. Nice to meet you also."

As Octavio and Tony walked back to their seats, Pat bent over and whispered to Claire. "Remember, stay until ten-thirty at least."

Claire nodded.

Pat straightened up. "Well, I've got more backs to slap around here. Are you guys having a good time? Tony, don't get excited; it's not always like this."

Tony gave a grim smile.

"Yeah, this is great, Mr. Sullivan," said Tony.

"Okay, I'll be seeing you guys."

Pat headed for the bar and took the last seat seat at the end. At the right time, he could slip out thru a long hallway that extended past the bathroom and out to the alley. Pat's ride would pick him up there, away from the eyes of Wiggin and anyone else. He sat and turned to the bar and ordered another beer; he would not be going anywhere, at least for another hour or so.

The TV monitors continued to display graphics with numbers and multi-colored bar charts, each comparable to the percentage of votes for that particular candidate. The 51st Ward results flashed on the screen. Eddie Byrne's bar chart was almost double Dale Robin's. The crowd gave an enthusiastic cheer, as these were the first numbers of the evening and certainly looked good despite only 37 percent of the vote having been counted.

This was going to be an early one tonight, thought Pat. Eddie will probably time his speech to the ten o'clock news to achieve the most live media exposure. He would come out just as the newscast started, and the live video feed would open the show, giving Eddie top billing across the city on election night. That was ideal for Pat. The whole room will be focused on Eddie or the TVs; that would be his time to slip out, ten minutes after ten.

Perfect.

Pat sat at the bar, drinking with anyone who strayed by. Everyone in the room had something in common and an open bar, so talking with strangers was not as tough as usual for him. Small talk comes easy sometimes when you have something in common. The room's noise level spiked with laughter and boisterous tales and war stories, and wafts of relief also hovered about. Pat partook in the revelry, passing drinks from the bar to those gathered about him and ensuring the bartender got tipped each time. He was acting as the keeper of the gates.

Suddenly, the crowd began to quiet. Everyone's attention slowly turned towards the main entrance, where the Reverend Zuko, in a conservative white shirt and black suit, entered the room, accompanied by his large head-to-toe black-clad assistant. It was certainly no big secret that Zuko worked for Eddie and turned in good numbers, but it was the first time anyone had ever seen him at an Eddie Byrne function. But the interruption was short-lived as the tone rose and everyone returned to their conversation. Zuko slowly circled the room, occasionally nodding at a familiar face, until he found a relatively quiet corner and stood silently with his assistant.

From behind his two-tone sunglasses, he scanned the room, looking at faces in the crowd. Occasionally, one would catch Zuko's stare and nervously look away. The more he tried to be unobtrusive, the more discomfort he caused. Finally, he whispered to his assistant, who made for the bar. In his absence, Warney approached and warmly greeted Zuko.

"Reverend Zuko, it's good to see you. Eddie will be glad that you're here."

"Thank you, Mr. Warney. I'm certainly happy about that; after all, he requested my presence."

"He sure did. He certainly appreciates all you've done for him; your numbers are outstanding."

"Well, thank you."

"You're the first one he wants to have a private audience with after his speech."

"Well, I'm here."

"Thank you, Reverend. Can I get you something to drink?"

"No, I'm alright. I just sent Carl to get me something from the bar; he'll be right back."

"Okay, and thanks again for coming. Eddie will be glad you're here."

Warney then disappeared into the crowd.

Joe stood at the bar among a group of precinct workers, telling stories regarding the day's events. Despite several easier and more accessible spots at the bar, Zuko's assistant, Carl, squeezed his way in next to Joe. It caused some irritation among the group, but a glance at the size of the intruder prevented it from going any further.

"Iced tea," said Carl to the bartender.

Carl leaned on the bar next to Joe, staring silently straight ahead, waiting. His massive frame hovered like an eclipse over Joe, making the most prolonged and most uncomfortable minute of the evening for him, as he tried to avoid any eye contact. The bartender returned, gave Carl his drink, and he was gone.

"Who the fuck does he think he is?" came a voice from the group.

"Yeah, I should have kicked his ass." said another.

The crowd began cheering again. The bar graphs on the TV monitors showed the 51st Ward numbers were even more encouraging. It sure looked like a romp now. Eddie will be out soon.

Pat was still at the bar, chatting with everyone who was nearby. He saw Zuko in the corner of the room, and once or twice, he thought he saw Zuko make a glance at him. If Zuko's in the room, he couldn't follow Pat. What was the old saying? Keep your enemies close. That was what he was doing, watching the opposition. It was all working so far. It was a little past nine-thirty now; he would take a leak, come back, and be ready. He turned to one of his new friends.

"Can you save my spot at the bar? I need to lean on something, or my arthritis kicks in?"

"Sure, old-timer. Just leave your glass there."

"Thanks, buddy."

Pat headed for the bathroom.

Zuko's attention was indeed on Pat. He slowly scanned the room, trying to be as indiscreet as a Wal-Mart cop, and sipped his iced tea. Left, right. Left, right. Left... where is Sullivan? He was just at the bar, and now he's gone. Zuko quickly gestured to Carl, who began to look for Pat. When Pat reappeared at the bar, Carl sat beside his boss, who leaned into his ear.

"My wife's stupid fucking family. I will personally do those two idiots if he gets away."

Carl nodded his head.

Just then, Warney approached the dais as the opening act to warm the crowd up.

"Okay, everyone. It looks good, it looks good."

The well-oiled crowd responded.

"We're shooting to be the lead story tonight, so Eddie will be out just a little after ten. And when he does come out, we need a strong welcome. But I don't have to tell you that. Okay, hang in there, folks. The food and bar are still open. Have some fun, and we'll be right with you."

As Warney walked off the stage, the crowd returned to party mode. Some of the crowd, wanting to be on TV, staked out spots in front, near the dais. The group began to thin, as Pat had anticipated.

Sitting in his unmarked Crown Victoria across from Kirk's, Wiggin lit a cigarette with a disposable lighter. Six butts lay about the pavement below his open driver's side window. He was smoking more now and didn't feel good about it.

His views of the front door of Kirk's Family Inn and Pat's Ford Taurus were unobstructed. Earlier, he had watched Pat and Claire arrive together and witnessed Zuko's entrance. This was an unexpected event, and it disturbed him that Eddie Byrne would have the reverend openly endorsing him at a public event. Was Zuko a leopard with different spots? Deep in his bones, Wiggin thought not. His intuition of human nature stirred at the thought of Zuko turning over a new leaf. No, this guy was up to something.

Wiggin looked at his watch. A few minutes to ten. He took a final drag from his cigarette, tossed it out the window, and looked at his watch again.

* * * * *

"CBS Channel Two will declare Eddie Byrne the winner in the hotly contested run-off election in the 51st Ward," a TV reporter announced. The Channel Two News theme kicked off the ten o'clock newscast.

"Good evening. Welcome to Channel Two News. We have our eye on all the local election results this evening, and some are far too tight to call at this point; however, we can declare that Eddie Byrne, incumbent alderman of the 51st Ward, will win his fifth straight term by a considerable margin. We'll take you live to his victory speech in a minute or two. But first, Mike, what did you think of the numbers?"

"Well, Carol, it's pretty close to what we like to call a mandate."

The crowd ate it up. A loud, boisterous yell went up after the word "mandate," drowning out the rest of Mike's commentary. Suddenly, the lights went down, and the spotlights showed on an empty podium. The crowd surged close to the front, ready to hail their conquering hero and possibly make it on TV.

Warney made his way to the mic. He tapped it twice.

"Alright, everyone, this it!"

Warney looked offstage at a TV producer beside his portable camera, pointing at his watch.

"Twenty? Thirty seconds? Okay."

"And now, I believe, we will take you to the Eddie Byrnes Campaign Party on the southwest side. Warner?" said Carol.

The TV cut to a shot of the reporter, Warner, standing off to the side of the dais where Eddie was to speak.

"Yes, Carol, the party is on tonight at the Eddie Byrnes Campaign, and it seems like everyone is letting off a little steam. There was concern from the Byrnes camp regarding the challenger, Dale Robbins. However, that concern has all but disappeared among everyone here."

The off-camera producer signaled to Warney.

"And now folks, Eddie Byrne!"

Immediately from a door at the rear of the stage, the smiling Eddie Byrnes walked in, waving to everyone and making the classic victory sign like a hip and young Nixon. The crowd ate it up as confetti flowed from the ceiling. The house DJ played "Don't Stop" by Fleetwood Mac at loud volume to accompany the entrance of the conquering hero. The party had reached its fever pitch.

Pat sat alone, sipping a beer and witnessing rather than experiencing the moment.

The celebration continued as Eddie bent over to shake hands with the front row of supporters. He was enjoying the rush of victory. The TV guys were all standing around looking at their watches, but screw them, thought Eddie, this is my time.

"It's my fifteen minutes," he thought as he continued to shake hands with anyone who would offer their hand.

Zuko tried to keep an eye on Pat, but the crowd blocked this line of vision. He craned and tried to peer over the heads of the well-wishers and still barely caught a glimpse of Pat sitting at the bar. Carl had a better view and looked down at Zuko with a slight nod, indicating everything was alright.

Octavio also eyed the bar and saw that Pat was still there. He turned to Tony and leaned into his ear, trying to be heard over the din.

"Keep an eye on him."

Tony yelled back into Octavio's ear.

"No shit, Sherlock."

"Don't be an asshole, man."

Eddie finally approached the podium while gesturing for the crowd to calm down, for he, the Conquering Hero, was about to speak.

"Alright. Alright, let's simmer down now. Thank you, thank you all."

The crowd obeyed, and Eddie started his speech.

'That was fun, wasn't it?"

A small and knowing chuckle rumbled through the crowd.

"You guys deserve a big hand. Give yourselves a hand; go ahead."

The crowd gave itself a loud back-slapping cheer and turned its attention back to Eddie.

"I think the people have spoken."

"Yeah, they want you, Eddie!" came an anonymous voice from the crowd.

"Well, I think they want good government. They want the continued service and economic development we've enjoyed in the 51st Ward for the past 16 years!"

Pat took another sip of his beer and looked at his watch.

"Yes, the people have spoken, and I have been listening. I listened to them for the last couple of weeks. I barely spoke; I just listened, and what I heard made me feel good, but I know we can do this better. The people of the 51st Ward deserve it!"

Eddie could give a speech with the best of them. He held his right hand high as if he was holding an invisible pointer and gestured as he spoke. His words came out like a roller coaster, peaking and dipping and peaking higher again, building the crowd up at the appropriate moments and bringing them back down with excited plunges that seemed to go on forever.

He could enthrall an entire room with not only his words, but also with his tone, pitch, and gestures. The room was entranced. Eddie was the focus of their attention.

Octavio glanced at the bar again.

Pat was gone.

"Shit!"

Octavio nudged Tony on the arm and bolted from the table to the bar area through the crowd of revelers.

"What's going on?" asked John.

Octavio ignored John.

A disturbed John watched Octavio and Tony wade through the room until they disappeared into the crowd. He turned to Claire, "I'll be right back." He followed Octavio through the crowd.

Behind Kirk's Family Inn, Pat emerged from amid the group of dumpsters and walked to a plain white van waiting for him. He opened the passenger door and got in.

"Thanks, Dave."

Behind the steering wheel was Stutterin' Dave, on loan from Mike McGurn.

"To the park, Dave."

"No problem, Pat."

CHAPTER TWENTY-NINE

Dave headed down the alley and turned onto 87th Street. The plain white van went unnoticed by Wiggin as it passed him on the street.

Octavio and Tony burst through the rear door of Kirk's just in time to watch the van disappear around the corner.

"Fuck, man! Go get the car!" Octavio yelled to Tony. For once, with no argument, Tony obeyed and ran to get the vehicle.

John came out the rear door.

"Hey, what's going on, man? You okay? I saw you run out of here. Do you need a hand?"

Surprised and a lousy liar, Octavio tried to recover.

"Oh, it's nothing, man; just go back inside."

"Where's Mr. Sullivan? Wasn't he at the bar?"

Stalling, Octavio looked into the open dumpster. He finally raised his arm and pointed behind John.

"Hey, he's over there."

When John turned around, Octavio hit him with a wine bottle. Glass shattered and blood flew. Octavio stood over John's fallen figure with the neck of the bottle still in his hand.

"Sorry, man."

Tony pulled the car into the alley. Octavio jumped into the passenger seat before it came to a complete stop. Tony stepped on the gas as they tried to catch up to the white van.

"He's on Pulaski, heading that way, a plain white van. Faster man, don't lose him!" yelled Octavio.

"Fuck you, man! We don't want them to know we're behind them. We lay back a bit. Think! Dickhead!" Tony replied as he turned onto Pulaski.

"Yeah, yeah. Good idea. Lay low."

"What the hell did you do to that dude back there?"

"I had to do him, man."

"Do him? You mean you killed him?"

"No man, but he's messed up."

"Wasn't he a friend of yours?"

Octavio paused to gather himself.

"Yeah, he was."

They drove silently as they spied the van about five car lengths ahead and cautiously followed for a mile when Octavio reached into his jacket and pulled out his cell phone.

Back at the party, Carl reached into his chest pocket, pulled out his cell phone, listened, nodded, and finished the call. He leaned over to Zuko and relayed the message, then awaited instructions.

"Call out the group and have them follow those two idiots," Zuko said. "They can finish the job."

* * * * *

"Man, he's gonna love us now! This old man's gonna lead us right to his kid. We have to keep Carl in on where we're at. He's got his people catching up to us now. We finally gonna get big time!" Octavio yelled at the top of his voice.

"Yeah, mother fucker! Who da' man? Who da' man?" replied Tony.

"I am mother fucker!" yelled Octavio. "Hey, he's turning."

Suddenly, Octavio's cell phone rang. He answered the call.

"Hello? Yeah, we're right behind him now. He's just turned off Pulaski on the 67th Street. Yeah, he turned right. East? Hold on."

Octavio held his hand over the cell phone and turned to Tony.

"Hey, are we going East?"

"Yeah, I think so."

Octavio went back to the cell phone.

"Yeah, east, onto 67th Street, we'll stay on the phone, no problem."

*****

Back at Kirk's, Claire sat alone at the table and tried to look attentive as Eddie was still spouting. She decided to look for John. She followed his route, past the washrooms and the kitchen, out through the back door amidst the dumpsters.

"John?"

She heard a groan from behind the dumpster where she was standing. She found John trying to stand up. His face and neck were covered with blood from the wound on the back of his head.

"Oh my God! John! John, are you all right?"

"Oh, this hurts. I didn't see anything."

Claire looked at the wound. "We've got to get you to a hospital. You're going to need some stitches. What happened?"

"I don't know. I followed Octavio out here, and the next thing I knew, I was hit over the head with something. Hard and glassy."

"Come on, get up. Can you walk to the car?"

"Yeah, yeah. You may have to lead me; I can't see too well, blood in my eyes."

"Fine, lean on me."

Claire put her arm around John and slowly led him from behind Kirk's Family Inn to the parking lot to her car. As he got in the car's passenger seat, she started around the car to the driver's side when she came face to face with Wiggin.

"I'm a cop. What happened?"

"We don't know. He got hit over the head and was knocked out. I have to take him to the hospital."

"Where's your dad?"

"I don't know. I... hey, who are you, and what do you care about my dad?"

"Listen to me. Your dad is in danger. They're trying to get to Tom through your dad, and they don't mess around. Take a look at your boyfriend there. Now you have to tell me, where is he?"

"I don't know if I can trust you."

"Claire, at this stage, you don't have a choice. These people will kill your father and your brother without a blink of an eye. If you know anything, you have to tell me."

Claire remembered her father's dire request not to reveal anything.

"I can't! I can't tell you anything! Leave me alone!"

Claire tried to get into her car, but Wiggin stood in her way. John continued to groan from inside the vehicle.

Wiggin looked her in the eye.

"Again, I need to know, where is your father?"

"Again, I can't tell you."

"Claire, you have to listen to me." Wiggin paused. "I don't believe Tom had anything to do with this."

"Tommy? You're looking for Tommy, too, aren't you?"

"To save his life. Both your father and your brother are in real danger right now. You have to tell me what you know. Now."

Claire looked into Wiggins's eyes. They were stern and rigid yet simultaneously reflected desperation and urgency. And they were true.

"He's meeting Tommy at Marquette Park. At the Lithuanian Monument. It's on 67th and..."

Wiggin ran to his car. "Get that kid to a hospital. I know where it's at. I'm a Lugan."

Claire stood and watched him speed away, wondering if she had done the right thing.

* * * * *

"Man, when this is over, Zuko's gonna love us! Maybe even get a piece of the action," Tony said as he drove.

"No shit, Jack. We'll be hanging in the bar with the playas," replied Octavio. "Slow down now, slow down. You're getting too close. Hey, man, you're getting too close!"

"Calm down, asshole. We're not too close; everything is cool."

"Stay in your lane, stay in your lane. We don't want to get pulled over."

"I can hear both of you assholes." said a voice from the cell phone on Octavio's lap. "Where are you guys now?"

"Still on 67th Street. Heading east." Octavio said while looking at Tony for an approving nod.

"All right. Keep the phone on."

Tony stayed about ten car lengths behind the van, ducking behind interim cars that flowed between them.

The voice on the phone spoke again.

"You should be hitting California soon. We will pick you up there."

* * * * *

"...and finally," said Eddie Byrnes from the Kirk's Family Inn dais. "The work will continue, and the Fifty-First Ward will benefit from this hard work. All of us will benefit. The black, the white, the Hispanic, the Asian, everyone will benefit!"

The crowd's enthusiastic response was long and loud. Eddie waved and shook hands with an onrushing wave of outstretched arms from below the dais. It was good to be king.

CHAPTER THIRTY

The white van continued on 67th Street until it reached its intersection with California, pulled over, and the passenger got out.

"Thanks, Dave. Tell Mike thanks also."

"Will do, Pat."

Stutterin' Dave drove off.

Pat stood alone on the darkened sidewalk, about a hundred feet from the monument. The streetlights and the convenience store on the northwest corner dimly lit the street corner. The park had a horseshoe roadway for automobiles but closed at 10:30 p.m., so it was currently void of cars. The road looked like an asphalt carpet leading to the monument. The surrounding trees prevented any light from appearing on the monument, making it convenient for a clandestine meeting.

Pat walked toward the monument.

A black Cadillac Escalade pulled into the parking space next to Tony's car at the convenience store and turned off its lights and engine. Two large men in the Cadillac looked at Tony and Octavio, sending a shivering charge through them both.

"Is that him?" the front seat passenger quietly asked.

"Yeah, man. That's him, Sullivan, walking to that monument." Octavio replied.

"Is the kid here?"

"I haven't seen him yet."

"We'll just sit here and watch. No more talking."

"Yes, sir. Yes, sir."

Octavio and Tony exchanged nervous glances.

Pat stood before the dark granite monument and looked up at the Art Deco design and its stark lines. The monument itself stood about 15 feet high and 10 feet wide. It was a solid piece of polished granite tapered off in the rear to about 30 feet and sloped to the ground. It looked like a giant, ominous playground slide and was indeed from a time long gone by. He read the inscriptions dedicated to the two Lithuanian aviators, Darius and Girenas, who made one of the first trans-Atlantic flights in 1933. They also died at the end of the flight.

He heard a voice behind him.

"Dad."

Pat turned to face Tom. He walked over to him, put his meaty Irish limbs around his son, and squeezed as if he could physically transfer his love.

Tom squeezed back.

* * * * *

Eddie Byrne sat behind a card table in the backstage room of Kirk's Family Inn. The room was mainly used as storage for the stage equipment and party decorations. When there was an event like tonight, it was used as a green room for band members. The lighting flickered occasionally from the fluorescent fixtures and cast a shadow over Eddie's face, reflecting his current mood. Despite the election win, it was a serious mood. A CD player sat on the table, plugged in and ready.

The Reverend Zuko entered the room, led by Warney and followed by Carl.

Eddie rose from his seat and extended his hand to Zuko.

"Reverend, it's good to see you."

"My brother Eddie. Congratulations on a stunning victory."

"Thank you, thank you. Won't you have a seat? I'd like to have a word with you."

"Surely, Eddie, surely."

Zuko took the seat opposite Eddie at the table.

"Do you guys mind?" said Eddie to Warney and Carl.

"It's okay, Carl."

Eddie waited until they left the room and sat across from Zuko. He wasted no time.

"Reverend, I'm going to get right to the point. You can't touch Tommy Sullivan. He's an innocent man."

"Well, Mr. Alderman, as we discussed before, there are certain things that I cannot control. The die has been cast, and the wheels are in motion."

Eddie reached over to the CD player and pressed the play button. Instantly, the CD player came alive, and from the speakers emanated a familiar voice, the Reverend Zuko's.

"We did what we had to do. Bedrun had to be shut up. He didn't

Listen to us, so we had to make sure that he never opened his mouth again."

* * * * *

Eddie pressed stop.

"Shall I continue?"

"No." The Reverend paused as if he was figuring out all the angles. "But you have as much to lose as I do."

"Murder? Not a fucking chance. I'll go down in flames, but I'll go down knowing for once that I did the right thing. What a concept, huh, Reverend?"

Zuko paused and stared into Eddie's eyes.

"I have to make a phone call."

"Well, you make it then."

Zuko slowly rose from the chair and walked out of the room.

* * * * *

The healing started right there. The wounds inflicted from years past would begin to coagulate and form a hard scab of penance that both father and son would do willfully. Pat knew that his kid loved him and that he was not such a bad father, or at least he could fix whatever damage he may have caused. His eyes welled and broke, and together, they silently sobbed into each other's shoulders, trying to relay 35 years in one desperate minute.

It worked.

Finally, both men composed themselves as best they could and separated.

"Tom, they don't think you did it. They have someone else at the scene."

"They'll nail me, Dad."

"No, no, they won't. We think they'll drop the charges."

"Who told you that?"

Pat answered hesitantly.

"The cop. Detective Wiggin."

"The cops? Of course, they'll tell you anything to get to me. I can't go to prison for something I didn't do."

"Tom, I've come to trust this guy. I can't say I know why, but I believe him."

"They'll still send me to prison. All these guys getting out after 20 years for crimes they didn't do; that shit happens all the time now. I can't risk it, Dad."

"Well then, what's the alternative? A life on the run? Nowhere to go?"

"It doesn't matter, Dad."

"And TJ?" What about him?"

The query choked Tommy up. He couldn't respond.

"Here, I've got some new pictures of TJ that Claire took."

Pat handed the photos to Tommy, who had difficulty seeing them through the teardrops. He tried to look at the pictures, but he could not make it. He started to waver and finally dropped the photos to the ground as he fell to his knees.

Pat knelt next to him and put his arms around him.

"We can make it right, boyo. We can."

* * * * *

"Let's move." said the Escalade driver.

The two figures exited the Escalade and began to cross the street. Octavio and Tony got out and followed behind.

Halfway across 67th Street, the driver's cell phone went off, and everyone stopped as he answered it.

"Yes? Yes sir. Okay." He closed the cell phone.

"Change of plans."

He turned to Octavio and Tony.

"You two. Come with us."

"What for?" asked Octavio.

"Yeah, does Zuko want to see us or something?" asked Tony.

"Yeah, that's it. Zuko wants to see you guys. We're to take you to him."

The four men turned and headed back for the vehicles. Octavio and Tony were ushered into the rear of the Escalade. The vehicle left the parking lot with two extra passengers being taken for a ride.

Wiggin approached from behind the monument. The Sullivans, huddled and kneeling. When he was 20 feet away, he cleared his throat to announce his presence. He didn't want any surprises.

When Pat turned to him, he knew his work was done. Tom would be coming with him.

"Come on, Tom. Let's go now. Your son is waiting for you at home."

Through red eyes, Tom looked to Pat for guidance, someone to trust, and the truth. Pat's paternal glare comfortably responded to his plea.

"All right. Let's go."

CHAPTER THIRTY-ONE

The crowd at McGurns was quiet. It was early on a Friday, and the place wasn't half full. Pat sat in his usual seat in the corner near the front windows. The sun was setting later now as April turned to May. Pat had promised Claire that he would come right home when the streetlights came on. Pat smiled at the irony, for he was in no hurry tonight.

As was his custom, he had taken a week's vacation immediately after the election to wind down from the work and drama associated with the democratic process. He felt he had a little more to wind down after this one. He was feeling better than he had felt in the past six months, so he ordered one more beer before heading home and basking in the glow of his new household.

"Here you go, Pat," McGurn said as he placed his order on the bar.

"Thank you, sir. You are a scholar and a gentleman."

"That's on me. You certainly earned it."

"Thank you again, good sir."

"So, when will Tommy be home? You excited?"

"Monday. Monday morning at nine o'clock. Monday morning at nine o'clock, this shit will be over."

McGurn reached behind him, took a bottle of Irish Times from the back of the bar, and poured two shots.

"Slainte."

"Slainte."

After they toasted, the shots went down the hatch.

"It's just a fucking shame that he did any time."

"Well, they don't like it when you skip bail, innocent or not, but he'll be all right."

"Any word on the dirtball?"

"Octavio? No, nothing yet. The kid fell off the face of the earth. Probably to Mexico or something. Who knows? Stupid kid. Stupid fucking kid. Smart, but fucking stupid. He had to be, but the kid fooled me, he really did." Pat paused. "He could have mattered."

"His partner?"

"No, nothing. Both just gone."

Dave appeared from the storeroom and leaned against the bar next to Pat. Pat gave him an ear-to-ear grin and put his arm around him.

"My man! Dave, how are you?"

"I'm glad T-T-Tommy's gonna get out. I can't wait to see him."

"Thank you, Dave, but you are full of shit."

"No. If you're glad, then s-so am I."

Pat paused, looked down into his lap, and sniffled loudly.

"Thank you, Dave. I appreciate that. I do. Thanks."

Dave returned a big smile and left the bar to return to his chores.

"He's a good kid."

"The best. You ready for another one?"

"No," said Pat. "I think I'll head home."

The bar's front door swung open, and Larry Wiggin entered. Immediately, he saw Pat at the bar and approached the vacant seat next to him.

"Is this seat taken?" asked Wiggin.

"No. Help yourself," responded Pat.

Wiggin draped his coat over the back of the stool and sat at the bar.

"Can I buy you a drink?"

"Yeah, I'll have a beer with you."

Wiggin signaled McGurn for two beers and turned back to Pat.

"I hear Tom will be home on Monday."

"Yeah. That's what they're telling me, too."

"That's good. Getting back to normal at the house?"

"Yeah, well, whatever is normal now. We'll find out."

McGurn arrived with the beers. Wiggin took a long sip of his and turned to Pat.

"I went and took my kid to the museum yesterday."

"That's good. That's good to hear."

"Yeah. I'm starting to think about this a lot more now. I got a ton of personal time in the bank at work, so I figure we'll even do a vacation this summer."

"Oh yeah? Where?"

"Vegas. Just kidding. I guess Disney's the way to go for a kid his age."

"That will be nice. I never got to take my guys to Disney. I was thinking of taking the little guys down there when they get a little older."

"You should." Wiggin took another sip of his beer. "Anyway, I just wanted to pop in here to see if you were around."

"Well, you got me."

"Well, it's just that, oh, I dunno. You're a good man, Pat. I think that's just what I wanted to say to you, that's all. I wanted to tell you that."

"Thank you, Wiggin. I think you're a good guy, too."

"I guess I have a lot to work on, but I'm going to really be at it." Wiggin finished his beer, rose from the bar stool, and put on his jacket. "I'm going to his basketball game; gotta go."

"Thanks for everything." Pat extended his hand to Wiggin.

They shook hands, and Wiggin left the bar.

Pat finished his beer and followed Wiggin out into the spring evening twilight. The sky was still blue with burnt orange streaks stretching from behind the newly budded trees like the finger of a departing fire god. The warmth from the day's sunlight still hovered.

He liked to walk when it was chilly. Not frigid, but chilly, spring-like. It had an inherent optimism that, most of the time, was a fool's gold, a cruel joke. He recalled many springs thinking precisely the same thing, like the false promises contained in the bud of a tulip, but he felt different now.

A burden had been lifted from his shoulders, and he came out of it all right, maybe even better. Pat's relationship with his son seemed to have taken on a deeper meaning, a more genuine connection. He hoped to be more of a part of everyone's life in whatever way he could. Earlier, he worried about how he would spend his retirement time, but that seemed so distant now, like a prior life.

As dusk finally infiltrated the chilly city, he approached his home and noticed that the light was out on his doorbell. He pressed the button but heard nothing from inside the house. Peering through the door window, he saw TJ and Jesse sitting on the carpet watching TV, neither moving a muscle when he pressed the button again. Their usual reaction to the doorbell was a race to answer it, with the winner usually embedding his face into the door.

Son of a bitch. My doorbell is broken.

His immediate thought was to head straight for the garage and pull out the tools to repair it. He turned to descend the stairs but stopped and turned back.

"Fuck it."

He knocked on the door.

* * * * *

Two hours later, Pat was tired but comfortable in his living room chair, slowly scanning the room. The kids were still in front of the TV but were scrubbed and in their pajamas, the homestretch of their day about to begin.

Claire and John, or Juan as he now wished to be called, were both on the couch, the end of the day also showing on their faces. Poor Juan sat there with a bandage tied vertically around his head like he suffered from a 1920s toothache rather than a severe cut to his head. Understandably, Juan had failed to see any humor in Pat's observation when he mentioned it at the dinner table. Still, Pat liked Juan. There was a tenderness he thought would be good for Claire, and for once seemed genuinely happy. His little girl had grown up big-time, and Pat felt proud that she passed the family crisis with flying colors. Her mother would also be proud.

Feeling buzzed and tired, Pat decided that, given the choice, he would rather fall asleep in his bed than in his chair, so he rose to call it a night.

"Good night, folks."

Immediately, both children arose and hugged Pat. "Good night, Grandpa."

"Good night, guys, love you both."

"Night, Dad,"

"Night, Mr. Sullivan."

"Good night, Claire, night John."

"Very funny, Dad. Now say it right."

"Sorry, forgot. Juan. Good night, Juan."

Pat walked to his room, undressed, and climbed into bed. He still slept on the left side as he had for the last fifty years. Lying on his back, he stared at the bare white ceiling, savoring and enjoying the current moment. He knew it would not last and wanted to experience and try to save, via one of his senses, the feeling he was enjoying.

He was safe, happy, and secure, at least for now. He knew this feeling could not last; things change, the elliptical ride of life would see to it, but things seemed to go right every now and then. Everything clicks as if some cosmic or spiritual force convergence settled on your head, and you wear it like a crown, a big, shiny, golden jewel-encrusted crown where the light bounces off it like a radiant star.

Pat knew this moment was fleeting and rare, as he now battled fatigue and alcohol to stay awake, but this was such a moment, and he hoped to lie and revel in it.

But he could not. His lids shut, his hands opened up like lotuses next to his still body, and he fell into a peaceful, deep sleep.

* * * * *

The projector shot a speckled and grainy white light on the screen. It was filled with the black and white image of Mary, mid-day, standing in front of what looked like a summer cottage and attired in her favorite dress, the green one, Pat knew it, despite the lack of color in the film. She smiled. Oh, how she smiled! A smile Pat had not seen in a long time, a smile of true happiness. And she waved. At first, fast and excited, and then she slowed her wave until she just held her hand in the air, but still smiling. Oh, how she smiled!

THE END

ACKNOWLEDGEMENTS

I wish to thank lots of friends for helping me put together this story. My family and friends' suggestions and constructive comments were extremely helpful.

To the Monadnock attorneys who helped me with some details over beers at Cavanaugh's.

John Linehan, my lovely wife Laura, Dan Byrne, and Bill Figel were my go-to readers. Each contributed wise and profound suggestions. My kids Lucy and Grace again acted as my techies. Jim Elsener also contributed with his vast editing skills, again.

Kevin Theis at Fort Raphael Publishing and Paul Stroili at Touchstone Graphic Design again provided top-notch skills in assisting my in putting this thing together.

Here we go again!

Bob Allen is a life-long resident of Chicago, mostly on the south side. He is the proud father of two beautiful girls, Lucy and Grace, with his lovely wife, Laura. The beautiful girls have left him and Laura alone with two rescue cats who let them live with them.

Bob's past involves making eyeglasses, stand-up comedy, loading airplanes, practicing law, and tending bar, among other things. In addition, he has authored a previous book, "Let It Be At That". His play, "Opening Day" was produced to exactly zero reviews, however a friend gave it a thumbs-up while smiling on the way out, so there's that. Also, just in case you were wondering, Bob likes the Sox over the Cubs, thin crust over deep dish, dry over wet, Stones over the Beatles and Ginger over Mary Ann.